ACCOMPLICES, YOU ASK?

CHARLES S. KRASZEWSKI

MONTAG

First Montag Press E-Book and Paperback Original Edition January 2022

Montag Press ISBN: 978-1-957010-01-4
Design © 2022 Amit Dey

Montag Press Team:

Author Photo: Aleksandra Kraszewska
Cover image: *Prapory* (Banners) by Stefan Tejk.
Editor: Charlie Franco

A Montag Press Book
www.montagpress.com
Montag Press
777 Morton Street, Unit B
San Francisco CA 94129 USA

Montag Press, the burning book with the hatchet cover, the skewed word mark and the portrayal of the long-suffering fireman mascot are trademarks of Montag Press.

Printed & Digitally Originated in the United States of America
10 9 8 7 6 5 4 3 2 1

DEDICATION

Uh… this book is dedicated to no one. In order to provide you all with plausible deniability.

ACKNOWLEDGEMENT

The author would like to acknowledge all the musicians and poets mentioned in this book, all of whom contributed to who he is today. Ray Verano is a fictional character, and his opinions are his own; our tastes are similar except for this: believe me, as I see it, none of you suck. I would also like to acknowledge the sacrifices made by all veterans (as, I believe, Ray would, too). You are braver than us both, whether you were kicking Saddam's ass or changing the oil on humvees. And I'd also like to acknowledge the service of politicians, who do have a tough job. On second thought, nah. Let's strike that last sentence.

JUST SO THERE BE NO MISUNDERSTANDINGS ...

A *ccomplices, You Ask?* is a work of fiction. A glance at its place of publication should convince you of the fact that the wonderful city of San Francisco is still as beautiful and peaceful as it ever was. Nothing that happens in the pages that follow here is historically true. Wixburn, Sanantone, and the Naxkohomen Valley are figments of the author's imagination. Although they are said to lie somewhere in Northeastern Pennsylvania (a lovely place of fresh air and green rolling mountains, just as real as San Francisco), they are not based on any real location. So don't nobody try to draw up a Wessex map of this novel, OK? Such a project would be doomed to failure. There may be Pelagians in the world, but there is no St. Pelagius, and no Pelagian Order. There is no such place as Hanskung College. All of the characters of *Accomplices, You Ask?* are completely fictional, and based on no real person, whatsoever. Any resemblance between them and any real, live person is pure coincidence, unintentional.

History does not arrange its products in bunches;
It is man who seeks to put order into the
disarray of history.

—Jacques Barzun

I s this thing on?

It's recording, yeah?

You don't have to say, like, *Testing, one two three* … the way they do in the movies?

OK then.

When you get right down to it, it all happened because he bought *Sgt. Pepper's* instead of *Abbey Road.*

Well, it's a little more complicated than that, but it can be boiled down to the fact that nothing evil or even awkward would have happened in Jason's life — or that of the world — if he had bought *Abbey Road*, as he had fully intended to, and not *Sgt. Pepper's*, which he already had on his iPhone — synced from a CD he had imported to his MacBook years ago. But let me explain.

So Jason Hughes, the unwarrantedly infamous Jason Hughes, is, or rather was, a professional writer. No, nothing sexy, not novels or plays or anything like that. He was a professional writer (you can get a BA in that, believe it or not) for a pharmaceutical company in Wixburn, Pennsylvania, right off of Pennsylvania Avenue.

It wasn't what he wanted to be; it wasn't what he ever thought he would turn out to be, although he might have foreseen it all, coming from a nowhere background with working-class parents who couldn't give him, simply *couldn't* give him any good advice about things like college and all, because they never went, and being from a nowhere backwater like Wixburn, Pennsylvania, where nothing ever happens that doesn't involve rust and dry-rot;

where I am sitting now, (as I have been since ever I was born);

where I met Jason Hughes in the Washington Avenue Elementary School when we were both eight years old, and where ...

But this isn't all about me, and anyway, I was supposed to explain how the Beatles are involved in all this, the dismemberment of the United States.

So let's try again.

Jason and I used to be in a band, together, back in high school. I know, I know, here "I" come again, but it has something to do with the story (as you know, right?).

So, I was the rhythm guitarist and Jason was the bass guitarist in a group called One Hour's Practise (the "s" was Jason's idea), so named because that was exactly how much time we had together before we got up on stage in the cafeteria of Bishop O'Rigen's (closed now, as just about everything else is closed around here, except the pharmaceutical company), and played so well that ...

All right, all right!

Jason wanted to be a professional musician. He wasn't good enough. Or, he could have been good enough, but he didn't slog away at it as musicians must do in order to become real professionals. He was talented enough; had a good ear, and could even sight-read, and improvise, following the left hand of the keyboardist (when — to our misfortune — we had a keyboardist). ... He was just lazy.

He never married. He never traveled. He never left the house he was born in. He grew fat and flabby. And farsighted. Yes, that's important to the story. As is the fact that he kept on playing bass, as a hobby.

So here we have this flabby unmarried, farsighted bass player without a band. *Are you with me so far?* as Don Henley once interjected ...

One day, Jason took himself in hand. He started to run.

At first, he couldn't make it down to Pond Lane, barely half a mile away from his door, before he was doubled over, panting. But he didn't give up; he kept on at it, gradually getting up to three miles round trip, down Maplehurst to the highway, up to the Tom Thumb's to buy his *New York Daily News* (the carrot), and then back home around Pond Lane. By the time he was up to six miles, he'd lost thirty pounds — down from 225 to 195, and, for a big guy like Jason, who was over six feet, this was positively svelte.

At forty-five / fifty or so, he was fit again, healthy and happy.

He kept at his six-mile jogs every morning, up to and around the track at College Miserabile Dictu — oops, that's

Miserabile Dictu University these days, but old habits die hard — before his daily "commute" (if you can call it that) into the dying city of Wixburn, some eleven miles distant.

The morning in question — the fateful *Sgt. Pepper's* morning — he got up at seven, brushed his teeth, took a leak, put on his sweats, and jogged up to the Miserabile Dictu track through a steady drizzle.

He had his iPhone on shuffle. System of a Down, the Smiths, Cream, and a band nobody's ever heard of called Prime Minister Benjamin Disraeli and the Victorian Parliament (shortened to Dizzy and the Primos — who knows why? maybe they couldn't fit the whole thing on the album cover?) that Jason once discovered in some trash bin at the Sound Arcade (he was always grubbing through the discard racks — that's how he first came across Camel and Russia, too).

It was a string of familiar songs, some of which he'd known since the seventies, and he was ready for a change.

I'll buy myself Abbey Road, he thought, pulling the iPhone out of his sweat pants pocket.

Don't laugh. Of course, *Abbey Road* is nothing new to Jason Hughes. He had a copy of that, too, sure, but on vinyl; he didn't even have a stereo to play it on, any more, and he didn't have it on CD like *Sgt. Pepper's*, so he couldn't listen to it on his iPhone and that's why he wanted to buy it.

And as part of his continuing love affair with the bass, he was learning the riffs of his favorite bassists, from start to finish. He'd just gone through Roger Waters and Andy Rourke, was casting longing eyes, tentatively, towards

Flea, and at the time about which we are speaking, he was working his way through McCartney. All of the songs on the *Beatles 1* album, to be exact. Now, the suite of songs on the B side of *Abbey Road* is not on that album, because they were never released as singles, to say nothing about charting at number 1.

Having heard McCartney's bass on that part from "Golden Slumbers" through "Carry that Weight" on WNKR 106.5, "The Rock" one night, he wanted to give it a closer listen, run it through Riff Master maybe, get a bass tab from Songsterr or whatever, but — to speak the truth — he just wanted the simple pleasure of having something new to listen to on a run when his forty-five/fifty-year-old knees were getting creaky and tired and he was getting cranky.

Oh, dear.

Do they have to show that?

What?

On the television across the hall. That little patch of green park near the Pike Place Market in Seattle. A pack of dogs pulling at the corpse — I hope it's the corpse — of a homeless person. And dragging it across the street, past the overturned police car …

What?

Of course, it disturbs me!

It's disturbing.

Must the camera zoom in on the radiation burns on that golden retriever?

Aren't you disturbed?

OK, so where were we?

Abbey Road. Yeah.

So, he pulled out the iPhone, as I said, and as he trudged around the track (trying not to crush all the earthworms that had crawled out onto the rubber surface under the influence of the warm rain), he keyed in "Beatles" — and was surprised when "Beatphreak" came up on the search screen.

What the hell?

But it was raining, and he was farsighted, and he didn't wear his glasses while he was running, after all … so he swept the rain off the screen, erased "beatp" in the search bar, and tried again, squinting.

"Beatles."

There they were, their long feud with Apple (that of Cupertino, not Saville Row) now over; finally, the most successful and influential musicians of the twentieth century, available for purchase and download.

He tapped "See all" under albums and when he did, there it was, on the list, from top to bottom, *1* (which he had, again, imported from a CD given him back in the 90s by his weird chum, Emily), *Abbey Road*, and, underneath it, *Sgt. Pepper's Lonely Hearts Club Band*. He clicked the $12.99 box to the right of *Abbey Road* and was prompted to confirm the purchase by TouchID. Which he did, and it didn't work. Again he touched, and again, nothing. Well, it was raining. So he dried the home button against the inside pocket of his hoodie, dried his thumb, and — *ching!* the blue checkmark. Purchase complete.

But when he opened iTunes and clicked Play on his Recents screen. … what a surprise, when the first two bars of McCartney's insistent A-A-A-A-A-A-A-A C-C-C-C-C-C-C-C G ... etc., came thumping through his earbuds. Turns out, his farsighted eyes had not caught his thumb clicking on $12.99 to the right of *Sgt. Pepper's*, that is, beneath where it should have been clicking: on $12.99 to the right of *Abbey Road*.

And this is what led to tragedy.

And brought us together.

If it's not love, then it's the bomb, the bomb, the bomb, the bomb, the bomb, the bomb, the bomb that will bring us together ...

You're right, you're right.

Bad joke these days.

Tasteless.

I'll try to be a good boy from now on, out of respect for the dead.

Anyway, because although he went back to the iTunes store and bought *Abbey Road* (intending to write for a refund of *Sgt. Pepper's* at the first opportunity later), had he not made the mistake, he would not have wasted the five minutes it took him to get back to the store, dial up the album list, purchase the right one this time, and turn it on; "Here Comes the Sun" or maybe even "Because" or "You Never Give Me Your Money" would have been playing when Alison got in the car, and all this mess, this horrid bullshit, this tragedy that the papers and TV, the internet and the pulpits, are now full of, *would never have happened.*

So here we have my friend, Jason Hughes, who is not the monster you take him to be, peacefully tramping around the maroon rubber track at Miserabile Dictu University, in a steady drizzle, the monotony of the *slap-slap-slap* of his Nikes on the track alleviated, if not lifted entirely, by the genius of Paul McCartney's *Boom Boom ba da BOOM Boom D-D-G-A-F-D* up on the tenth and twelfth frets (what a master Paul is with those upper bass registers) that signal the oh-so-familiar first bars of "Come Together."

No, I'm not being a smartass! But thank you for listening so carefully. May I pull out my phone? Thanks ... So here are the lengths of the various songs on Side A of *Abbey Road:*

Come Together: 4:19
Something: 3:02
Maxwell's Silver Hammer: 3:27
Oh! Darling: 3:27 (another great bass part, by the way)
Octopus's Garden: 2:51
I Want You / She's so Heavy: 7:47 ...
Together, this gives us, what ... 24:53.

Now, in order to understand how the silly, random circumstance of wasting the first 4:19 of the album by the above-detailed sequence of mistaken events can lead to so great a tragedy as the assassination of the President of the United States and the subsequent nuclear annihilation of San Francisco (a far more fetching city than Wixburn, by the way; pity that the continent couldn't have been flipped by some sort of mammoth computer program like Photoshop, just before the missile struck!), we must understand that it is somewhat over a mile from Jason's front door to the

Miserabile Dictu track. He used to make sixteen laps of the track, which would get him up to five miles (with the run-up), at which the mile home from the track would get him to his goal of six before he showered, grabbed a cup of coffee from the battered percolator that remembered his mailman daddy and his own childhood years, locked his front door and trotted out to his car to begin the commute to work.

He'd decided on buying the album on the last quarter mile but one; he'd completed the purchase and began listening *Boom Boom ba da BOOM Boom* on his last one, slipped through the gate, jogged up through the parking lots and down Pond Lane, back up Maplehurst, arriving at his front door (he ran more or less a twelve-minute mile) just as "Oh! Darling" was coming to an end. There he paused the album, unlocked his door, pried off his sneakers in the mudroom, trudged up his stairs and into his shower.

At the exact same time, Alison Prickney was calling her Dad's cell phone.

Aha.

Alison Prickney worked with Jason at the pharmaceutical company (which said it would sue me if I mentioned it by name in association with Jason Hughes, so I'll just call it "the pharmaceutical company" or "the pharmaceutical company on Pennsylvania Avenue"). She was in Layout — no, I don't know why that made me chuckle just now, or then again, maybe I do; later, later … and so she worked in the same general department as Jason, Advertising and Design, headed by Billy Kowalski.

Billy?

Yeah.

But more about him later, too.

Alison's car had a flat. Two flats, as a matter of fact. She was sure it was the neighbors' kids who had let the air out of her rear driver's side and front passenger's side tires — because how could something like that happen all by itself? — but she couldn't prove it.

Why would they want to do something like that, you ask?

Well, because …

But let me tell you about that later, too.

We have to stick to the story, right?

So Alison had *flats*. Adding to that, she had never changed a tire in her life, but her Dad lived just a few miles away in Macktown, so she called him, but — of course! — he was at the Burger King in Raserville with his cronies, as he was every morning, and — of course! — he left the Tracfone she bought him in Walmart back home, and there was no use calling the landline because nobody was home since her Mom had left so many years ago, and … so she put on her overcoat and locked her front door and trudged down Hodge Lane in a black mood to Autumn St. and then down Mitchell to the bus stop at Finney's Pharmacy to catch the bus into town.

"The bus into town."

"Town" being Wixburn.

It's Wixburnese, or whatever you choose to call it.

Other local phrases are "tree" for "three" as in "Gimme two or tree a dose kilbassies, heyna?"

"Heyna" being a catchall phrase for "Will you?" or "Isn't that true?" or "You agree with me, don't you?"

It should also be pointed out that Wixburnians go "up da mall." Or, used to, before the opportunistic terrorist bombing that's got everybody quaking under their beds. As if there weren't more pressing matters to worry about.

But I'm getting away from my story again.

By the time that Alison Prickney got down to the bus stop outside Finney's Pharmacy, Jason had poured himself a large cup of that percolated coffee (way too strong, as always), grabbed his copy of *Bass Aerobics* that he'd taken to reading over lunch, stepped out into the drizzle, locked his front door, stepped out, I say, onto the flags leading to the garage, spun on his heel, returned, unlocked the front door, went back into the kitchen to make sure he'd turned off the gas under the percolator, and had time to notice the odd way that the house looked at him as if everything had become animated now that the master had left, and — *What's he doing back here?* the clock on the wall ticked to the radiator in the strange peaceful silence which belonged to them, and not to him; *Damned if I know* the radiator pinged back — spun again on his heel, exited and locked again the front door, traipsed down the flags, lifted the garage door without spilling his coffee, got into the Corolla, backed down the driveway pitted with old crumbly asphalt that he knew he should fix but never seemed to get around to (and now, of course, it's too late), and glided down the hill to lurch out into the traffic in the space between a Rav4 with a Rottweiler hanging out the back window and a Sheetz tanker truck rolling slowly upgrade as the Bluetooth located his phone and the first notes of "Octopus's Garden" began to bounce through the speakers.

I've already mentioned that Jason was unmarried, right? You should have intuited that the same holds for Alison Prickney since she always calls her father when something goes wrong — like flat tires in the morning, or a pilot light in the boiler that goes out, or the odd cockroach that, incongruously for such a clean person living in the semi-rural area of Sanantone (yep, that's what they named it back in the middle of the 19th century — "Our plans are as big as Texas!" is the unofficial town slogan), suddenly spills out of a pile of laundry pulled from the hamper — rather than a husband or live-in boyfriend (Oh, God Forbid the latter! But more of that later) armed with jack or matches or heavy boot, as the situation requires. The only beings she truly loves are her dogs. Hunter, and Dale, two long-suffering boxers whom she dresses up on every occasion — black masks and Superman costumes for Halloween, bunny ears and puffy tails (which Hunter spins around at in frothing fury, trying to tear off his butt — I'm told it's hilarious — for everybody except poor Hunter, that is — when the tail slips out of his grip and comes slapping down on the small of his back thanks to the elastic strap) for Easter, elves' caps or reindeer antlers for Christmas ...

Maybe it wasn't the neighbor's kids after all, who punctured the tires, but poor Hunter and Dale, taking out their revenge, at last, in this futile, but potentially satisfying manner?

Now, don't get me wrong. I love dogs as much as anyone. But dogs should be treated like dogs. Dogs *want* to be treated like dogs. No clothes, no booties, no fancy shampoos, and doggy beds — they want to roll around in crap and eat disgusting things and smell like themselves; they want to wear the fur coats God provided them with, and nothing else, which makes all sorts of immoral activity so dear to their hearts all the more easily performable, and not to be dressed up like those poor psychically abused little Southern girls at under-five beauty pageants.

Do I mind that shopkeepers set out bowls of water on the sidewalks outside their doors?

No.

Do I mind dogs being allowed in supermarkets?

No.

Do I mind hotels that cater to dogs?

Well, no, as long as it's not an all-room-dog-friendly sort of place, and I have to risk waking up in the morning with flea-bites.

But of course, I'm exaggerating. Americans are so nuts about their dogs that there's a better chance of *them* having fleas than their canine companions …

And the tone for that nuttiness is set by the Head Honcho down in DC, right?

I mean, dearly departed 48 hiring a long-distance doggie limousine service whenever he traveled by car — at how much of a cost to Joe Taxpayer?

I mean, sometimes, he wouldn't even take his wife (who could ride by his side); but he always took Ol' Beau along, and you and I were paying for it, bucko!

But that's another story.

I need to tell you about a different chauffeur and a different chauffeured, right?

So Jason caught sight of Alison through the wet thumping of his wipers as he pulled up at the light, right before the bus stop. He recognized her and wondered if she saw him and if she hadn't if he should just ignore her and go on his way when the light turned green ... I mean he had done so, several times in the past when he saw her standing there (and she didn't, or pretended not to, see him) ...

The thing is, Alison wasn't — isn't — bad looking. She's about five-four, with a tidy body, and a face ...

But I won't describe her.

That's what I learned from Lord Byron (on whom I wrote my dissertation at CUNY oh, twenty-five years ago, is it now?) If you remember, in *Don Juan* he never really describes Gulbayez. That's because he wants each of us to see in her our ideal of the most sexually attractive woman possible, and thus our wonder, or shock, or admiration, at Juan's refusal of her bed will be all the greater.

Yeah. I'm an egghead.

As you already know.

You know, you should work on that slight deprecating sneer when looking over a person's history in the files between your fingers. Or was that intended to be intimidation?

Anyway, when I got my degree, I made the fatal mistake of coming back to Wixburn to teach at Hanskung College — where I, and Jason, and Alison for that matter, all went to school — but later, later about all that …

Anyway, would Alison be your sexual ideal?

I. Don't. Know.

But — after Byron — picture her thus: a trim young woman with a pretty face, who wears skirts short and tight enough to turn the heads of balding men with flab spilling over their suit pants on sunny Thursdays on the Rondo in midtown, when they're at the funnel cake wagon and she's browsing the farmer's market.

If that's the case, why *isn't* she married?

Later. Later!

Today she was dressed in a short skirt, which could be seen since her pinkish raincoat was open (it was a warm day, if drizzly).

Is that why Jason decided to offer her a ride? Rolling down his window as he pulled up alongside the bus stop, and shouting out, "Hey, Alison!" and almost getting rear-ended by the Range Rover behind him (he stopped rather suddenly, while the light was green), "You want a ride in?" and the Range Rover beeped long and sharply and angrily before swerving around and bellowing out a dopplered, "Asshole!" as it swung past the Post Office and down 390.

A better question is, why did Alison get in?

Well, why wouldn't she, you ask, not knowing what I know, yet …

Was it because of the blare of horns? Did she want to put an end to the awkward situation, in which maybe the anger of the drivers behind Jason would suddenly be directed at her, somehow?

Or was it something else?

At any rate, she made a jerk-step forward, then back, and then plunged forward again, opened the passenger door of the Corolla, and got in, closing the door behind her, but first pulling down the hem of her skirt which had got hitched up a bit when she sat down, and covering it all with her pinkish raincoat.

"Thanks," she said.

"No problem," said Jason, lurching forward again, just as a car opposite was starting to make a left up the road towards Sanantone Hardware — again the angry blare of horns.

I should point out that drivers in Sanantone, in Wixburn, actually in the whole of the so-called Naxkohomen Valley of NEPA like to blare their horns at:

— Other drivers
— Joggers
— Cyclists
— People in Wheelchairs
— Mothers with strollers
— The Handicapped
— The Blind

and generally, any human being who dares to even attempt to share the road with them.

Animals have it worse. They just run them over. It must have something to do with their pent-up frustration of having to live in Sanantone, in Wixburn, or in the so-called Naxkohomen Valley of NEPA which Morrissey might as well have had in mind when he spoke of the (seaside) town that they forgot to bomb.

Well, at least that town of his had a sea.

Come, come, nuclear war …

Ah, but that joke isn't funny anymore, is it, to quote him of his Smiths days. Poor San Francisco …

She got in the car and "Octopus's Garden" was still playing.

Now, I wasn't in the car with them. And you, certainly, weren't. But you might suppose that the following happened:

"Oh, I like this song," Alison may have ventured, knowing it her duty to be polite, and make conversation.

"Do you?" replied Jason.

"Yeah. That and 'Yellow Submarine' are my favorites."

"Hmm," Jason said, also trying to be polite, and biting his tongue to stifle the urge of coming back with *Those are both Beatles throwaways, don't you think? You wonder why even Ringo would agree to do that sort of shtick. I mean, come on. They don't even have the Vaudeville cutesiness of 'When I'm Sixty-Four …'"* because whatever you or I think about Alison, (am I sexist? talking with you as if you were a heterosexual male? Be that as it may, let's let that be, let that be, for now at least …) she was lonely, and Jason was lonely, and she was (as we have said) decently attractive, and he was back in shape, tall, and decently attractive, could carry a tune (he sang all the Clash stuff we did way back when and a creditable Ronnie Van Zandt on the obligatory "Freebird, Freebird!").

"I'm more of a *White Album* person, myself. But anything the Beatles did is all right by me," and since he was stopped again at the light by Ferguson, he said as he turned to her and flashed her a smile.

I won't describe him either, ladies, though I know him since back when he would share the fries that his Dad brought him from Stop'n'Go for lunch when we were in the third grade.

You wouldn't be far off if you saw a young Brad Pitt around the mouth.

Think *Dark Side of the Sun.*

Without the skin condition.

Not that I'm queer or anything, as if that matters.

But I have a good eye for beauty, I think, and I'm not ashamed of it.

The light turned green, and on they went, as Alison (for who knows what reason?) turned a little red and let that pink raincoat slide open and reveal those knees, those three or four inches stretching from the kneecaps to the hem of her dress … and both of them thinking if it would be out of line to ask what the other was doing for lunch? Or how one should go about asking the other out for dinner? Or …

And you might well suppose that this is what happened, but (as we now know), it wasn't.

Alison said nothing about "Octopus's Garden."

She just sat there, nervous, her nostrils flaring at the very faint aroma of Gucci that Jason had sprayed on his cheeks after shaving that morning, and Jason himself was turning a bit red, with a girl in his passenger's seat, a girl from work that he knew, but didn't really know, that was kind of cute but, *crap! He should have just driven on!* And, as it turned out, he *should* have just driven on, tensing his stomach muscles to suck in the flab that remained with him after sloughing those thirty pounds, and hoping, praying, that there would be no more red lights and he could skim into Wixburn and into his slot and turn off the car and get her out of the passenger's seat, himself out of the driver's seat, and both into work (he holding the door open, or not holding the door open, for her), his good deed done, and nevermore to drive this way to work, or at that hour, or …

I want you.

I want you so bad.

I want you.

I want you so bad, it's driving me mad, it's driving me mad, John Lennon began to sing, and out of the corner of his eye, Jason saw Alison tense and cock her head slightly towards him, her eyes wide, her body shifting farther away from him, up against the door, as they stopped at the light at Ferguson …

And Jason didn't quite know what to do. More or less out of habit (as he'd always press the fingertips of his left hand against the hard edge of his desk, or the table at lunch, to keep working up the callouses), he started going over an imaginary fretboard, the wrist of his left hand set against the steering wheel, those funky skips over the top three strings from the seventh to the ninth frets beginning around the twenty-eighth bar, and trying to fill in the dead air with.

"God, he fingered well."

Alison's eyes got bigger, moving from those four swaying fingers of his left hand like so many fat wriggling worms, to his eyes and his mouth (oh, why did you have to let your saliva pool at *that* moment, Jason my friend? He sucked it in, he thought, silently, but *she noticed* and interpreted it as *she would* — but more of that later ...)

"I wish I could finger as well as him."

The light turned green and Alison was just getting up the courage to say something like *I don't feel very comfortable with this conversation*, getting up the courage, I say, because she'd just accepted a ride from a coworker, and it wasn't like he'd placed his hand on her knee or anything,

"Oh! Do you hear that?" he asked, with authentic enthusiasm now, as the pattern repeated, reaching out and *giving her a nudge with his right wrist against her knee!* (something that he did so often with a friend in the passenger seat, or at the cafeteria, or on a park bench ...) but situation, situation, you innocent fool, my friend, poor Jason *you raver, you seer of visions, you painter, you piper, you ... prisoner ...*

She was saved from it all — (it was courageous nonetheless, wasn't it?) when she caught sight of her father's Lincoln Continental in the Burger King parking lot one light down 390 and said,

"Pull over into Burger King, please."

"What?"

"Pull over into the Burger King!"

It was hash-tag-me-too assertiveness in her voice now; this girl was *not* going to be a victim.

And he did.

"You, uh, you want me to wait?" he asked, leaning over to the open door, as she got out, wrapping the pinkish raincoat tightly around her torso and waist and thighs and fastening the belt.

"No."

And without a word of thanks, she strode across the wet macadam to the doors, beyond which she could see her father laughing with Arnie Lucchesi (who para-legaled in sneakers with Velcro straps) and John Simonovich, a third retiree who always had six PowerBall tickets sticking up out of the breast pocket of his coffee-stained Arrow shirts, sagging left under the weight of the plastic pocket-pen-protector from Howie Duke Wayne's Chrysler Dealership … which like everything in this dying, rotting, decrepit area had been closed since just about the flood of 1972.

The door had been slammed.

The door of the car, that is.

What, she don't like the Beatles? was the only thing that came to Jason at that moment.

He straightened up, drove around the drive-thru onto Center St., turned right down 390, and drove the rest of the way to work, alone.

And then.

He had just returned from his first coffee break at 11:45 when Billy Kowalski showed up at his desk, with two uniformed security guards (one of whom was obese and wheezing, the other thin, with exceptionally long nose hairs) and said: "Jason, take your things and come with us."

I see that now they're showing those horrible images of the destruction on Market St. on the TV across the way. The black greasy shadows that used to be people, splattered against the lower piers of the TransAmerica pyramid … I really ought to apologize for quoting "Every Day is Like Sunday."

I mean, not now.

It's like how they stopped playing "Chop Suey!" after 9/11.

What?

Yes of course I do expect you to believe this. I wish you would appreciate the fact that I am not explaining away the surprise North Korean attack as a mere coincidence, totally unrelated to the unfortunate, premature death of the President of the United States, which is what has brought us together here today. I am explaining a sequence of events, perhaps convoluted, but nonetheless logical; a *chain* of events of which, had any one of the numerous links been ruptured, the present Western border of these shrinking United States of America would not be wavering somewhere along the Ozarks.

It is all very clear to me and so I will thank you for not using that expletive of yours. I certainly do not have sh … excrement for brains — if you only knew how that *one* vulgarity, that *one and only* vulgarity, causes a veritably physical revulsion in me, and when launched at me unawares can have unexpected consequences, well … Thank you. I am no prude when it comes to the odd vulgar expression, but … As I said, everything is linked together. And if you will allow me to continue, doing your best to pay attention as I follow the thread that is passing through my fingers, all will become clear in the end.

That's why we're here, right?

So then.

What was it that freaked her out?

She would say, she *said*, that Jason made an unwelcome sexual advance to her in the car.

And that was that.

Of course, the Beatles were a part of it.

I should also say that I know for a fact that Jason was hesitating between *Abbey Road* and *Magical Mystery Tour* (a better all-around record, when you come right down to it). Had "Penny Lane" been playing (again, *excellent* bass opening — starting with the sixteenth fret on the top two strings! Brilliant!) instead of "I Want You," Coit Tower would not be lying on its side today.

Lennon is a bad boy, all right, but McCartney?

Who can get mad at Paul?

I read somewhere that someone said "Apple was thought up by Paul. Fresh, good for your teeth, your circulation, keeps the doctor away," to say nothing of ICBMs.

But Lennon is a bad boy.

At least to people like Alison Prickney.

I've never seen anyone so hypersensitive to music in a *bad* way. I mean, we all don't have to like the same things, right? but can you imagine a fifteen-year-old girl delivering a theme paper in AP English — with a straight face — suggesting that "The diabolical element in rock 'n' roll music is not a myth. It has been scientifically proven that the insistent beat of rock 'n' roll music subliminally encourages sexual promiscuity and that urban neighborhoods with high concentrations of record stores and rock 'n' roll venues have been shown, statistically, to suffer from a disproportionate amount of criminal activity."

I can.

I was in Mr. Easton's AP English class at O'Rigen when the paper was read aloud. And on deck — me, with an *explication de texte* of the entirety of *Dark Side of the Moon*. "The papers hold their folded faces to the floor / And every day the paperboy brings more."

Dude.

That's poetry no matter how you slice it.

Take it from me.

It's my job to tell people what poetry is.

Or, it was …

Oh and then later — don't ask me why — I surfed onto a local chatroom on PAHomeboys.com, where clicking from here to there got a person onto a section called "Contemporary Christian Music." And one of the posts — signed "Queenswoman" — was excoriating Peter Townshend (twenty-five years after *Empty Glass*, for God's sake, no pun intended) for "And I Moved," which (in her opinion) "blasphemously associates the Good Lord with liberal homosexual permissiveness." Now, however, she came to understand the subject of the song who is described as

[…] standing in the doorway
His figure merely filled the space

to be Our Lord and Savior Jesus Christ I never will understand (one of the reasons that it's dangerous, really dangerous, for the uninitiated to discuss the literary merits of pop lyrics), and why He — nor I, nor I dare say Pete Townshend would ever suggest this — would be the person spoken of as having "lain [the narrator] back just like an empty dress," and why that gorgeous line must be indicative of sexual promiscuity, liberal or conservative, homosexual or missionary, well, I just haven't the foggiest. But then the strange thing — maybe, in retrospect, actually logical, for don't we excoriate publicly our private longings? — she went on to say "and it's a pity, really, because it's a catchy tune, and I'd like to listen to it, but, I just can't. It's sinful."

There followed a series of posts from the like-minded in support of her, with references to similar passages in the work of Townshend, from "Rough Boys" on the same album to "Tommy, can you feel me?" and the obligatory "Well, there's nothing wrong with music and you shouldn't be too hard on yourself. It's like dieting. Replace. Toss the chips and replace them with rice cakes. Get rid of the Who (who needs 'em?) and have a listen to Raze, White Heart, Dogwood …"

I couldn't resist. I tried. But I signed up to the list, under the name "Queen," and wrote "Can you people grab some vaseline already and slide out the stick you've got jammed up your ass? It's only music! You think Jesus has nothing more important to worry about than Peter Townshend's lyrics? Time for you all to lay someone back like an empty dress and unblock your neuroses."

It wasn't published. Got a pink slip at the email alias I had specially created for the purpose, informing me of its inappropriate content.

So these are all just bricks in the wall, so to speak, leading to the radioactive contamination of the Embarcadero, and if we're looking for whose fault it is that Alison Prickney played her irreplaceable role in that chain of events, we also ought to blame Damon Albarn.

Or Morrissey.

To show you why I've got to take you to the Christmas party. The one that Jason played at.

I wasn't there.

Not on stage I mean, and I did come to regret it, but that's the way things turn out, after all. But I was *there*, in the crowd.

He called me in November. November 1 to be precise.

Creepy, no?

In hindsight?

"Hey," the voice said.

"Hello?" I ventured.

"Ray? It's Jason."

"Jason?"

"Jason Hughes. Remember me?"

"Ooohhh yeah, Jason! What do you mean, man, 'do I remember you?' Shit, Jason, how's it going? How's it *been* going? How long has it been, man?"

And other such stuff that you might think insincere, but it was a nice surprise, in a weird sort of way, after almost thirty years. I didn't find out anything about how it had been going with Jason, of course, because that's the way Jason is. He gets right to the point.

"You wanna get back together?"

"Back together? Like in, for a drink or something?"

A knock came on my office door. It was a kid from my freshman comp class with a Nirvana t-shirt. I motioned him to sit down.

"Nah, man. I mean the band!" Jason explained. "I got a gig for us, whaddya say?"

"The band?" I said, "Our band? A gig?"

Any other person would have thought I was deaf. Of course, I was just putting on the Ritz for the Kurt Cobain wannabe with his illegible first draft of a paper he didn't want to write and I didn't want to read.

I often have the urge to say to my students, or at least to some of them, *Hey. You want a diploma from Hanskung College. I want to be able to buy my groceries. Let's set aside all the bullshit about the humanities and making you a better person by writing a 500-word essay on your first job in something we with temerity refer to as the language of Shakespeare. You keep having your Daddy pay the tuition, I'll give you the A you want, and we're quits, OK? I'm sure we both have better things to do with our time …*

But that's another story altogether.

Our band? a Gig? like, me on guitar again? anybody else would have thought I was simpleminded. But not Jason …

Patience. There is a point to all this.

"Yeah, man! One Hour's Practise, stepping into the New Century!" he laughed. "I talked to Dave and Rick, and they're on board."

"What sort of gig?"

"Just fun, you know. I'm working at …" *Ahem.* "… the pharmaceutical plant on Pennsylvania. We're having a Christmas Party on the 18th of December, and I offered to play it. Well?"

"For nothing?"

"What, you hard up for money or something? It says on LinkedIn that you're a professor. Just for fun!"

"Gee, I dunno," I said, milking the situation in front of a kid who — far from staring open-mouthed in awe (*Duuuude — you rock out?!*) was clacking away in boredom at his telephone screen, exhaling little puffs of smirky laughter from time to time at a joke only he was privy to, "besides, it's bad luck to add a new member to the band. Remember what happened to us when we added Ron Bednina before the gig at —"

"You're so fucking superstitious. And anyway — it wouldn't be adding a new member. You're an *old* member. You're a *founding* member!"

"Nah, I don't think so, man. I've forgotten just about …"

"OK then, no problem. Me and Dave and Rick can do it as a trio. It'll be like it was when you left the band."

Ouch.

But he's right. That was what they did when I left the band. And they got on pretty well for a couple more years until Dave knocked up Sarah and Rick got so deep into drugs that he would only play left-handed, and that, of course, could only end up one way. A baby and a curfew are one thing, but Jimi Hendrix, there's only one Jimi Hendrix. *Nascitur,* you know? ...

He said it matter of factly, no, in the same happy tone he was using when he first called.

I've often wondered if Jason was autistic. But that's also another question.

"Look though," he said, "anyway if you want, drop over on the 18th. Tell the guy at the gate that I invited you. There'll be a crowd, not just us drones with the badges. I know the guys would love to see you again ..."

And I did go. I don't know why. Or maybe I do. Let's just say that I put my Epiphone in the trunk, *just in case,* but wasn't bold enough to take it in hand when I headed off to the rec area in the pharma factory.

There was a crowd. A lot of people. Most of them in jeans or outside clothes that you wouldn't wear to work, guests I suppose, and rocking under the crazy sway reflectors as OHP, my boys, were cranking out a very creditable rendition of "Rock the Casbah."

As soon as I caught sight of them, I was glad I came. Dave was in the back walloping away at the kit that still had OHP scrawled in green glitter across the front of the bass drum; Rick — *holy shit!* In a dog collar, open at the throat? — Not a Sid Vicious dog collar, mind you, but a clerical collar.

Turned out that he cleaned himself up, and did a Dave Hope.

Who?

The bassist from Kansas ...

No, not the state, the band ...

He'd been ordained a priest of some Anglo-Catholic church down by the hospital and had come right over after an Advent meeting with his bishop. Still whanging away at that stripy Van Halenesque Frankenstrat and pounding his legs in Vs like Tommy Shaw ... And Jason was there, stage left, with the biggest surprise: a midnight blue Rickenbacker 4003 he'd always lusted after back in the day when he was playing Kents and the most affordable P-Bass knockoffs ... There he was, paddling over the upper registers on the chorus, every inch a Topper Headon (Yeah. That's his bass riff, not Simonon's).

They went through a whole repertoire of stuff that I remembered we did, from REO's "Back on the Road Again" through the Jam's "Eton Rifles" and Badfinger's "No Matter What" — which used to be *my* song, and by then I was so psyched that I was about to go out to the car and get the ax and ...

But then, after the briefest of pauses, Jason started playing the handspan stretching bop of Blur's "Boys and Girls," and Rick and Dave joined in seamlessly, and I felt old, so old. They were no younger than me, of course, but they were a group, a team, together ... It was obvious that they were miles ahead of me ... Like, there weren't any keyboards up there with them, and it still sounded *good*. It wasn't just that they'd had more than one hour to practice since Jason's November

1st brainstorm …They were tight. Caught a ghost, all three. And wailing away at stuff that I didn't know. I wasn't about to get up on stage and look like an idiot. I was even debating whether or not I would go up and say hi to them at all.

That's when I saw her.

She was standing right next to me.

Well, one girl over.

We were at the bar, in the back; I was waiting on my Bloody Wetback.

What's that?

A local drink. Four parts rum, two parts tequila, a spritz of lime and sriracha — served warm. Traditionally, the bartender turns his back on you before serving and gyrates his hips — using his Johnson as a swizzle stick.

No, not kidding.

Not sure how the tradition got started, or what it means … and of course, it's probably not *really* done. Not *always* done … But that's another story.

It was Rick singing:

Looking for
Girls who are boys
Who like boys to be girls
Who do boys like they're girls
Who do girls like they're boys
Always should be someone you really love …

"Well, *theeyyyy* haven't changed, I see," I heard her say.

No mistaking that nasal whine which, — believe it or not, in Alison's mouth is fetching in an odd sort of way.

Could that be her?

And if it was, did I want to make my presence known?

It was crowded enough; I didn't have to. I tilted my head a bit past the taller girl with the straight black hair who was standing between us, and, yep, no mistaking it: Alison Prickney.

Just like Jason, I'd known her since third grade at Washington Ave. school.

Come to think of it, is there anyone still around here, slowly dying, in this slowly dying city, that I *don't* know since third grade?

I was once at a birthday party of hers when she lived in Countyline and we were about fourteen ... but more of that later.

There she was, still short and thin and tight in all the right senses of that word — which might have led you to believe, those of you who *didn't* go to Washington Ave. grade school and are just passing through the strip mine known as Northeastern Pennsylvania — that sparks might have flown between my two old schoolmates at that rainy bus stop.

See, I once had a thing for Alison Prickney.

Back at O'Rigen.

I mean, she filled out real nice when she was sixteen. All the curves in all the right places, and thick curly hair, a pretty foxy-shaped face ... No, I'm not going to describe her.

Again, she is *such* a contradiction, that I ought to let you picture your *donna ideale* here, to make that contradiction all the more baffling. But I can remind you of what she looked like in her school uniform. Doesn't take too much imagination. She wore that grayish-blue plaid skirt a few good inches above her knees; it was tight around her shapely ass, as tight as that white blouse around her nice full tits, that hourglass figure only all the more accentuated when she had a tight blue cardigan buttoned over it (reaching only to her slim waist) — the perfect fantasy of the Catholic school girl — perfectly appropriate for Catholic school boys, and criminally creepy for Dad-age baldies.

Remember that video with Britney Spears when she's dressed in that schoolgirl uniform?

She was on the cover of *Rolling Stone* back in the day; this must've been in the '90s, and I was driving to work, listening to WNKR 106.5 "The Rock," and the DJ misspoke with "Britney Spears and the Rolling Stones," and then *ahem* "extricated" himself with something like "Britney Spears on the cover of *Rolling Stone*, I mean. Not Brittney Spears getting it on with the Rolling Stones ... But then again, I mean, in that schoolgirl getup maybe? Hell, I'd pay to see that ..." Welcome to Northeastern Pennsylvania.

> Avoiding all work
> Because there's none available
> Like battery thinkers
> Count your thoughts
> On one-two-three-four-five fingers
> Nothing is wasted

Only reproduced
You get nasty blisters
Du bist sehr schan
But we haven't been introduced

Yep, that was her all right, and she hadn't changed much, although my tastes, of course, had. And that reminds me of the last time I saw her. We were about four years out of high school; this was, maybe, that long-awaited year 1984, when everything could have changed, we thought, but no bangs, only whimpers ...

Yeah, sorry. I just keep putting my foot in it, right?

Inappropriate, what with "our boys" retreating on all fronts in the Southwest, as the Mexican government takes advantage of the recent chaos to nullify the treaty of Guadalupe Hidalgo ...

So, 1984, we're all, what? twenty-two? And me and Rick and Jason have eight beers each in us and we pull into the parking lot of a place called Station A up by the old Schweinharn brewery, on Pennsylvania Ave, not far from where they built the pharmaceutical company I'm not sup-posed to name — Station A (so-called because it was in a refurbished railway station) was this bar with a dance floor that stayed open for, like, a month and a half (Wixburnians having no idea what a night club is for) — and who do we see but Alison Prickney, done up — like half the other girls in Wixburn in 1984, like Madonna as photographed by Helmut Werb (the other half would dress up like Cyndi Lauper ... no, who am I kidding? this is *Wixburn* after all), like Kate Bush on the cover of *The Dreaming*, only, Alison Prickney could pull it off, man.

And so I disengage from my bandmates and shamble over to Alison who catches sight of me and sends a frown-smile in my general direction with something like "Which are you tonight? the middle man?" And that didn't bother me, because I'd had eight beers already and she really could pull off the Madonna look back then and ...

I was thinking about this at that moment, sipping on my Bloody Wetback, wondering all the time if I should reveal myself to her or not, and if not, maybe I should go, when OHP made a quick turn into "You Handsome Devil," which *was another of my songs!* and maybe if I had accepted the invite from Jason on November 1st it would have been *me* singing up there, as I used to do in the old days, and not Jason, and then, of course, Tucson would not have been overrun within six hours of the Ejército Mexicano crossing the border, and San Diego within forty-eight, after the tense standoff at the Naval Base when Admiral Bronson, faced with overwhelming odds, did what he had to do and surrendered to General Cabrera, saving in this way untold lives, civilian and military ...

All the streets are crammed with things
Eager to be held
I know what hands are for
And I'd like to help myself
You ask me the time
But I sense something more

And I would like to give
What I think you're asking for
You handsome devil
Oh, you handsome devil
Let me get my hands
On your mammary glands
And let me get your head
On the conjugal bed

Jason sang, doing a decent job of it (he is the most musical of us all, but lazy, God so lazy!) although it should have been me ... and the people on the linoleum of the rec hall are bopping and swaying beneath the reflectors and the sound is churning out of the Peaveys as it ought to be and the chick next to me is also starting to jive and over the sound of the band I hear her say to Alison, "They're not bad, are they?"

"Not if you like perverts," came the reply.

"You don't like the Smiths?"

"If you're asking me whether I like the subliminal glorification of perverse sexual permissiveness, then, no."

(See? I was right. She *was* "Queenswoman." Plus ça change, plus c'est la même chose, as Geddy Lee would screech). That made up my mind.

"Hey Alison," I said, turning to her, and smiled to see her eyes grow wide in recognition.

But instead of "Hey, Ray! Long time no see! What're you doing here?" and stuff like that that you or I would say to somebody in this situation, she stifled her initial surprise or whatever was elicited by my sudden materialization, and re-found her sea legs.

She said, "Well. Gray. Speak of the devil. Suzy, this is my ... This is Gray."

Freudian slip with that unfinished "this is my ...?"

I said she was conflicted.

But it's pure Alison Prickney to unapologetically use the nickname applied to me in middle school.

Gray. Gay Ray, get it?

Can't say she's not smart, in a devious sort of way. She was just baiting, just waiting for black-haired Suzy to say something like "Gray? That's an odd name" (although really? Remember Gray Davis?) Didn't work, though. All Suzy said, extending her hand was, "Hi! I'm Suzy." And then, to Alison, wittily or not, "a *handsome* devil, at least." "Don't bother," grinded Alison, "he's not interested in girls." But still, Suzy was unfazed. How times have changed. "You're gay?" she asked.

"O, like that subliminal glorificator of sexual permissiveness," I smiled, nodding towards the stage, "I'm what you might call humasexual. I'm attracted to human beings."

"Oh!" said Suzy, with a pretty smile, and (I'm not imagining things) she barely, but perceptibly, shifted her body closer into my personal space.

What would have happened had Jason tapped *Suzy* on her thigh in the passenger seat of his Corolla to the tormentedly yearning strains of "I Want You / She's so Heavy?"

Well, for one thing, the Governor and State Legislators of Utah would *not* have committed mass suicide in Mormon underwear beneath the Rotunda of the state capitol in Salt Lake, surrounded on the exterior by the divisions commanded by Colonel Obregon, determining "never to cede the sacred soil of Deseret to the forces of Mexican oppression."

But Alison was not giving up.

"How come you're not up there with your boyfriends?"

"You're a musician too?" Suzy smiled.

"Guilty. Used to play guitar with them. Jason and I — the bass player — went to high school with Alison here. We were tight once."

"Gray here and Jason, that is," Alison hastened to interject. "Real tight you were, weren't you?"

"Only once," I said, getting pissed off already, but keeping the smarm in place. "Jason didn't cotton to it, but I, well, I just can't forget …"

And Suzy laughed, and put her hand on my forearm, and was about, I bet, to share her number with me or ask me for mine, or … When, all of a sudden, Jason had the band do another sharp turn on a dime and the rhythm shifted from 160 bpm British new wave to Tex-Mex (Jason was in his element. I don't know if OHP were "back," but if so, he was now the leader and was getting to do what I didn't let him do way back when: those tight asymmetrical turns-on-a-dime during sets. Always bugged him that anal way I liked to order things, so frightened of improvisation … Dear God, do I

have more in common with Alison Prickney than I'm willing
to admit?) and it worked, I must confess … Maná, another
find of Jason's, and he letting his Hispanic side loose:

> *Ya me gritaron mil veces que me regrese*
> *A mi tierra por que aquí no quepo yo*
> *Quiero recordarlo al gringo*
> *Yo no cruce la frontera la frontera me cruzo*
> *América nació libre el hombre la dividió*
>
> *Ellos pintaron la raya*
> *Para que yo la brincara*
> *Y me llaman invasor*
> *Es un error bien marcado nos quitaron ocho estados*
> *Quien es aquí el invasor*
> *Soy extranjero en mi tierra y no vengo a darles guerra*
> *Soy hombre trabajador*

But further invasion of private space Ray-ward or even
Suzy-ward was precluded right about then, by Alison of
course.

Yeah, it was this bouncy tune, originally by Los Tigres
del Norte that turned the trick. Even though it was dark
in here — they had hung the windows with drapes for
atmosphere — I saw the blood flush into Alison's face.

But before I go any further with this, I ought to explain
why Jason was singing in Spanish, and just as fluently as if
he were Fher Olvera himself. There are a lot of Hispanics
in NEPA these days (and even though President Paz has

publicly stated that "the Mexican Government is committed to respecting the territorial integrity of the traditional Anglo core of the United States of America, and has no plans of readmitting any territories to the United Mexican States save those which were torn from her living body in the nineteenth century," you're probably going to be seeing a lot more, and very shortly), back when Jason and Alison and I were in high school, there weren't many of us.

Yeah, us.

Of course, you know me as Ray Verano — my parents came here from Guadalajara by way of Papi's route to citizenship through the U.S. Army, which brought him at one point in the late fifties to Hannatoto Army Depot, and Jason's mother is named Verano, too. (Yeah, we're cousins).

There weren't many of us back then, I say — along with Gray, another of my tender middle-school nicknames was The Spic who Licks Dick — and we were either cool, or funny, or exotic, or dangerous, depending on who you're referencing here; in the last case, that group would definitely include Alison Prickney's mother, but more of that, later.

I don't want to get too far off track.

So this will serve to explain why Alison turned crimson at the strains of "Somos más Americanos," even though Spanish was never her strong suit.

No, I stand corrected.

She aced Spanish.

I know, because she was in Spanish with me all four years at O'Rigen. Jason and I took it (still not sure how they let us) for an easy pass, it being something of a maternal language to both of us, but Alison worked at it, like she did everything else, and honor rolled herself into the State Foreign Language Olympiad as the difficult hormonal years of high school rolled by.

You should also know — although I must make a slight digression here — that she actively campaigned on the Congressional staff of Lolo Vendetta (*Go, Lo!* remember? Sometimes lengthened to the unofficial *Make'm all Go, Lo!*), former alderman of a nearby city that was experiencing an influx of Hispanics, documented and otherwise, who ran (and won) on a platform of "these people are coming into our area, not paying taxes, overburdening our social services, putting an extra strain on our police ..." etc., etc., etc.

She was also an early and fervent supporter of the 45th president of the United States, and (according to Billy Kowalski, said Jason — Billy, who shared Alison's suspicions and, yes, would have liked to share even more than that) *cried for three days* when number 46 began dismantling the border wall that had been constructed at such enormous cost to the American taxpayer, and had quickly become economically unfeasible to finish, police, or maintain.

"White guilt!" Alison suddenly cried out towards the stage over the melodic hubbub, to which a crowd of presumably guilty whites were bopping happily over the dance floor.

Because no one had heard her, she turned to Suzy (who, at her friend's outburst, had discreetly raised her eyebrows in my direction), and said, "This stuff I can't stomach! Eleven million illegals in this country! And you know why these bleeding-heart liberals are letting them in? Because they're easy. Yeah, that's right, you heard me right, they're easy. Did you know that girls as young as fourteen are forced into prostitution in Mexico by their parents?"

So, I was about to say (against my better judgment), *is it them who are the rapists? Or is it us who are raping them? Which victim do you want to blame here?* But then the crisis (so, it's Enrique Valencia's fault!) happened, as Jason reached the refrain, which even those with less high school Spanish than Alison could understand:

> *Y si no miente la historia,*
> *Aquí se asentó la gloria la poderosa nación*
> *Entre guerreros valientes, indios de dos continentes*
> *Mezclados con español*
> *Y si a los siglos nos vamos, somos mas americanos,*
> *Somos mas americanos, que el hijo del anglo-saxon*

That was too much for Alison. She fumed her way through the song, pulling on her coat (which she had draped over a chair and patting down her coat pockets for her keys, and chattering irritatedly at Suzy about "I'm off. If you still need that ride, let's go," and Suzy shrugging and making eyes at me and wanting to stick around and looking for me to offer her a lift instead of Alison when suddenly the music stopped, right at maybe the wrong moment for Alison? or the right moment? because in the pause between the last thump and the applause she screamed out:

"REBUILD THE WALL!"

and everybody heard her (some clapped, one or two booed, somebody said "Right on!" and tried to get a chant up "Wall Wall Rebuild the Wall!" which died out anemically after one or two halfhearted choruses.)

Jason heard the voice (though he didn't know who had shouted it) and he responded with spirit

"Good morning, worm your honor!"

Some people laughed, but I saw (as she grabbed Suzy by the hand and dragged her toward the exit, precluding my offer of a ride, which I would have tendered) … I saw Alison shiver.

The band then launched into "The Handler" (which makes absolute sense, what with those *gorgeous* runs around bar 30 from the seventh to fourteenth frets) and I knew there was nothing else for me to do here.

So, Alison shivered, as I said.

It's about the worms.

I'll tell you why in a moment.

Because even after she'd pulled Suzy away, I was about to follow them out and offer Suzy a ride home if she wanted to stay and listen to the whole set and have a few drinks and maybe get my Epiphone out of the trunk anyway and get up on stage and convince Jason (why not? an invitation's and invitation, isn't it?) to reprise "This Charming Man" and "William, it was Really Nothing," when Billy Kowalski (who had seen who it was who called out "Rebuild the wall" (and maybe was the one who tried to start the chant), also saw the hubbub around us and ran out himself, shouldering me aside and jostling my Bloody Wetback all over my shirt front.

Wetback on Wetback I thought involuntarily.

Alison would approve.

But before I do tell you about those worms, I need to point out that Billy Kowalski is also to blame for Cuba's lightning-quick annexation of the Florida Keys, Miami, and the southern portion of the state up to and including Route 70 (which, if not with the prior knowledge of Mexico, was at least facilitated, and tacitly condoned, by their invasion of the Western and Southwestern States — or Alta California and El Norte as they are now known, again), all of which was triggered by the assassination of the American president — something directly derivable from a rainy day in Sanantone, Pennsylvania, and an enthusiastic bass guitarist with hyperopia.

Why?

Because if Billy Kowalski didn't knee-jerk his response to Alison Prickney's hashtag-me-too-moment — no, if Billy Kowalski hadn't *hired* Alison Prickney in the first place — no, it's all about Billy Kowalski's neurotic OCD compulsion to *do the right thing*. As always, his devotion to doing the right thing is the direct result of once having done the wrong thing; in his case, a very wrong thing, and then spending a lifetime trying to cover it all up.

It happened this way.

No, I didn't go to school with Billy Kowalski. He's four years older than us — me, Jason, Dave, Rick, and

Alison — and was already two years past a terminal degree (AS) in Service Industry Management from that august institution of higher learning listed as Lanstrome County Community College in the tome *World of Learning* (which lists every institution of higher learning on the planet, from Cambridge to Lanstrome County Community College); the latter of which is known to the Gibbons-and-kielbassy denizens of NEPA as LCC, and, most aptly, to the snarkier amongst them as Last Chance College.

I met Billy when I was working part-time at a supermarket that was periodically flooded by a garbage-clogged creek out back.

No joke.

And when it flooded, we would close down temporarily while those of us who cared to get "time and a quarter" (right. Not even "time and a half," stingy bastards!) would cross the sloping shallow asphalt lake in a rowboat, hand-towel dry all the products we could reasonably still salvage (from canned soup to oranges and pears) and restock them for sale, once the dirty waters receded.

Billy Kowalski worked in the meat department. I remember once going back there on break to grab a soda from the meat cooler when he approached me with a long knife.

"Hey, Ray, c'mere. Lemme show ya sumpin."

And with a little more narrowing of the eyelids than I would consider quite healthy, he proceeded to plunge the knife into a side of beef hanging on a hook (his menthol cigarette dropping ashes down his white smock all the while), up to the hilt, again, and again.

"Feels just like you're stabbing somebody," he said. (*Did he have a hard-on?* I wondered, my eyes inadvertently dropping to a more pronounced bulge in the general region of his white-smocked groin).

"Here, give it a try," he said, offering the knife.

"Uh, no thanks, Bill," I said, grabbing my Dr. Pepper and going off to the Deli, where a girl named Lolita (again, no joke) worked. She had model-quality looks that couldn't even be marred by the red and white polyester spacesuits she was made to wear by the company back in the '80s, and so fucking stupid that I still wonder why she never made it big on the runway to become an advocate for elephants or land mine removal or elephants made to remove land mines.

At this time in my life, I pined for her, with passion unrequited.

Now, Billy Kowalski was passionate about more than one thing: his Corvette, Hall and Oates, Great Britain (more about that later), Hustler magazine, Barely Legal magazine, and, believe it or not, *acting* …

But more than anything else, he loved weaponry.

Bow hunting.

He could talk your ear off about communing with nature by skulking in some misty corner of the Pennsylvania woods and ending the life of this or that creature of God by hurtling an arrow at it from a distance and puncturing a skull or breast or any other appropriate quarter of its defenseless body.

Is Billy Kowalski a dick?

Indubitably.

A harmless dick?

I suppose that question is better posed to the odd doe or squirrel or side of beef.

Or, you judge for yourself.

After all, he *is* directly responsible for the fact that Cubavision Internacional now has its main broadcast studios on Calle Ocho, not all that far away from Marlins Stadium (today's Estadio Fidel Castro).

What has this got to do with my story?

I've just told you.

I'll make the connection clearer in a moment, but you've got to be patient.

When I first met him, Billy Kowalski was one of those ("wunna dem") denizens of NEPA who would "go up da mall" to buy "two or tree tings" at Sears or JC Penney's, and wash down his daily "kelbassy sammich" with a Gibbons or two. *Except* when he was on the boards of the Wixburn Little Theatre on West St. or the Gramophone Playhouse in Perryville. Then his diction would get sharp and take on a slightly indefinable quality that might, just might, be that of a British speaker trying to disguise his Britishness on this side of the Atlantic.

The greatest of his passions was (I kid you not) Shakespeare. His great dream was to play Shakespeare. His great disappointment in life was that the "theatrical" life of

NEPA was restricted to a revolving schedule of *Don't Drink the Water* and *Guys and Dolls*, with the NEPA ballet (yes, such a thing existed) breaking up the monotony, so to speak, with their annual Yuletide performance of *The Nutcracker Suite*. Which constituted their entire repertoire.

He always had a Penguin edition of one of Shakespeare's plays sticking out of his back pocket — even, I imagine, when he was stabbing the odd side of beef in the freezer — and always quoting the Bard like some idiot savant or strangely classically-wired sufferer of Tourette's syndrome.

The second great disappointment of his life was that he had to dress in fluorescent garb when stalking and piercing to death the animals of the Pennsylvania woods. How he would have liked to don his leathern-jerkin and green hose and stalk the timid deer!

No, I am not kidding.

He had jerkin and hose.

I've seen him wearing them.

At the time we're talking about (again the eighties, maybe 1988?) he was nearing the end of his career in the meat department of the swamp-musty supermarket, renting a small house on a triple lot in the Yonder Mountain area. He had neighbors to the left and right of him, but the houses were distant by nearly a quarter-mile in each direction. His front yard sloped down to a newly paved road (which once had been a dirt road, which once had been an Indian track), while his back yard stretched out into a dark copse of wood in the Yonder Mountains. There was a dirt road there out back, sometimes used by runners, sometimes by underage drinkers, between the woods and his yard, running parallel to the road in front of his house.

When the mood struck him, Billy would dress himself up in his Robin-Hoodesque costume, skip out into the back yard where, far away from the front road, he had set up a succession of targets, from pockmarked deer and bears to police-range thug targets — which on long winter nights, he spent hours adapting with acrylic paints into approximate semblances of sixteenth-century worthies.

"We must have bloody noses and crack'd crowns," he would exclaim, "And pass them current too. God's me, my horse!"

Thwack!

The arrow which had left his bow would bury itself into the breast of a square-jawed villain wearing a painted-on picadillo — or into the long grass and soft earth somewhere beyond its faux-velvet shoulder.

O war! thou son of hell,
Whom angry heavens do make their minister (he would orate when he was sure no one was listening)
Throw in the frozen bosoms of our part
Hot coals of vengeance! Let no soldier fly.
He that is truly dedicate to war
Hath no self-love, nor he that loves himself,
Hath not essentially but by circumstance
The name of valour.

Thwack!
Ftwhip!
"Uughchth!"
What the hell was that?

It was growing dark, about seven o'clock on an unusually warm early April evening, and probably a bit too dark for bows and arrows, *real* bows and arrows, especially for a marksman of the quality of Billy Kowalski, 60-65% of whose slings and arrows missed the mark entirely.

The third arrow in question that night — that which elicited the *Uughchth* after the first *Thwack* and second *Ftwhip* — had sailed blithely over the angry crest of a goon bearing the clumsily approximated arms of Medina Sidonia and buried itself in something solid, the sound of which (had he been close enough to hear it) would have reminded Billy of the *kschlipp* sort of sound emitted by the odd side of beef when punctured by his butcher's knife.

Instinctively, still gripping his bow, Billy rushed toward the dirt road running alongside his back yard and to his horror found that —

But you know what's ironic about it all?

At the time that it happened, he ought to have been 30,000 feet in the air, out over the Atlantic, on course for his first personal invasion of that demi-paradise, that fortress built by Nature for herself against infection, that precious stone set in the silver sea.

England, dude.

And why?

Well, that was Jason's fault.

Or, it would have been to Jason's credit, rather.

That's right.

The man who precipitated the entire chain of events leading to the first nuclear strike since 1945 and the dismemberment of the continental United States, was the very person who might have kept the status quo alive and kicking. How many chains of events have there been in the history of the world, which led to the *avoidance* of catastrophe? So many, perhaps. But — obviously — we will never know about them. In this case, however, I can tell you with perfect clarity and certainty how one such chain *might* have, *should* have, occurred.

At the time when Billy Kowalski was skipping around his backyard at dusk, urging on his imaginary troops, we all, Billy, me, and Jason too, worked in that supermarket. There was a breakroom upstairs that we never used, except when it was raining outside and the drain in the front of the main doors was clogged, effectively barring dry-shod passage to the Arthur Treachers across the lot, closer to the highway. (I'll always remember that place for once having eaten lunch there with Dora, a 40-odd bottle blonde dressed in the powder-blue and white polyester spacesuits of the cashier corps, who was skinny as a rail and looked to be 50-odd from all her chain-smoking, but who was happy all the time and once asked me "Do you think my tits are too small, Ray?"

Well. What do you say to that?

Dora smiled "Ah fuck it. More than a champagne glass is a waste, anyway.")

So, I'm sitting up there with Jason, who, on his first attempt at going meatless, had bought a slab of tofu and was trying to eat it, just like that — not knowing any better yet.

"Shit. Tastes like soggy styrofoam."

He was already in a bad mood (he had no more pocket money, was too proud to steal, and we only had twenty minutes to eat anyway).

"Here, let me have some of your …"

Pretzels, he was about to say, and I would have given him even half the pack, had he asked in time. But it just so happened that I had popped the last one into my mouth at that very moment and — in quite an unplanned way, but so seamlessly that it might have been a skit — had just crushed up the paper package and tossed it into the garbage can next to the soda machine.

I couldn't help but snort with laughter.

"Shiiiittt …" he groaned.

And just at that moment up the steps and into the breakroom comes Billy Kowalski in his white tunic, splattered with blood and smudged with cigarette ash.

"Hell is empty and all the devils are here!" quoth he, expansively.

"Fuck you, Billy," quoth Jason.

"Now now," he said, sitting down and lighting up a Camel, "God has given you one face, and you make yourself another!"

"I'm out of here," said Jason, rising.

"Then I too shall part," Billy went on, in a weirdly good mood, "For you draw me, you hard-hearted adamant; But yet you draw not iron, for my heart is true as steel. O, leave you your power to draw, and I shall have no power to follow you!"

"Speak English, you asshole!"

"English? that's *Shakespeare*, YOU asshole," Billy replied (now both of them were speaking the Wixburn dialect).

"Oh yeah?" said Jason.

"Yeah!" said Billy.

"Oh yeah?" said Jason again. "If you're so gay for Shakespeare, what the fuck are you doing, slicing cold cuts in Wartella's Market? Why aren't you somewhere being an actor or something, William Shakedick!"

"I do act …"

"Oh yeah. *Guys and Dolls*. And then *Don't Drink the Water*. And then *Guys and Dolls*. What a resume. The Laurence Olivier of shantytown!"

"You don't know nothin' about me!"

"I don't?"

"You don't."

"I know all I want to know. Why don't you go to fucking London or something where everybody's gay for Shakespeare and act *there*?"

Billy turned crimson, but then shot back,

"Where do you think I'm going on my vacation?"

"What?"

"Yeah. Next week. I'm taking a week next week. And I'm going to London. I'm going to meet with an agent."

"Horseshit!"

"Not horseshit. Honest to God truth!"

"Yeah, fuck you, Billy."

"Fuck you, Jason. I'll send you a postcard."

"I'll believe it when I see it."

"You want to see my ticket?"

This was becoming surprising.

"You have a ticket?"

"Yes."

"To London?"

"Yes."

"On you? Show me."

"Not on me, prick. It's at home. You working tomorrow?"

"I am."

"Well, I'll bring it in and show you, then."

"Hah" snorted Jason. "Right. Just don't fucking call in sick and hope I'll forget about it, Richard the Turd. I gotta punch back in."

And he was off down the steps to the timeclock.

I looked at Billy; Billy looked at me. He smiled a crooked sort of smile and gave out a little peep of a hiccup; Billy was in trouble.

So after work (having first organized a week's vacation with Bill the Manager (who once waved a glue-trapped mouse in front of my face "nya-nyaing" me, after word got to him that I would set off the traps so as to not see the mice he caught suffer — the springs were never strong enough to kill them at one go, and that bothered me), lying that his Uncle Leonard in Tampa was mortally ill, and only he out of all the nieces and nephews could possibly make his final hours bearable), he got in his white Corvette and screeched out of the parking lot doing a left on red to blaring horns

(Wixburnians most like blaring horns at other drivers), he tore a quarter mile down the road towards Edgarsville, screeching to a double-parked halt in the parking lot of Cameras Galore, and racing through the glass doors (a car turning into the Gateway Theatre i.e. movie house blared angrily at him — is that a record? getting flipped off twice, in the space of five minutes, once as a driver, and once as a pedestrian?) and threw himself into the Cameras Galore travel office five minutes before five; startling the cat-eyeglassed but for all that sexy Milly Tifflin who was dressed in a way too hot woolen skirt suit, blonde hair piled up over her still-fresh, thirty-five year-old oval face just as she closed her Rolodex.

"Phew!" said Billy, plopping down uninvited into the gray aluminum chair facing the family shot of Milly and John and little Michael and Jessica Tifflin. "I need a ticket to London."

"Can you come back tomorrow?"

"I can't. It's an emergency. A funeral."

Milly put her purse back down and sat down again, sympathetically.

"When will you be flying?" she asked, clicking on her white Tandy 1000 TL again, which was so big it hardly left room for anything else on her desk.

"April 2."

"That's a week away," said Milly, among the beeps and whirrs of her desktop computer and dot-matrix printer. Now that everything was powering up again, she'd stay and get the ticket for him. But she was just saying …

"He's not dead yet," Billy responded.

And Milly raised her eyebrows.

"But he will be," Billy riffed on ahead. "The doctors can't stop the bleeding. They can only … slow it down. All they're doing, me Mum says" (slipping into the most unconvincing British accent he could muster) "is pourin' buckets of it down the bog. Five days, a week, tops, and he's goin' to the angels …"

A fare is a fare, thought Milly.

"Name …?"

And less than fifteen minutes later, Billy Kowalski walked out of Cameras Galore travel, a fresh PanAm ticket from JFK to Heathrow in his sweaty hands.

"Watch where you're going, asshole!" beeped a punk in a brown Ford Pinto as Billy stepped off the curb in front of the store. (Actually, the punk in the Pinto had speeded up as soon as he saw Billy near the curb).

But Billy didn't mind.

He closed the driver's side door of the Corvette and sat in the hot interior (it was an exceptionally warm spring) for a moment before turning the key, putting it in drive, and joining the traffic flow up the back way home, "Fool for the City" blaring through his JBLs.

Thwack!

Ftwhip!

"Uughchth!"

What the hell was that?

Instinctively, still gripping his bow, Billy rushed toward the dirt road running alongside his back yard and to his horror found — "Holy Fuck! Holy Fuck! Holy FUCK!"

I bet if Alison Prickney had stuck with her plans to become a surveyor, she could have sized up the problem of the dip in the parking lot in front of Wartella's and advised the best way of leveling it out. It wouldn't have solved the problem of the creek out back flooding in the more torrential downpours, but she could have eliminated the lake out in front, which kept retirees and shoplifters — 83% of the population of Wixburn when taken together — away from Senior Citizen's and Five Finger sales days at the market.

Because that's what she wanted to do with her life — become a surveyor, not a layout artist — ha, ha! sorry, sorry! — in a pharmaceutical company in a department run by Billy Kowalski. She was always good in math (rumor had it, that she would entertain herself waiting for an appointment at the dentist's, or waiting on the bus, by mentally running through square roots) and she was especially good in geometry and geography. In the seventh grade, she once made the History teacher, Mr. Wallace, blush by correcting him: "Only a part of Russia is in Asia, Mr. Wallace. Eurasia is one continent, divided in two merely by convention. The Ural range splits Russia into a 'European' and an 'Asian' portion."

And she was right.

Even in fourth grade, she knew the capital of Burkina-Faso.

Do you know the capital of Burkina-Faso?

Look it up.

Yeah, that's what she wanted to do; that was her dream — to become a surveyor. And had she done so, I can guarantee that the United States of America would not have had, for the first time in its history, three presidents within the span of six months.

And she would have done so, if not for the worms.

But I was talking about the lake that would collect in front of Wartella's Market on especially rainy days, and the day in question was just such a rainy day: enough water had collected on the dippy macadam to keep most of the clients away, but not enough to close the store. There was nothing to do for Bill the Manager but to keep checking his glue traps and other instruments of rodent torture (they too were staying away); there was nothing for the employees on break to do but to eat in.

Jason had learned his lesson with the tofu. He was still sticking to his meatless thing, but this time he asked Lolita to fry him up some french fries down in the Deli, and thus was in a better mood when Billy came bounding up the steps and with a loud

"Holla, ye pampered jades of Asia!"

slapped the PanAm ticket down on the table in front of Jason, next to the sweaty white styrofoam container with the cooling and ever more soggy fries.

"What do you think of that?"

"I still think you're an asshole."

"But …!" he said grandly, "I'm an asshole with a ticket to London for the 2nd!"

"And your passport?" asked Jason.

His face draining white, Billy snatched up the ticket from the table, mumbled something incomprehensible, and ran back down the steps, as quickly as he'd run up.

It wasn't like he was even planning on going to London anyway.

As soon as his shift was over, he drove down to Cameras Galore again, leisurely this time, as he got out at four.

Have you ever tried to pull open a window or a door that you assume is open, but it's locked? If you're trying to pull up the plastic ledge of the window, or pulling against the slanted aluminum handle of a glass door, chances are your fingers will slip against it, your nails will catch at the edge, and it will be painful — so painful that chances are you'll kick against the door or punch the sash — and hurt another limb in the process …

That's what happened to Billy at Cameras Galore — it was a Saturday and the owner was Shomer Shabbat.

But he still had five or six days to try for a refund.

What with work and his bowling league at Chuckie's, though, and other little problems including a visit to a doctor who didn't know him, up in Caseytown (for a nasty rash in an embarrassing place), he wouldn't get back to Milly Tifflin until March 30.

"I thought you had a funeral in London?" she said when he told her what he had come for.

"I do. I did. I mean he didn't die."

"Well, that's good news."

"So, can I get a refund?"

"I'm sorry," Milly frowned, tapping her pencil's eraser against a Rubik's cube. "It's not our policy, it's the airline's. All sales final."

"But I don't need to go anymore!"

"Yeah, I understand. But look at it this way. Your uncle didn't die. That's good, right? So now you can go and visit him. I'm sure it'll perk him up. I mean, you must've been close, the way you were so panicked about buying the ticket in the first place …"

Billy left the store in a dejected mood, ticket in hand. He got back in the car and closed the door. He turned the ignition and punched off the cassette player with an angry fist when "Cat Scratch Fever" began to blare. He then drove home.

It happened on April 3.

Billy was on vacation.

At home.

He had to eat the 800 bucks for the ticket, but at least he showed that fucker, Jason. And now he had a week to do what he wanted. He pulled on his green tights — gingerly (the cream was starting to work, but the rashed skin was still tender) — and the leathern jerkin, and the cap, and bounced outside into his yard, jauntily whistling "What is a Youth," from Zeffirelli's *Romeo and Juliet*.

"We must have bloody noses and crack'd crowns," he exclaimed, stepping out onto the greensward, "And pass them current too. God's me, my horse!"

Thwack!

An arrow from his bow buried itself into the breast of a square-jawed villain wearing a painted-on picadillo.

Ftwhip!

The second one missed its mark and buried itself into the earth beyond a goon bearing the clumsily approximated arms of Medina Sidonia, whom Billy threatened with an angry address to Mars:

O war! thou son of hell,
Whom angry heavens do make their minister,
Throw in the frozen bosoms of our part
Hot coals of vengeance! Let no soldier fly.
He that is truly dedicate to war
Hath no self-love, nor he that loves himself,
Hath not essentially but by circumstance
The name of valour.

Again he strung his bow, again took aim, again he missed the mark.

"Uughchth!"

What the hell was that?

As you probably remember, the third arrow in question that night — that which elicited the *Uughchth* after the first *Thwack* and second *Ftwhip* — had also sailed blithely over the head of lucky Medina Sidonia and buried itself in something solid, the sound of which (had he been close enough to hear it) would have reminded Billy of the *kschlipp* sort of sound emitted by the odd side of beef when punctured by his butcher's knife.

Instinctively, still gripping his bow, Billy rushed toward the dirt road running alongside his back yard and to his horror found — "Holy Fuck! Holy Fuck! Holy FUCK!"

There had happened to be a stoner passing down the dirt path between Billy's back yard and the woods that evening, and instead of his panicked imprecations, Billy might have said, in the words of his favorite author, "I have shot mine arrow o'er the house / And hurt my brother."

Killed him, actually.

By the freakiest coincidence, the arching trajectory of the missile coincided perfectly with the vertical space occupied by the stoned kid; what is worse (or maybe better for him? the poor kid, that is?) it came into contact with him just as he was turning his face toward the sounds coming from Billy's direction. The arrow punctured his head, just above his right eye, through the soft flesh under the eye socket, entering his brain, and killing him instantly.

"Shit! Shit! Shit!" Billy said, spinning around and around on his axis, now looking down the dirt road, now up the dirt road, now into the woods, now back to his yard, now down at the corpse of the boy he'd just killed, and I mean *just* killed ... the rear wheel of the toppled white K-Mart ten-speed still spinning.

"Fuck man, fuck man!" said Billy, jostling the boy, "You dead? Are you dead?"

Although the boy in question couldn't make an answer, the evidence was irrefutable.

"Mother fucker!" said Billy, grabbing at his head.

What to do now?

Well, there are quite a few things a normal, upright, good person might do at such a tragic fork in the road.

But this is what Billy did.

He ran back home.

He ran up into his room.

He stripped off his Robin Hood costume, hopping on one foot as he pulled off his hose over his soft leather boot, losing his balance and falling hard onto his butt-cheek next to his bed, then pulling on (in this order) Jordache jeans, a too-small Keep On Truckin' T-shirt (over his feathered cap, he was in such a hurry!) and his python boots, without socks (*bad decision!*)

Then he opened his desk drawer and pushing through unopened Trojan ribbed condom packs, an assortment of unused rolling papers, and beer bottle caps, he pulled out his ticket to London.

"Fuck!"

It said, right there, "April 2."

He looked at his watch.

5:30.

He got in the Corvette and screeched out onto the street that led to the highway that led to Cameras Galore.

He was in luck. It was Monday, and this was the one night that the store was open until 9, to make up for the closure on the weekends (Saturday Sabbath, Sunday blue laws).

Milly Tiffin's mouth dropped open when she saw who rushed in.

Again.

"I need the ticket! For tomorrow! He's dead again!"

"Again …?"

"I mean now. I mean for the first time. I mean he's really dead! And I didn't go, but now I need to, tomorrow, tonight if I can! Here's the old ticket. Can I turn it in?"

Milly took the stiff crumple of paper gingerly in hand, turned to her computer screen, and clicked away.

"Well, the policy is that flights can only be changed before the original date of departure … But you're in luck. PanAm will allow you to reschedule, within forty-eight hours of a missed flight,

for a fee of two hundred and fifty dollars …"

"OK, OK!"

"But ah! You're in even better luck. Fees are waived for personal emergencies, among which are … funerals of close family members … All you need to do is to show me proof of your uncle's passing …"

"No time for that!" said Billy, pulling out of his back pocket the checkbook that he had, even in his panicked state, remembered to bring with him. He wrote out the check, and in a trice, had a new ticket to London.

"You mind if I ask you something?" said Tilly, barely repressing a titter as Billy stood up to leave.

"Huh?"

"The funeral … Is it in … Sherwood Forest?"

And Billy, following her eyes with his hand, pulled from his head the pointy green woodsman's cap with the flouncy feather.

"I'm an actor!" he said. "And anyway, it's not nice to make jokes about a personal tragedy!"

He spun on the heel of his python boot and marched out the door.

Tilly reddened behind her desk, because she was a polite person, and because Billy was right about that stupid joke.

It was dark when he pulled back up to his house. He shut off the headlights as he came up the freshly paved road and pulled onto his gravel drive. He left the ticket on the passenger's seat of his Corvette, stuffed it into his checkbook, and closed the door as silently as possible. He walked up the yard, slowly, and moved close to the dirt path. The boy and the bike were still there. No one, it seems, had come across them.

Billy went into his house through the back door. He put his hand on the kitchen light switch, but kept it there, hesitated, didn't turn it on; then he went up into his room with a green contractor's bag he'd taken from the kitchen pantry. Opening his closet, he pulled out all of his archery gear: the two other bows, the *crossbow* (sic), arrows, broken arrows, blunted arrows, wristguards, and spilled them all into the bag. He lugged this out into the hall, then paused, and returned for his costume, which he jammed in on top of it. What else? What else? He'd left the murderous bow and the quiver with the unused arrows out by the kitchen steps. He got them too and put them in the bag. Then he put the bag, tearing already, in the trunk of his car.

And then he thought — the targets?

And he ran up the yard again … But what could he do with them? They couldn't all fit in his car. And all the neighbors knew he was a bowhunter. Everyone who drove up the road saw the targets, the fake deer and bears, the goons modified to look like Spaniards from the Armada … He went back into the car, put the key in the ignition, and paused.

Shit. Fingerprints.

He went back up through the yard for the third time. He approached the black mass of slain humanity. Gave the cold right knee a little nudge with his foot — as if the fresh night air could have revived a person with an arrow sticking out of his right frontal lobe.

Still dead.

Billy took a deep breath and reached out for the arrow. He placed his foot against the boy's forehead and pulled. The arrow came out smoothly.

Fighting back an urge to retch, Billy turned on his toes and hastened back through the dark yard, dodging the targets like a ghoul darting amongst tombstones.

He was about to get into his car when another thought struck him. He went back to his back door, made sure it was locked, and then kicked hard against the door handle.

Nothing happened. *Oh fuck.*

He backed up, and kicked it again, harder; the jamb gave way this time, and the door swung open at a crazy angle.

Then he got in his car, turned on the ignition, and without turning on his lights or stepping too loudly on the gas, pulled out on the road and set off for Queens.

As he drove through Sanantone, he passed through Sanantone Corners. This is where, that same day, Alison Prickney's career as a surveyor had come to an end.

It had been decided — this was back in 1988, '89, mind — that the stoplights at this intersection of five roads should be replaced with a roundabout. It would only take six to eight months, the town planners said, to get this done. After all, who can get big things done, if not Sanantonians?

First, the area had to be surveyed. Alison, who was in her second semester in the AS Surveying Program at LCC, was out with a crew getting some practical experience under her figurative belt.

She tried to fit in. She was the only girl in a crew of guys — all of them old enough to be her father, and dumb enough to be, well, Billy Kowalski — so she smiled and did whatever they asked of her, which in the main was to be a flagger (getting beeped at and flung the finger at by angry drivers when she'd stop traffic to have the transit or level kits moved to another part of the road).

She drove up from Potocoke in the passenger's seat of a Ford truck driven by Mattie, a forty-five-year-old with a hairy belly and outie belly-button that was never completely covered by his dirty T. She smiled and laughed at his jokes and didn't mind the Marlboro smoke that made the windshield practically invisible (he didn't crack open his window, so she didn't hers, either) nor did she even wince when the first thing she caught sight of upon entering the cab was the row of Hustler cutouts pasted on this side of the passenger's sunscreen. So determined she was to become a surveyor. She tried to make small talk.

That day (remember, it had rained earlier), she mentioned to Mattie as he walked past her flagger's station with his level tripod, "My, look at all the worms!"

And there were quite a few of them on the asphalt that morning, poor stupid blind things (just like the ones Jason tried, on that much later fateful day at the track, to avoid crushing).

The sun got warm about eleven that morning, and it was almost time for lunch.

"Hey, Allie!" called Mattie from the panel truck parked near the Sunoco station. "C'mon over here, will ya?"

Alison put down her flag and trotted over to where the group of men were standing between the open doors at the rear of the truck, with their backs to her. It seemed as if they were looking at something.

"What's up, Mattie?" she said in her chummiest voice.

"Come here closer — I wanna show ya sumpin'," he said over his shoulder.

And so she did.

When she was about two feet away from them, Mattie said, "Look at all da worms!"

At which all the guys turned around and Alison's eyes grew large at five pricks, of various lengths and hues.

Mattie's was stiff as a rover rod.

Speaking of stiffs, they're still talking about the preparations for the president's funeral, I see.

The things Americans get heated over.

I mean, should there be a riderless horse, with the boots turned backward in the stirrups? Since ol' 48 wasn't in the service ... He was the commander in chief, we hold sacred (to use a hackneyed phrase) the civilian control of the military, but because he "didn't serve," there's this debate going on over whether somebody should lead a poor animal who has no idea about why it's being led down the broad avenue between the rows of so many people lining the way (I hear there's also an argument going on about how many people are going to line the way; number 45 supposedly — supposedly — said that the US Park Police had assured him that if it had been *him,* the crowds would have been huge. Gigantic).

Is the funeral of a celebrity even a real event? I mean, does it even revolve around a real person? When someone we know dies, our reaction is real, visceral; whether it's astonishment, or anger, or simply grief, it's real. A person we knew, talked to, kissed and smelt and tasted, felt … is gone. But when it's a person that *People* magazine features on its cover? I mean, for example, when one of the Kennedys — the recent Kennedys — be it Jackie with her anemia or Ted with his tumor or JFK Jr. thinking down was up and ascending into the concrete surface of the Atlantic, dies, isn't it like the end of a fairy tale? Don't we kind of *expect* it to happen? How else might it have ended? That's not a *real* person there, in the caisson-borne, flag-draped box, is it?

But there was a real person at the receiving end of Billy's arrow.

His name was Jason (— yeah, coincidence,) but it was a popular boy's name back then — Jason Bartosz. He was fifteen years old, and he owned a Fender Jaguar. I know that because I bought it from him a week before he died. For 150 bucks. Can you believe it? It's true. He had a girlfriend and his girlfriend was a real girlfriend, which means that she had flesh and bones (not like those supposed celebrities made out of newsprint and radio waves), which means she was actually born and had a birthday. She had real feet that needed to be covered with real shoes and she didn't want any sort of shoes, she wanted Gucci. And for her birthday, he needed 150 more bucks, and he loved her so much (so he thought, stupid fifteen-year-old kid) that he (I mean, it was a *forever love*, wasn't it?) decided to sell a Fender Jaguar for 150 bucks. And I bought it. Exploitative prick that I am.

That's not the only connection I have with Jason Bartosz.

I was an altar boy at St. John the Baptist church in Swallowsville with his brother Bob.

Here's where the link which is Bob Bartosz becomes soldered to the chain that leads to all this hand-wringing about boots turned backward on riderless horses and greasy nuked stains in the City by the Bay.

Bob, unlike me, his brother Jason, my friend Jason — unlike almost everybody on the planet Earth — hated music. Well, he may not have hated it, but it was incomprehensible to him. Or better, not incomprehensible, but something indifferent. To him, there was no distinction between Eric Clapton's solo on "While my Guitar Gently Weeps" and Andrew Lloyd Weber's score for *Cats* and the music piped into the elevators at Trump Tower. (That is, if there is music piped into the elevators at Trump Tower. I don't know. But if there is, I bet it sucks. I bet it's like Sade dipped in chocolate and rolled in gold dust and then eviscerated to sound like a barbershop quartet singing a song by Sade arranged by Kenny G. Sorry Sade, but it's what comes to mind. You deserve better).

When Jason turned fifteen — which was one month before he entered eternity, thanks to Billy Kowalski — his brother Bob, wanting to buy him a birthday present which would make him happy, walked into the Sound Arcade at the Gateway Plaza in Edgarsville and was stymied by the music on offer. There were so many of those square sleeves containing LPs. Which one to buy? He went for something in the middle. The Ms. He picked up an album by Mitch Miller called *Sing Along with Mitch*, and then put it down, and picked up another double album by Mitch Miller called *Sing Along with Mitch Miller and the Gang* (I mean, double the music, for only a fraction of the price more? How could you go wrong? containing heart-thumping classics like, "That Old Gang of Mine" and "Down by the Old Mill Stream," "I've Been Working on the Railroad" and "Be Kind to your Web-Footed Friends,") asked the guy at the cash register (with a skunk stripe in his Vapor-style do, the fingernail of his right pinky grown out and painted black) if they do gift wrapping? and gave it to Jason, who was rather into Santana and David Bowie and Kiss (he was eclectic, but definitely electric and post-1946), and Jason …

… was so moved by the clumsy kindness, the real, disinterested effort of his clueless brother to make him happy, that he nearly cried upon receiving it, set it down on the table by the Pepperidge Farm Chocolate 3-layer cake with candles dripping wax onto its brown surface, and gave his brother a big, real hug from the heart, as we all should do. Later, he filed the LP away between Metallica's *And Justice for All* and Motörhead's *Nö Sleep at All*.

This is the person, the real person, that Billy Kowalski killed with his stray arrow, and left to be found — by stray pedestrian, rat, or earwig — on the dirt road between his back yard and the woods.

When he was found, bewept, and buried from St. John's, Bob decided to do something else for him. To carry on his legacy. For Jason (like my Jason, and so many of us all) wanted to be a rock 'n' roll star. This dream of his was effectively brought to nothing by the arrow of that dimwit Billy Kowalski. While Bob could not do a Johnny Van Zant and live out the dream for his dead brother, he could at least help forward the dreams of other brothers who wanted to play their Fender Jaguars and other mysterious combinations of wood and nickel … He became a promoter.

Thing was, as tone-deaf and clueless as Bob Bartosz is, thinking (as he did) that music was music and that a band was a band, he developed a stable of local garage bands and other such groups, kept their numbers in a Rolodex ordered, not alphabetically, but by date of their signing with his company, InaPo Music (named for his mother, Ina, and his father, Porfiry, Bartosz), and when any gig came his way, he would send a band there — not based on stylistic affinity, but rather, in the order of their being signed to the company. In his mind, this was the most equitable way of going about it all.

What happened, of course, was what you can imagine happening without my having to explain it.

Meyer Steinmetz was celebrating his Bar Mitzvah. Bob Bartosz sent along a group called Führerheiligesturm, which specialized in völkisch pagan metal. The Altar and Rosary Society of St. Anthony's Church was holding a "purse bingo and polka party;" next up was Götterdämmerung, which did Ted Nugent and Scorpions covers — and so they were dispatched to the parish hall.

The upshot ... was something no one could have expected. The skinheads of the neo-Nazi death metal band invited the guests up on stage to whirl with them through a crowd-requested five-string bass version of "Hava Nagila" and everybody partied like it's 5759; down the road at St. Anthony's, plush mumued blue-haired Slovak hausfraus and loinclothed long-haired boys skipped to a grungy version of the "Beer Barrel Polka" that was screaming out of Flying Vs and Explorers, and everyone had, as the soundtrack to *Dirty Dancing* puts it, "the time of my life" ... God bless him, Bob Bartosz could have, if the stars had only aligned themselves as they ought to have, inaugurated the thousand-year reign of peace foretold by Isaiah.

Soon, InaPo Music became known as Inappropriate Music amongst the cognoscenti of Northeastern Pennsylvania, Bob Bartosz made money hand over fist (50% of which he donated to the National Shrine of the Immaculate Conception for annual Masses for the repose of his brother's soul) ... but — alas— all this success merely led to the state of anarchy and the rollback of the manifest destiny of these United States of America, which we are living through today, but which Genevieve Watson foretold with uncanny prescience at her daughter's fourteenth birthday party in 1976.

Yes, I did mention a fourteen-year-old's birthday party — Alison Prickney's.

And that's exactly where I'm taking you now.

It's where the breadcrumbs lead us.

Genevieve Watson is Alison Prickney's mother. She was forty-five at the time, garishly made up — long fake eyelashes, coal-black brows, and lips painted with orange lipstick that stained the multitudinous Cool filters that littered the ashtrays and half-filled water glasses in the shotgun house on Roosevelt St. that she shared with her second husband, her only daughter, and an evil polydactyl tabby cat that liked to chew crayons — all set off by a face caked in powder. Behind her back, we kids called her Esposito — for Tony Esposito, the gifted goalie of the Chicago Black Hawks. Poised on her naturally-colored neck, that white face of hers looked just like his old-style face mask.

Esposito — that is, Genevieve Watson, Alison's mother — was also gifted. She had second sight, I mean.

Really. I used not to believe in such things, but then I met her.

About a month before this party that I'm talking about, I was walking up Roosevelt, returning from school, on my way to Swallowsville, lugging my black cardboard guitar case in which my Greco Les Paul knockoff loosely rattled with each step I took, trying to act cool. Anyway, just as I got near the top of the hill, at more or less 60 degrees from Alison's house, Esposito materialized on the porch. I mean *materialized*. I didn't see any door open, and I swear that no one was sitting, or standing, on the porch a second earlier (I know this because I always sort of glanced longingly at that house as I trudged up the hill in my blue blazer) — this is where Alison lived, and, as I told you, I once thought she was kind of cute, and there's something special about the house where a cute schoolmate lives, isn't there? Especially when one is shy? It is an ally and a fortress. An ally, because it separates the beloved object from the group of *her* allies, the cool girls in school, who she hangs out with, and who call you the Spick who Licks Dick, so that you daren't even approach her; that ally of a house, though, makes *her* vulnerable — it's the place where she takes a bath, eats cheetos in pyjamas watching *Welcome Back, Kotter*, crawls into her mommy's bed at night when she's scared — well, maybe not *that,* maybe not *that Mommy*, and certainly not *that bed, what with Tommy Watson next to Esposito* (but more of that later), you know what I mean, right? But it's also a fortress, kind of like the tabernacle over the main altar where the ciborium with the Blessed Sacrament is kept, which no one can approach but Father Chrypa — O, how the whole church whooshed with an intake of scandalized breath when the Host fell to the floor from old lady Primus's lips and our Jason — just like that! — laid the paten down on the communion rail and bent down and picked it up with his own, unconsecrated fingers! But to get back to where I was at, here I am trudging up Roosevelt and glancing over at the tabernacle, sorry, the front porch, and nobody's there, and then suddenly, *somebody is!* It's Esposito, and she calls me over.

"Boy!"

"Me?" I say, pointing at the fat loose tie hanging around my white shirt with the sweat stains at collar and armpits, and looking over my shoulders.

"Yes, you! Come here!"

And such is the eerie power of adults, that I dutifully cross the road, approach the cracked, steep concrete stairs leading up to the sloping porch, and begin to ascend them, catching my patent leather (yes, sorry) shoe toe against a mid-step and tumbling to my knees, whacking the guitar case against the upper step, at which the Greco gives out an irritated whine.

"You see that man over there?" she asks, pointing with long bony fingers from which a Virginia Slim is upwardly sticking, across the street, to the top of the hill.

"Him? The man on the porch?"

"Yes. Him. Go and approach him."

"Approach him?" I say, the little hairs on the back of my neck pricking upwards.

"Go and talk to him!"

"I don't know him …"

"Go, boy! He has something important to share with you. And you must go now! He will not be there tomorrow when you walk by at the same hour."

"Wha …?"

"Tomorrow he will be *gone*! Go, go now!"

Jeepers. Creepers.

And yet down I went.

And I went up the hill.

In the direction of the old man on the porch, as I would have anyway, as I always turned left in front of his house and went down the road to where it meets Jackson St. Before I got there, I looked over my shoulder and saw that Esposito was watching me. She shooed me on quickly with her hand. I walked on, and, just before I got to the steps leading up from the sidewalk and through the old man's front yard to the porch stairs, I turned around again — and Esposito was gone. Phew. I'd dodged that bullet of weirdness.

Go and approach the old man who will "be gone" tomorrow …

I shivered and was about to turn up the street when the old man spoke.

"Whatcha got there, brother?"

"Me?" (I was an awkward child; always kind of feeling invisible, or, when seen, visible at precisely the worst moment; Me? You talking to me? Why me?)

"Yeah, you, bub. That a geetar you got there?"

I looked down at the scruffy case.

"Yeah."

"You know how to play it?"

"Kinda."

"C'mon up here an' show me."

And up I went, such is the power of the adult command. But back in the 70s, kids never thought twice about stuff like this. There were no creeps to be warned against. Or if there were, you never met them. Or they were creepy in a harmless way like Esposito. So I opened the green painted metal gate fashioned of old water pipes, scuffed my *other* patent leather shoe *Shit!* against the stubbly concrete step, and trudged up onto the porch, the floorboards of which were painted battleship gray.

The old man was thin, but wrinkled, maybe sixty years old. Ancient he seemed, and now here I am, closer to sixty than fourteen myself. He looked like an emaciated Jack Kerouac, but with a thicker black quiff. He was sitting on a blue slatted porch swing, smoking a Lucky Strike. At his feet panted a large mongrel of uncertain parentage.

"What's your name?"

"Ray."

"Siddown, Ray. I'm Al. This here is Buster."

I sat down next to him on the swing and patted the dog, who licked my hand and farted.

"Just et," said Al with an apologetic smile. "Let's see your geetar."

I set the case down on the battleship gray floorboards next to Buster, who was already snoring contentedly on his side and pulled out the Greco.

"A Les Paul man!" Al smiled. "What can you play me?"

I'm always nervous performing in front of people. I was especially so back then. So I tried something simple. Second finger on the fourth string, second fret, third finger on the third string, second fret, let out a sigh and … *Ba da dee da, da dee da, da dee da, da datta* … three or four times through the opening riff of "Don't Fear the Reaper." I only stumbled once with my cross-picking, so, gaining the courage to smile, I stopped, said,

"I can do this too," gripped a Dsus4 and picked my way, more or less, through the opening sequence of "More than a Feeling," which was big that year.

"Not bad," said Al. "But you're a little outta tune. You mind?"

"No, sure," I said, handing the Greco over into his outstretched hand.

"Buster," he said, giving the dog a nudge with his foot. "Gimme a low E."

Buster dutifully growled, a long, drawn-out growl, the kind you hear a dog do in the middle of the night when the moon is full and he suddenly gets his wolf on. Squinting, Al tuned to the howl.

"Agin," he said, and Buster growled agin. "Atta boy. Go back ta sleep."

Buster flopped down on his side again, and Al got on to his relative tuning, after which he laid on the few opening bars of "The Wind Cries Mary," before squinting again and handing me back the pick.

"Too stiff," he said.

Pulling his own pick out of his pocket, he laid into it again, smiling and nodding,

"That's better!"

And then he went off onto a fretboard excursion such as I hadn't seen or heard before, doing a few double Hendrix bends (was he really doing "All Along the Watchtower?") and segueing into a jazzy sort of rendition of "Greensleeves," seamlessly. Was that *my* guitar that sounded like that? You could almost hear the Greco sighing, *At last. Somebody who knows what he's doing. Leave me here. Please.*

"That's cool!" I said, and I meant it.

"You know how to solo, brother?"

"N-no, not much."

"It ain't that hard. You know your pentatonics?"

"Uhhh …"

Al smiled.

"Look. There's five patterns here. You learn these, and you learn how to solo. Most of your blues and your rock and roll fellas base their riffs off'm. Here. Give it a try."

And I did, with him writing out the tablature on the inside of his torn open Lucky Strikes pack with the nub of the pencil he'd been doing his crosswords with.

"You learn them, Ray. They'll come in handy."

I patted Buster, shook Al's hand, packed up the Greco (while my guitar gently wept, tacky, but true), and walked down those steps, *floated* down those steps as if I'd just discovered the philosopher's stone.

As I turned up the street towards Jackson, I looked back at Al's porch and smiled. He waved. I waved back and went on.

How many times had I walked up that street, turning in front of that house, never knowing who lived there?

I mean *who* lived there?

This dude with guitar wizardry in his nicotine-stained fingers?

It became a different, totally different neighborhood from that moment on. Who lives next door? What if it's Ginger Baker's twin, separated at birth? And what if the guy across the way, up from Esposito, is Stanley Clarke's brother, and when the sun goes down they all tune relatively to Buster's pristine low E and jam like there's no tomorrow?

Yeah, that's what I'm getting at!

There wasn't.

Not for Al; just like Esposito said.

The next day, at the same hour, I'm trudging up the hill, and there's this big black car out in front of Al's house; and down the steps come two soberly dressed gents in black suits, one on each end of a stretcher, on which is lain a body, completely covered in a blue sheet, strapped on at torso and thigh. And from the end of the stretcher waved the tips of a thick black quiff.

The black car was a hearse from Stuhr's Funeral Parlor (why do they call them Funeral Parlors? Do they have Funeral Kitchens too? Funeral Bedrooms?), and before I tell you more about how Esposito predicted, back in the presumptuously-celebrated Bicentennial year of 1976 what you see unfolding in real-time on that television of yours (Idaho is back in the Mexican fold. The self-proclaimed civilian militias around Coeur d'Alene shat their pants when the SF Corps para battalion poured in crying *Todo por México!* giving new meaning to the term Minuteman, after which they meekly marched down the main street to the jail), you should also know that Stuhr's are the ones who prepared Jason Bartosz for his final journey, and that should remind you of good old Billy Kowalski.

This is important. Because if it weren't for a well-meaning British immigration officer with a fondness for R. Crumb and Zap Comix, the state capital would never have been moved from Sacramento to Monterey (they'll move it back; it's just sentimental posturing) and aid for the stricken citizens of Marin County would be delivered by FEMA, and not by the Armada de México and the Ejército Mexicano.

His name was Alfred Prickney, the immigration officer.

But before we meet him, you will remember that Billy was leaving his house, as surreptitiously as possible, with all of his archery gear in the trunk of his car.

He had a plan.

Sneaky people, and cowards, often do — even in a panic. This is why he kicked in his back door before he left. He was hoping that someone would come across the forced entry in his absence, and assume that he, too, like poor Jason Bartosz, was a victim, in this way deflecting suspicion from himself. And if no one would venture down to his house to knock on the door and ask questions after the discovery of the murdered boy, (let's call a spade a spade, even if Billy, or his lawyers, would object to that term) he would be able to feign shock and surprise after returning home next week, call the cops himself, and — if he kept his cool, but he *was* an actor, wasn't he? — this would be even better. Because not only would he have the kicked-in door to point at, but his PanAm ticket from Heathrow, as well.

This must've happened while I was away, far away, in London, for a week. What? Somebody was killed on the dirt road back there? Oh, God! When? You mean when I wasn't here, but far away in London? Oh, what a shame!

Cowards are good at tying up loose ends. It was this prescient instinct for self-preservation that held him back from cleaning up the outdoor archery targets. A crook just *might* have broken into his house to steal his archery shit, and it's even *conceivable* that he would have started fooling around with it, inadvertently shooting the boy on the path, but there's simply *no way* that he would have piled those archery targets into his car as well. And besides, everyone roundabout where Billy lived knew about those targets on his lawn. They were a local landmark. And, what would the fletchery aficionado have been shooting at, when he made his horrible mistake? Isn't it plausible that he'd have wanted to test out one of the bows, and where better to do it, than by pointing at one of those targets, sending the arrow flying and … I mean, it was as clear as *Thwack! Ftwhip! "Uughchth!"* The first rule of lying: tell as much of the truth as you can. And here, we have, well, the whole truth, except for the door and who really shot poor Jason Bartosz.

There was a dumpster in the woods behind one of the dorms at College Miserabile Dictu (that's what it was called back then).

Billy knew about it because that's where he tossed all his copies of *Barely Legal* when, one Saturday afternoon Jenksy Wilcott, Dave Wilcott's dad (and one of two cops in the Sanantone Borough P.D.) showed up at his door with a tin can taking donations for the March of Dimes, and seemed to glance into the room over Billy's shoulder when he answered the door, with *B.L.* and other questionable paraphernalia strewn over the coffee table …

It was there that he dumpster-dived to retrieve them, too, when he realized that, after all, barely or not, those girly mags *were* legal, and maybe he was just a tad too jumpy?

And so it was here that he dumped his archery stuff, which was logical enough: let's say that the "burglar" sent that test arrow flying, and then discovered what he'd inadvertently done? Wouldn't his delight at the haul turn to horror, immediately? Wouldn't it make sense for him to pull the arrow out of the head of the poor bastard, wipe it down, along with everything else (*Shit! Forgot to do that! Whew! That was close!* muttered Billy to himself, climbing clunkily into the fetid interior of the green dumpster with a chamois cloth …) and get himself as far away from the evidence as possible? Maybe even as far away as the UK? (Stop! The first rule of lying: tell as much of the truth as you can … without *implicating* yourself …)

The car seemed to leap forward as if suddenly unburdened, when he pulled back out onto Pond Lane and then headed up the Cross-River Highway to the turnpike. It was only as he approached the ticket machine at the gates that his heart jumped. In the little parking lot off to the right, there were three staties in their cruisers. But he kept his calm (he was an actor, after all, wasn't he?) and when the gate opened (*There* was *no APB out after me, after all!*) he drove calmly onto the exit spiraling down onto the southbound lanes and drove on … glancing into the rear-view mirror from time to time until he got to the exit giving onto I-80 East … staying *at all times* under 55 —'cause that's all he'd need, right? To get pulled over for going 60-65 and, when he handed the license over to the guy in the Smokey Bear hat, to hear "Kowalski? William Kowalski? Of Upper Drummond Road in Sanantone? Behind whose house a boy was murdered by an arrow to the head? Step out of the car, please, and keep your hands where I can see them …"

There would be another "checkpoint" before he got to JFK, well, three, actually: the toll plaza at the Delaware Water Gap, and then the gates at the GW Bridge and the Whitestone Bridge ... but there's no toll entering New Jersey, so he breezed into the Garden State without a second thought, and no one was looking for him at the bridges either, it seemed ... he arrived at the long-term parking lot without the slightest problem.

Believe it or not, it was only then that he noticed how bad he smelled. When he got to the shuttle bus stop nearest his car, the other passengers (a Hasidic Jew with side curls and three overstuffed Louis Vuitton suitcases, two punks, one with violet hair, the other with green, each of indeterminate gender, linked together by a chain of paper clips stretching from one safety pin-pierced cheek to other safety pin-pierced cheek, and a young family with three small children) grunted and shied away from the new arrival.

"Mommy, that man smells like poo-poo," the youngest of the children said to the bob-cut female parent.

Well, what do you expect?

He had been dumpster diving, after all.

Fortunately, Billy always carried an industrial-size bottle of Brut cologne in his glove compartment, next to an (unopened, since 1983) box of Trojan ribbed condoms, breath mints, and a paperback copy of the *Kama Sutra*, which he thought would be a lot less boring than it turned out to be. And even though he missed that shuttle, he was able at least to mask his pungent aroma by dousing himself liberally from the green and silver bottle.

Unfortunately, Billy did *not* carry his passport in the glove compartment. He didn't have one (Jason's hunch was right). He'd even forgotten that he needed one until he got to the check-in counter.

"Smoking or non-smoking?"

"Smoking," he replied.

"Smoking …" affirmed the little Latina with her black hair pulled back into a bun, clacking away at her terminal.

"How many bags do you have?"

"Uhh … none," Billy replied, reddening.

"None?" she shot her eyes up at his, without moving her head. "You're going to London for six days …"

"Yeah, I, uh, I have a place there. Here and there. With clothes. So I, you know, I travel light, and I just dress there in the stuff I have in my, er, flat and here, in the stuff I have here in my, er, pad …"

"Carry-on?"

"Hmm?"

"Do you have a carry-on?"

"Just, uh, this," Billy said, holding up his packet of cigarettes.

"Well, at least you'll have room in the overhead bin," she said.

"Is that, uh, is that where I have to stow them?"

"I was just joking," the girl said, with the slightest, just the slightest, shake of her head. "OK. You're all set up. May I see your passport?"

"Oh, God! Passport?"

"Yeah. It's a different country, you know. Has been for more than two hundred years now …"

"Oh, wow! Oh, nuts!" Billy said, the coward in his brain scurrying about from here to there, looking for an answer, not to the question, but to the existential, or rather investigative, problem.

I mean, he could book himself into a hotel at the airport for a week, right?

But what would that do to his alibi, which was tenuous at best already?

I mean, the farther away, the better, right?

The dates might not match up *exactly* in his favor, but if he just showed the cops the return ticket, and bluffed a bit, I mean he was an actor, wasn't he? That would be convincing.

But if all he had to show was a hotel receipt?

From Queens?

I mean, that would look like a cover-up, wouldn't it?

He just happened to want to spend a week at an airport hotel in Queens, right after a kid was shot with an arrow behind his house, and his kitchen door was kicked in? Oh, this was cutting things much too close to a very, very, inconvenient truth …

"Sir? Sir?"

"Yeah?"

"Did you forget your passport?"

"I … Yeah. I must have. At home. Or at London. At home in London, I …"

"Please step aside," she said, handing him a form and a pen. "Fill this out, and give it to that man over there —"

Shit! Billy's python boots seemed to leap two inches up off the linoleum when he noticed that the man he was supposed to give the paper to was wearing something that looked like the uniform of a cop ...

"Sir? If you wouldn't mind stepping down a bit? There are others behind you waiting to check-in ..."

"Yes ... Sorry ..." he said, taking the form and the pen into his trembling hands and shuffling over a step or two.

"Thank you. When the form is stamped, come back in line, and we'll process your boarding pass."

It was a simple immigrations form — more than one person showed up for international travel without a passport, it seemed. Billy let out a sigh of relief. *Loose, loose, like before a show.* He rolled his head around on his neck, took five deep breaths, shook out his arms from shoulders to fingertips, raised himself up on his tip-toes three times (noticing for the first time that he'd pulled those python boots on over naked flesh, no socks, and that his feet had gone sweaty, and swelled, and he was probably in for blisters tomorrow), and began filling out the lines with the aid of that ingenious coward inside his skull.

Name: Archibaldo McCracken

Address: 4658 N. Riverside Square, Houston, Texas. 81762

Nationality: Argentine (OOh! That coward was a bit too ingenious. He scratched it out. And then blocked it out, almost tearing the paper), writing after it American, with the "ican" winding upwards along the right margin of the card, as his sudden, unthought-through avowal of citizenship to the land of the Albiceleste had left him little room on that line.

Telephone number: None.

Passport number: (He left that blank).

Father's name: Sigmund McCracken.

Mother's maiden name: Lucinda Sigmundo *(Shit!)* But it would be too much if he inked out *another* mistake.

He rolled his neck again. Despite his calming exercises, the little paper card was growing mealy under his sweating fingers. But, in for a penny, in for a pound … It was time to see this game through to the end.

Signature: William Kowalski *SHIT!*

This Freudian slip turned out to his advantage, anyway, as it were — for right beneath Signature and Date was a note instructing him to present the completed form to the agent along with a driver's license or other forms of identification … *Archibaldo must go.*

There was nothing for it.

He approached the Latina again, nudging in front of the father of that family from the shuttle stop.

"Mommy!" said the little kid, "That's the man who smells like poo-poo!"

"I'm sorry," Billy said to the Latina. "Can I have another form? I made a mistake on the one you gave me …"

"How could you …?" she said, her eyes growing wide. But instead of finishing her sentence, she just shrugged and passed a new form across to him and went back to the family from the shuttle stop.

"He stinks like Grampa," the little kid said.

Phew.

A few more neck rolls and Billy took himself to the task again — pulling out his driver's license and placing it down beside the form so as to make no mistake this time.

The guy in the uniform seemed bored, and therefore harmless. The nameplate on his navy blue shirt said, Greene. Billy's eyes locked onto this, for some reason.

"What kinda car you drive?" he asked.

"My car?" Billy said, snapping out of the reverie. "Chevy Corvette."

"What color's your house painted?"

"My house?"

"Yeah. You live in a house?"

"Yeah. Green. No, white, white. Sorry."

"White? You sure?"

"Yeah. White. Sorry. I'm nervous."

"What're you nervous about?"

"Flying. I don't like flying."

"Where you going?"

"London."

"Why?"

"My child is being christened."

Shit!

"Congratulations," said the agent, and *whack!* he stamped the form, handed it back along with the driver's license, and Billy joined the queue again. In less than a half-hour, boarding pass in hand, he was through the metal detector and off to the plane to Heathrow.

His place was towards the back of the airplane, in a window seat, next to a short man in a gray suit reading a book in some language Billy didn't recognize.

Did the little man in the gray suit sniff and recoil as Billy squeezed past him?

Was the Brut wearing off?

Billy lit up a smoke just in case and listened to the paper crackle as he inhaled deeply, looking out the window into the blackness of the tarmac as the other passengers boarded. When the cigarette was almost down to the filter, he crushed it out in the little rectangular ashtray in the armrest, and immediately fell into a deep, deep sleep.

"What is your name, young man?"

It was Esposito speaking, to me, in the tiny parlor of the house on Roosevelt, in 1976, a month after Al's death. A young family was living there now, in the house behind the porch where I was introduced to the pentatonic scale. I saw them washing the car and listening to the radio and falling off a tricycle as I walked down the street.

It made me sad.

So I was on my way to Alison's fourteenth birthday party.

Esposito — Mrs. Genevieve Watson — took one last drag on her Virginia Slim and doused it in a half cup of Fanta orange soda.

"Ray Verano."

"Verano," she said, her eyes floating up to a chintzy print on the wall depicting Jesus in the Garden of Gethsemane, kneeling at a boulder, while an angel hovered above him with a chalice in his extended hand.

"Verano," she repeated, rolling the R this time. "Your people come from Jalisco."

"Guadala– Guadalajara …" I stuttered, those little hairs at the back of my neck pricking up again.

"Guadalajara is in Jalisco," she smiled, condescendingly. "You're Mexican."

"I'm American," I said, firmly, a little pissed off.

"And that boy? Your friend?" she said, ignoring my comment and nodding towards Jason, who was standing over a pile of LPs near the console stereo topped with a candelabra in which sickly green bayberry candles had been stuck. Jason was shaking his head at Patsy Cline and Eddy Andrews and Bing Crosby.

"His name is Jason Hughes."

"Aha. Miscegenation, I suppose ..." she said.

I said nothing, not knowing what that word meant until much later.

"He's so dark. He's Mexican, too."

"He's my cousin," I said and opened my mouth again to ask her what problem she had with us being *Americans* of Mexican descent when she suddenly shot out her two bony hands toward me and tightly gripped my forearms with her white, white fingers. Then her eyes rolled upwards until I saw their tiny red veins and she uttered a little groan and swayed slightly, back and forth.

Cripes!

Did nobody see this weird shit but me?

But as I glanced around, I just saw four of my classmates — three girls and a boy — desultorily playing *The Game of Life* on the sticky green short-shagged carpet, Jason shaking and shaking his head as he fingered on through Mitch Miller and Burl Ives while Patsy Cline crooned "Crazy" in the background, and Alison entering the room from the kitchen with a bowl of Charlie's Chips in her hands, and Tommy Watson — her stepdad — sitting in a recliner under a framed needlepoint embroidery of the twelfth and thirteenth verses of Psalm 69, knocking back and refilling, knocking back and refilling, glass after glass of Old Grandad.

"C'mere, little sweetheart," he said in a gravelly voice, face flushed, grabbing at Alison's arm. "Come and sit on yer Daddy's lap!"

But all he succeeded in doing was jerking askew the bowl in her arms causing some of the chips to fall onto the floor. (The polydactyl tabby pounced on the white flakes, tried one, *cacked* as if expelling a hair ball, and retreated to her box of Crayolas).

"Look what you made me do, Tommy!" said Alison, jerking her arm free of his grip. "And you're not my father!"

"Kinda, kinda … ummm," he said, sizing up her ass as she bent down to clean up the spilled chips. She *felt* his stare and quickly squatted down on her haunches.

I'm crazy for trying and crazy for crying …

Meanwhile, Esposito stopped her swaying. Her eyes swiveled back and locked onto mine with an unblinking stare.

"You will be among the victors. A Conquistador!" she cried aloud, and *nobody fucking noticed!* shot her hand up in the air like some angry Rintrah prophet painted by Blake.

"The time shall come, though I shall not see it, when the shame of 1848 will be avenged. Your people … (*What "my" people? The old Slovaks from the upper end of Swallowsville?*

The Welsh Methodists up there on Mountain Road in Cwmdwrcymru?) Your people shall restore the grand sway of the empire of Iturbide! I see a great Armada docked near the Presidio! I see the Golden Eagle soaring aloft, toward *la frontera con Rusia!*"

And … well, how about that? Isn't that exactly what happened last week, as the Ejército pushed up the Pacific Coast while His Imperial Majesty Vladimir, Emperor of All the Russias, re-annexed Alaska, "in order to stabilize the situation and protect Russian interests" and the ten or so people with names ending in "sky" and "ov" grouped around the Transfiguration of the Lord Parish in Ninilchik?

Not so crazy, huh?

"Until then, Paco," she said to me, drinking down the half glass of Fanta *along with* the fag-end of her spent smoke, "you and your amigo there stay away from my daughter."

Putin and Medvedev. Medvedev and Putin. Like two brothers. Igor and Vsevolod. Laurel and Hardy. Jekyll and Hyde. It always comes down to two brothers, right? Cain and Abel.

I mention this because, as I said, the guy who let Billy Kowalski into the UK and helped on the chain of events that led to the nullification of Seward's Folly was named Prickney. Alfred Prickney.

Related to Alison?

Of course.

Distant, distant cousin.

Real distant.

Both of these Prickneys came from a Protestant family that emigrated to England in the mid-seventeenth century; both of them descend from the original immigrant, Stanley (Stanisław) Jajcarz, a craftsman from the Raków area, and thus a member of the (Arian) Polish Brethren, who were forced by the Polish Sejm in 1658 "to convert to the One True Catholic Religion of our Lord and Saviour Jesus Christ, or to dispose of their goods and emigrate from this Polish Kingdom within the space of three years, on pain of death."

So Stanley Jajcarz disposed and emigrated, settling in the region of Silver Street (some say Monkwell) in London, where he met and married Isabelle Duhamel, a "maker of tires and wigges" of French Huguenot stock. They had only two children who survived infancy: twin brothers, Simon (named for that great Polish Arian, Szymon Budny) and Michael (for Michael Servetus), of whom Michael, who begat Henry, who begat Shadrach, who begat William, who begat ... you get the idea, remained in England and finally begat Alfred, while Simon emigrated to the New World and (begat and begat and begat, etc., etc.) Mike (ironically enough) Prickney, who begat Alison upon the body of Genevieve, his wife (before she left him for Tommy Watson).

But, how do we get to Prickney from Jajcarz, you ask? Well.

Jajcarz, which is easy enough for Poles to pronounce — it sounds something like *Yeye-tsarzh*, is rather a tongue-twister for English speakers. Stanley (Stanisław) had his ears assaulted from day one of arriving in Baroque Albion with Jadj-kars and Yay-cuss and Bloody Prat of a Polack; soon after marrying, he had had enough. It was time to become British. And that meant getting a British name. Stanley was the easy part. Jajcarz — O, there's the rub. Now, he liked his wife's last name — Duhamel — and might have adopted it were it not for the fact that it too, though melodious and relatively easy to pronounce, also sounded foreign. And, from time to time, apprentices or unemployed pikemen or good old beef-eating Englanders would get fed up with the foreigners in their midst, who were taking the food from the mouths of their children, so they claimed, and making London resound with the clatter of foreign tongues, making parts of the city unrecognizable and like a foreign land, and, sometimes this developed beyond the mere ethnic slur into the threat of violence. And with Isabelle gravid — I mean *really* gravid, preggers with the twins Simon and Michael in her womb, it was time to pop out of the barrel of nails and hide oneself amongst the hammers.

Stanley even conformed to the Church of England, although this required his acceptation of the dogma of the Holy Trinity, which a practical sort of thinker like himself could never quite understand, mystery or not; but as this posed no great obstacle to his Calvinist wife (her ideas on predestination were also kind of weird to him, but she was a good woman, and he loved her), he went along, made his profession of faith before the priest at St. Bride's, was admitted to communion and confirmed on the same morning, and was entered into the parish rolls as *Stanislaus*

Iaicarius (which was to have serious repercussions for some of his descendants in the eighteenth century, but, more of that later), and that was that.

It was harder with the name change. It was *supposed* to be harder with the name change. Local statutes were designed to make it difficult, not easy, for the foreigners in London to assimilate (something that number 48 was also proposing in this country, if you remember, in the months before his sad demise). It wasn't supposed to be easy for foreigners to Anglicize their names. But, then as always, there's nothing that money can't do. And Stanley Jajcarz had a lot of money, being a tradesman in great demand during his lifetime (and setting his family up on such stable financial footing, as to see his great-great-grandson — of Michael's loins — raised to the dignity of Earl of Sandrington, an eighteenth pale ancestor of the royal family, believe it or not. But — wait for it — after begetting the second earl, the family fell from grace in a scandal involving the smuggling of jade and opium from China — that was to be the prerogative of the Crown, don't-ye-know — and devolving to the point that Alfred found himself working long hours at immigrations at Heathrow terminal 3).

Back in the halcyon days of the seventeenth century, the palm of the requisite official was properly greased, and Stanley Jajcarz was able to leave Poland behind him, once and for all, absconding under the British cloak of the name Prickney.

Prickney?

Why Prickney?

Well, why not?

It's an occupational surname.

You've heard of Fabergé eggs?

How prized they are, were, by the Russian Tsar and museums around the world?

Well, at the time of which we are speaking, London was gripped with a frenzy for *pisanki*.

Pisanki?

Gaudily colored and decorated Easter eggs. During Lent, these fragile little centerpieces might be sold for ten shillings — that's half a pound — apiece. Now, considering the fact that in the old system there were twenty shillings to the pound, Stanley, who could produce up to twenty *pisanki* a day, would make one pound sterling for every two eggs sold. One pound sterling in the middle of the seventeenth century was the equivalent of about 230 dollars today. So, do the math. Twenty eggs bring in 2,300 dollars a day; there are forty days to Lent (the busy season for *pisanki* in seventeenth-century London) — so, during the "lean" season of the year leading up to the anniversary of the Lord's Glorious Resurrection, Stanley Jajcarz would make the equivalent of $92,000 — quite a sum, no?

Prickney, Prickney, yes, I'm just getting to that.

I said that it is an occupational surname.

Now, the way you make *pisanki* is to take a raw hen's egg and *prick the egg* at both ends with a needle, after which you gently blow out the contents onto a plate. When only the hollow shell remains, one can begin the delicate task of painting the egg in bright colors, decorating it with gold thread and seed pearls (*92,000 smackers each Lent, remember?*), and start making cash.

One day, during the run-up to his decision to make himself as British as he might, Stanley was sitting at his workbench when, through the open window, he heard two jealous ancestors of the National Front griping about, "pricks like that egg-sucking Dutchman there turning this England of ours into a Flemish whorehouse where all you hear is *Ya mine hair* and *Goody Margery!*" And as he had been tossing over and over in his head various possibilities for his new British monicker — *hmmm … Stanley Coburg? Stanley Jones? Stanley Battermount? Stanley Windsor?* it suddenly hit him like inspirational lightning: *That's it! That's who I am! I'm the Stanley who Pricks Eggs! I'm Stanley Prickegg! Stanley Prickney!*

Pretty impressive etymological linguistics there, for a Jajcarz new-come to Lud's town, but that's where you get "cockney" from, you know? Cock (rooster) + *ey* (the old Germanic root for "egg") — Cockney, so … Prickney!

And that's how Alison, and Alfred, got their name.

"You haven't a passport?" asked Alfred, when Billy Kowalski approached him, smelling faintly of dumpsters, Brut cologne, Budweiser, and Benson and Hedges cigarettes.

"I forgot it," Billy lied. "They gave me this in New York."

And he held out the immigration form with bored Officer Green's energetic stamp.

Alfred Prickney looked at the paper, turned it front and back, then sized Billy up.

"How long will you be in the United Kingdom?"

"A week."

"Where are you staying?"

"Uh, with … uh, with relatives."

"Where do they live?"

"In London."

"Where in London?"

"I don't know. It's the first time I'm here. They're picking me up. I'm coming in for my grandmother's wedding and …"

"Your *grandmother's* wedding?" asked Alfred, with raised brows, thinking *but, that's so bloody unbelievable, he just can't be tellin' me porkies!*

"Yeah," riffed Billy. "She married young. And then she had me Dad, who moved to the States after the war, and her husband, my Granddad, well, he died in the Blitz of Britain, he was this pilot, see …?"

"You mean the Battle of Britain? or the Blitz?"

"Well, both."

"Both?"

"Yeah he, uh, like, when the … those … them enemies were coming over here? and Blitzing, you know?"

"The Germans?"

"Yeah. The Germans. Blitzkrieg and all that. They're coming over here trying to destroy England, and my Grandfather, like, he's this pilot and, and they shot him down, you know?"

Alfred looked down at the paper he held in his hand. *Kowalski. That's a Polish name. There were Polish pilots here, during the Battle of Britain. And some of them died for this country. They've got that stained-glass window there in St. Paul's.* Alfred's heart was warming. There was an old tradition in his family that they were kinda Polish too, though he couldn't quite understand how that could be. *Being from Battersea and Mum's folks from Brixton from age on age. But they said it was a long time ago …*

"And when he died, she, you know, she married this guy — a German paratrooper who fell into her back yard …"

Billy saw Alfred seize up, the pleasant smile on his face slacken and harden into a glare; oh, that too ingenious coward in his head!

"… who was escaping from the rest of the Nazis in the bomber, he was against Hitler, you know, and took the opportunity to bail out, they were gonna kill him! That was back in forty-six …"

Alfred turned red.

"… I mean fifty-six, yeah, after they let him out of the stalag. Or, whatever you call it over here. And then he died in sixty-four, and then my gramma didn't marry nobody, but she's always wanted a companion, and now she met Roy. Roy Benson, you know? Of London? And they're getting married, and I forgot my passport and …"

And Alfred was hesitating between stamping his *own* paper admitting this strangely yammering Yank into the Realm and calling for security to lead him over to the holding room prior to deportation on the next flight back to JFK when his eyes fell upon Billy's sweaty and grimy T-shirt.

"Zap Comix."

"What?"

"Keep on Truckin'. Robert Crumb. Zap Comix."

"What? Oh, yeah, yeah! Robert ..." said Billy, at a loss, "Love him, man."

"You're not from San Francisco?"

"Sort of."

"Sort of?"

"That's where my other gramma lives. She's dead now. Lived, lived I mean ..."

But Alfred wasn't listening anymore. He had been to San Francisco (where Billy had never); back in the Summer of Love (or, rather, shortly thereafter), and had never been back since ... It had been a grand expedition, *the* grand expedition of his youth, remembered fondly, and literally anything that came from there, be it sourdough bread, Rice-a-Roni, the smell of Patchouli, a Lawrence Ferlinghetti poem, or Zap Comix, melted his heart.

Alfred, bless him, was sentimental.

"Here you are," he said, thumping the entrance stamp onto that finger-worried and damp piece of paper that served Billy Kowalski for documentation. "Welcome to the UK. But you get this sorted at Grosvenor Square first thing, yeah?"

"Umm ... yeah, for sure," Billy said, wondering where, and what, the hell was Grosvenor Square (and how it was spelled, in the first place).

"Congratulations to your granny," said Alfred with a smile, letting Billy pass through.

"What?" Billy said, "Oh, yeah. Yeah! Same to you!"

And with that fatal exchange, Alfred Prickney opened the way for Billy's second-wind (after Shakespeare) love of Great Britain, which led him to embrace Anglicanism like Alfred's Arian ancestor so long ago, which led him to meet Alfred's unknown cousin, Alison, back in Sanantone Pennsylvania, and give her a job, and cause a great crush of Gringos recoiling north and east from the shrinking borders of their once monolithic superpower, in fear of a Latino wave pushing up the Florida panhandle and through the Rockies, snarling interstates and straining shelters and emergency supplies and the patience of their unsympathetic Gringo compatriots whose neighborhoods were now hip-deep in the backwash of manifest destiny.

Brothers?

Oh yeah.

None of this would have happened if it had been Michael, and not Simon, who had been forced to emigrate to the New World after an (unproven, but circumstantially probable) physical insult committed upon the person of the Lord Mayor's wife. For Michael had inherited the good, sentimental nature of his Jajcarz forefathers (the name in Polish, also derivable from the word egg — *jajko* — is slang for "good-hearted jokester,") a trait he passed down the generations to Alfred (unconsciously responsible for the nuking of his favorite city), while Simon, who begat and begat until Alison came into the world, inherited the rather unhandsome traits common to his line of the Prickneys — distrust of the foreigner, Calvinistic strictness, and a fanatical adherence to the letter of the law; right — Simon (like so many of his descendants) was a Prick.

Just think — here's one of those chains of events that *didn't* happen, unfortunately.

Michael goes off to these colonies, Simon stays at home, and instead of good-natured, sentimental Alfred there at the immigration desk at terminal 3, it's *Alison.*

"No passport?"

"I forgot it," Billy lied. "They gave me this in New York."

And he showed her the immigration form with bored Officer Green's energetic stamp.

Alison Prickney would have looked at the paper, turned it front and back, then sized up Billy.

"How long will you be in the United Kingdom?"

"A week."

"Where are you staying?"

"Uh, with … uh, with relatives."

"Where do they live?"

"In London."

"Where in London?"

"I don't know. It's the first time I'm here. They're picking me up. I'm coming in for my grandmother's wedding and …"

"Your *grandmother's* wedding?" Alison would have said, sharply, with raised brows, *You tellin' me porky pies?!*

"Officer!" she would have called someone over, after stamping "Entrance Denied" on the paper with a nice big thump of righteousness. "Escort this man to the holding area, in preparation for his deportation to the United States on the next flight to New York."

"But … but! …!" Billy would have babbled over his shoulder as he was being led away.

"And open a window when you get there, yeah? Bloke smells like he's been rolling in a skip."

Which, you remember, he had been.

And Billy would have been sent back home to New York, where his little house of cards would have fallen apart, and he would have been arrested and tried and convicted of the death by manslaughter of Jason Bartosz, and (more importantly) Alison would never have got into that car with Jason Hughes, and — who knows? Her unknown American cousin, Alfred Prickney, might have been walking down Market St. towards the Embarcadero today, in peaceful, American San Francisco, stopping in at the Peet's off Battery St., in a country unravaged by war.

Did you know that today is the anniversary of Flip Wilson's death?

While you were out of the room, the talking head on CNN interrupted the live stream of the standoff between the (unmothballed) Mexican destroyer *Manuel Azueta* and two nuclear-powered North Korean submarines just off Pier 39, to announce it.

I mean, not like it was "breaking news" or anything; he had this kind of weary, whimsical smile on his face when he came back on as if he wanted to say, *Dear Jesus, weren't they the good old days when this was what we would announce as newsworthy?*

I think we're all tired of the tension, aren't we?

So this little piece of anecdotal trivia about the "first African American television superstar," who brought us

Geraldine Jones and "Here Come the Judge," brought
a smile to the otherwise (one always supposed) inhuman
mask of the newsman, and drew him back, perhaps, to
his childhood filled with riding his banana-seat chopper-
handled bike down the dusty arroyos of Chowchilla, or
wherever he spent his after school hours, returning home
to watch the *Brady Bunch* and *Sanford and Son* and the
Rockford Files and … *Emergency!*, so ironically calming a
show, because the two EMTs always found a way to get a
cat safely out of the very top of a huge eucalyptus tree, and
the old man who collapsed on the sidewalk from a heart
attack, amidst so much panic, was always stabilized at the
right moment and transported to the hospital just in the
nick of time, where the dark-haired doctor with the deep
voice and the sexy nurse fixed him up just fine and the last
scenes of the episode were him smiling in bed, hooked up to
this tube and that tube, but well on the mend, holding the
hand of his equally beaming granddaughter who listened to
polite music, like The Monkees, or, at the wilder end, maybe
Shaun Cassidy? And California, and America, was as safe
and stable and eternal as we always thought they would be.

Flip Wilson. "The devil made me do it." Remember?

He had a point, you know, as all comedians do. I'll get
to that in a moment, but first, about that Conquistador quip
of Esposito's. She wasn't wrong about that, either. At least,
as far as my family tradition goes.

Juan Carlos Verano y Bobadilla. That was his name. He
accompanied Hernando Cortés on his fateful journey into
the interior of Mexico — according to my father, according

to his father, according — you get it, it was Juan Carlos Verano y Bobadilla who suggested to Cortés:

"Burn the boats. When the men see there's no way back, they'll follow you, and fiercely, out of necessity."

Cortés took his advice (if it was he who gave it), and the rest is history.

Somos más Americanos!

If anybody has a right to say that, it's me and my cousin, Jason.

"And my father told me that his father told him," he would say, and back, and back, as far as you choose to go, "that it was our own Juan Carlos Verano y Bobadilla who suggested to Cortés, 'Take him prisoner, this Monteczuma fellow or whatever they call him. The natives think he's a god. If you grab ahold of him and don't let him go, they'll see that you're a stronger god — so to speak.'"

And that's what he did, right?

He went and took Montezuma prisoner, and all the Aztecs went, like, *Shit, man. And I thought that dude was a god. Next thing they'll be telling us is the sun don't need blood sacrifices in order to rise in the morning. And then what?*

No, I don't mean to be culturally insensitive. And after all, I'm talking about my bros, remember. But that's what happens at cardinal moments in a culture's history. Everything gets knocked askew.

Who's talking about American power these days?

Who's singing that song they first ran up the flagpole for Ronnie Reagan back in the eighties or was it the first of the Bushes? "God bless the U.S.Aaaaaaaaay"?

Right now half the country's trying to learn Spanish, quick, and the other's trying to get into Canada — for all the good that'd do!

Is anybody still wearing those "Back to Back World War Champion" T-shirts?

Anybody driving around in F-150s with Confederate battle flags pasted across the back cab window? "The South will rise again."

My ass.

Billy Bob in Little Rock and Jim Bob in Jacksonville folded like wooden chairs when the preacher didn't show up for the tent revival.

Remember those bumper stickers with "These Colors Don't Run?"

Well, run they did, backed up as they are now in traffic, from the Rainbow Bridge to Rochester. Beeping.

"He fought his way out of Tenochtitlán with Cortés. Right at his side. And," my dad would pause, "Returned with him in triumph a year later."

"If that's true," said my mother, always the skeptic, "why was Old Pedro" — Old Pedro was my grandfather — "working for peanuts in the farms around Santa Maria when you were a small child?"

And dad would have nothing to say to that. For it was true. Cortés, despite being more than a tad arrogant in his dispatches to his liege lord the King of Spain, was appointed "Governor, Captain General and Chief Justice of New Spain of the Ocean Sea," and as for Juan Carlos de Verano y Bobadilla? You'd think he'd get something out of it for all the good advice he gave old Hernando? Even if just an appointment as Alcalde of Nueva Venta de Pantalones?

Well, it's a pretty family tradition anyway. But Juan Carlos de Varano y Bobadilla or no Juan Carlos de Verano y Bobadilla, if it wasn't for Old Pedro begetting Dad and Dad begetting me, well, you know the old song.

While we're on the topic, there is another family legend; this one is more believable. Before Old Pedro thumbed or hoboed his way to the Central Coast, he washed dishes in New Orleans. This was in the thirties.

"Your abuelo killed a man in New Orleans," my mother told me one night when my dad returned from the NCO club, drunk, with a welt under his left eye. "That's why I worry when your father comes home late," she said to me, half in apology, half in explanation of the frantic row that woke me up — and entirely in defense of her anger (for she saw the look on my face; I always took my father's side).

"Yes. That old bastard Pedro. He was a dishwasher in New Orleans, that descendant of the glorious conquistador Verano y Bobadilla! And one night, popping out the back door of the bar he was working at for a smoke, he said something bad to a woman who was walking home with her gringo husband. And he was already married to your abuela," she nodded self-righteously as if that was an aggravating circumstance to the crime of which she'd already convicted him. "And the gringo, stupid as he was — maybe he had a bit too much to drink — went up to your abuelo and gave him a push. Which is something one should never do to people like Old Pedro, and your father — and maybe you, too, for all I know." And she nodded. And I reddened. Because the way she tilted her head aside and looked at me from the corner of her eye when she said that, meant *she knew, all right.*

"'Let it go, Charlie, he didn't mean it,' the gringo's woman said, and Charlie, well, he wouldn't let it go. 'No ... dago is gonna talk to you that way,' he said, calling Old Pedro not only a *dago*, but using another term, too, which I can't say because it's a real bad word which you can't never use."

"*Pinche dago?*" I asked.

"Something like that," she nodded solemnly. "But an English word. One that reeks of brimstone. And he went up to your abuelo and he pushed him again! And what does your grandfather do, the son of perdition, but he pulls out a switchblade and he stabs Charlie, right in the heart! The gringo crumpled down in that back alley just like that. And the gringo woman starts screaming 'Help! Police! Murder! Murder!' And off he runs, Old Pedro, that is, because the place he worked at was on Bourbon St. and there had been somebody else killed on Bourbon St. the night before, and the night before that — and who knows if that wasn't Old Pedro at his evil tricks again?" she said, and spat to the side, "and there were police all around the bars, and the strip clubs, and the sorcerer's palaces" (this is how she referred to the tarot card and psychic storefronts, which to her were not just hucksters, but godless hucksters) "and they heard her screaming, and before you know it, there were police whistles squealing on all sides, and the sound of policemen's boots thumping on the cobbles ..."

I was never sure how policemen's boots sound different from other people's boots, but my mother knew how to tell a story. I was already under her spell; no longer mad at her for her being mad at my Papi.

"And the cops saw him as he ran up in the direction of Esplanade and they were gaining on him, but he escaped them by jumping in the garbage."

"The garbage?"

"The garbage. A more fitting place could not be found," she said, spitting to the side again.

"One cop was chasing him up Bourbon St. Another was running parallel to him on Royal St. And a third was coming at him along Ursulines Ave. But that's when the devil appeared to him."

"The devil?" I gasped, my feeling my hair rising on the back of my neck, and the crown of my head.

"Yes. It can have been no one else. Just as your old abuelo (who is probably eating hot pitch in Hell today) got to Governor Nicholls St., he passed a fat black man on the corner with a guitar. He was sitting there with an upturned hat in front of him, looking for fools to toss their hard-earned money in it in exchange for his blasphemous songs of adultery, and — your abuelo always remembered this — he had a bag of ice on his foot."

"Why?"

"Because it was hot, Old Pedro used to say. It was late May, and it was in the eighties even at night. And muggy. He was keeping himself cool that way, Pedro said, but I know, he was just hiding his black cloven hoof underneath that bag of ice," my mother said, and again my hackles rose. "The devil said to him, quite calmly, 'Go left. Use the garbage chute.' And the old shaggy brother of the fallen angels did just that. As he ran down the sidewalk, he saw a manhole cover with a handle in the middle of the sidewalk, and on the cover, it said 'Garbage.' And so he lifted the cover and jumped in. He was so small — you know how small your Papi is? Well, Pedro was even smaller than that. He fit in without even having to squeeze, and there he stood, straight up, in the filth, with his hands straight up over his head. He pulled the cover closed, and that's how he disappeared. He even heard the cops walking up overhead, asking each other, *Where could he have gone?* and nobody knew. He heard them walking back and forth, looking over fences, rattling doors and shutters, for fifteen minutes. He said the hardest thing was not to laugh. He wanted so much to laugh."

"To laugh?" I was shocked. Like it or not, I inherited my mother's moral umbrage. Believe it or not!

"Yes! He didn't care about the man he'd murdered. He didn't give a second thought about the woman he'd made a widow, or if any children were orphaned and would have to beg for food now that the breadwinner had been slaughtered. He wanted to laugh at the trick he'd played on the cops!"

I must have looked sideways at my mother at that moment. She always told really good stories, but I knew how much she hated my Papi's father, and, even though I believed that the devil existed, I didn't think that he had a cloven hoof, or that he could appear to a person like that, with a bag of ice on it. So I must have looked sideways at her at that moment because she got that offended look that all Mexican women get when they feel that they're not being believed or respected.

It's the look that must've come over Medea's face the moment when she decided that there was nothing else for it — she just had to kill her children to show Jason what a lying son of a bitch he was, and that such behavior as his was simply not acceptable.

"You don't believe me?" she said.

"I do …"

"Because Old Pedro showed me the paper."

"What paper?"

"There was a story about it in the New Orleans newspaper. I don't know how he got out of the garbage chute, but he did. I don't know how he got out of New Orleans, but he did. I don't know how he kept up with the New Orleans newspapers. But he did. And one day, he saw what he was looking for. A clipping on the inside of the newspaper about the unsolved murder of Charles Smith, a banker from Tennessee, who had been killed on a business trip one night. The woman — she was not his wife after all, but … a friend of his, told the whole story to the reporter, and this reporter even interviewed two of the policemen. And do you know the thing Old Pedro was proudest of? The line where it said 'the blow to the heart was delivered with precision.' Yes! 'Like a professional killer,' he said to me, when he showed me the clipping, one night when he was drunk and your father …"

"Papi, what?"

"Never mind. But he showed me the clipping, which he kept folded in his wallet like it was a holy relic. And that's why I get mad at your Papi when he drinks. He fights! And what if he were to kill his own Charlie? And you? Do you have Old Pedro inside you, too? Is there a Charlie waiting for you someplace? Remember Axel Ross!"

Oh yeah.

There it was!

Axel Ross.

That's another story.

But right now, the point is, whether I have a Charlie or not.

I do have a conscience.

Really!

And the thing I could never understand, even more than that devil with the guitar, was … how could my abuelo live with himself after having killed a man? That was more incomprehensible to me than his laughter at the policemen, his having fooled the policemen, or his pride at having delivered that blow with precision — that was something like that "seven at one blow" fairy tale — yes, but how could he live with the guilt of knowing that he had taken another man's life?

Which brings us back to Billy Kowalski, of course.

After an unsuccessful attempt at negotiating a bus ride into London, he went back into the terminal, exchanged the thirty-three dollars he had on him into the confusing thickish coins (all the wrong sizes and weights) and odd-colored banknotes with the Queen's picture on them, and then jumped the taxi queue outside (he didn't notice the line, and the British were either too polite or Billy's strange mélange of sweat, dumpster grime, cigarette smoke, and Brut too pungent, for anyone to protest).

"Where to, guv'?" smiled the cabbie.

They really say things like that! was the first thing to cross Billy's mind.

"Ro —wo — " Billy faltered, the postulate *Grosvenor Square* being completely new to him. "Ro — wa — no ..." he tried again, swallowing the *k* at the last minute, knowing full well that Roanoke was not on this side of the big water.

"Wanborough?" asked the cabbie, pulling out of the slot.

"Yeah," Billy nodded. He had no idea where Wanborough was, but he'd got a cab, was moving off into England from the airport where cops still sauntered around in their funny helmets and caps with checkered bands. This was a step forward. He'd figure it all out when he got there. The most important thing was to fit in.

"You'll want Paddington for Wanborough then," the cabbie smiled, winking in the rear-view, and they were off.

The cabbie was a pleasant enough fellow and tried to make small talk. But after ten or so 'yeses' and 'nos' and other one-syllable grunts from the murderous punter in the back seat, he gave up. In short order, he pulled up in front of the hotel on Praed St., took the fare and a none too extortionate tip from Billy, who extended his crumpled notes, pound coins and shillings in his moist palm, and directed him:

"Right down there, sir. The ticket office is on the left, right after you pass the chemist's, yeah? You take the train to Reading, where you'll change for that going to Gatwick. Passes right through Wanborough. All right? Cheers."

And there Billy stood, the part-time butcher from Wartella's market who dreamt of playing Coriolanus, first time abroad, in the heart of London, uncomprehendingly transferred from Sanantone, Pennsylvania, as if by Prospero's staff.

What. The. Fuck.

Crowds were pouring out of the tube station across the road leading down into the iron and glass arched barn that is Paddington Station. He looked across the street — over which all the cars and buses were driving the wrong way — at the line of souvenir shops and other mercantile flotsam between Spring St. and London St.; there was a young woman crouched on the pavement, begging alms. It began to rain. One person, then another, jostled him as they hurried toward, or from Westbourne Terrace. He was alone and no one knew him here. Not a single soul knew Billy Kowalski. He was as transparent as a ghost; had he been immaterial, they would have walked right through him. The thought was comforting, somehow.

Where to go?

No one was waiting on him.

He shrugged, put his hands in his pockets, and minced down the pavement on aching feet (no socks in the python boots, remember?) into Paddington Station.

No one knew him in London, that was true. But everybody knew him on Upper Drummond Road, and, unless the impossible happened, and John Gielgud caught sight of him walking down the street and said, "Look! The one there in the python boots! He shall be my Puck!" he would be flying back to that general region of the world in but a week's time where — he shivered — the boy he'd killed would still be dead, the back door of his kitchen would still be swinging open (if it were not already x-ed over in yellow police tape) and

Tremble, thou wretch!
Thou hast within thee undivulged crimes,
Unwhipped of justice!

— the clever coward in the reptilian portion of his brain took over; he spun on his blocky heels and trudged back up the incline to Praed St., crossed into one of the cheap stores across the way, pulled some 2p picture postcards indiscriminately from the rack and asked for a

"Pen?"

"A Biro?"

"Pen?"

"A Biro?" repeated the Pakistani clerk with a melodic bob of his head.

"A pen?"

"You want one of these?" he said, holding up:

"A pen! Yes!"

Then, after successfully completing the transaction and learning where the Post Office was, he shuffled back up

Praed St. toward St. Mary's Hospital, and soon addressed and mailed three postcards to the United States,

1) To "the gang" at Wartella's market, with "a big cheerio from the old sod"

(*good grief*) "wish me a broken leg," (*oof*) "tomorrow I'm off to a Macbeth audition" (*words fail me*);

2) To Dave Wilcott: "Hey, Dave! A big cheerio from London! Been here since the day before the first of the month" (*Sic. He couldn't remember what the last day of March was called*) "Thinking of you" (here he had to think real hard to make up a reason to write to someone he'd neither seen nor spoken to since high school) "because remember when in that geography test you played a joke on Ralphie Spencer and told him 'London' when the answer was 'Tokyo?'" (Never happened. The thing was, to get a postcard with an alibi into the letterbox of Jenksy Wilcott, the cop);

and 3) To Milly Tifflin (he could think of no one else to write to, but a third postcard wouldn't hurt, would it?) "Hello, thanks so much for the other night; the funeral was great!"

He wasn't much wrong there. Jason Bartosz's autopsy didn't take too long for the Lanstrome County coroner to complete. His body was released to his grieving parents, and the lines of well-wishers who came to bid farewell to the poor kid during the wake at Stuhr's on Wilson St. stretched past St. Anthony's and down Pacer St. one way and up past Lurking Lane and toward Swallowsville Corners in the other direction. It was a great comfort to the family.

Among the mourners were four members of a British band that Jason particularly loved, who drove up from a concert in Philadelphia after Bob had written a heartfelt letter to their manager.

It was a very nice thing to do, wouldn't you say?

But I won't mention who they were. They were so very image-conscious that, fifteen years later, they would refuse induction into the Rock and Roll Hall of Fame as "the antithesis of all that rock and roll has always been about." Well, they used other words, but that's the gist of what they meant.

Still, what a nice gesture, eh?

Which only confirmed Bob all the more in his incongruously chosen profession as the Brian Epstein of Northeastern Pennsylvania.

I know all about this because I was there too.

As was Alison Prickney.

No, not at Jason Bartosz's wake.

Her mother Genevieve had died a day after Jason, and the funeral was being conducted from Stuhr's too. Her body lay in another room at the funeral parlor, with much sparser grieving throngs passing by the open coffin. In fact, it was just Alison and Tommy.

Tommy was drunk. So drunk as a matter of fact, that Jenksy Wilcott, who was at Jason's viewing assuring the parents that "we'll do all we can to get to the bottom of this ..."

("Tommy, *stop* it!" came the girl's voice from across the hallway)

"... and whoever is responsible for this terrible, terrible tragedy ..."

("Keep your hands *off* me, you pervert!")

"... excuse me ..."

... So drunk was Tommy, that Jenksy had to take matters into his own hands, springing across the deep plush carpet and into the other room with that tread particular to coppers, and escorting Tommy Watson out the side door leading to Orchard St.

When I went in to pay my respects to Esposito ... (believe it or not, she had foretold the day of her own death. But being off by a year — so the story goes — she rescued her honor as a prophet by downing an entire bottle of Nembutal 365 days later. Can you blame her? Two years in a row and she'd have been a laughing stock, like Harold Camping. She left it all on the field. Whaddaya say to that, tarot card hucksters of Jackson Square? Which one of all y'all got the cojones for that sort of money-back guarantee?) When I went in to pay my respects to Esposito, only Alison was there. She flushed crimson and turned away.

"Well, I'll be fucked," said Jason (Hughes, bassist, and fellow sufferer at Wartella's Market) the next day, at lunch break. He was standing at the bulletin board, ramen noodle cup in hand, as I trudged up the stairs with my Philly cheesesteak.

"What is it?"

"He went."

"Who? Where?"

"Billy fucking Kowalski. To London. Look at this."

He unpinned the postcard and handed it to me.

"Why he sent a postcard of the Arc de Triomphe, though," he continued, "that beats me. But the stamp's genuine. The little shit actually went."

Billy Kowalski? thought Dave Wilcott right about the same time. *What the hell's he writing to me for? And what geography test? I didn't take no fucking geography in high school. Prick's playing some kind of practical joke?* And he crumpled up the postcard and tossed it in the trashbin.

"Who is Bill Kowalski!?" fumed John Tifflin, flinging open the front door as soon as Milly pulled up in the driveway after her shift at Cameras Galore.

"John!" wailed Milly, "You're hurting my arm!" she yelped, as he pulled her inside, roughly.

"And what's this shit about a funeral? That a code or something? Fu–neral? Code for another word that begins with F U?"

And he slapped her so hard across the face that she stumbled against the radiator cover, knocking to the floor a brass vase incised with intricate Persian designs that her uncle had brought back from pre-Ayatollah Iran, where he'd been sent on an oil junket by Esso.

"You want a funeral? What about a double funeral, bitch!? Who is Bill Kowalski!?!"

Slap!

Howl, howl, howl, howl!
Oh, you are men of stones.

So, it seems that the riderless horse and the backward boots are in play after all. 49 is quoted as saying, "Although our nation is at a crossroads, sorely tested by unprovoked aggression and armed invasion on multiple fronts, by enemies united against freedom, among whom are treacherously ranged forces who used to be our friends, we shall not only prevail, with the help of God, in our fight, but we shall not be diverted, at gunpoint, from the decorous honors we owe to our fallen leader. Our heroic troops, preserving our freedom on the western and southern fronts ..." etc., etc. The heroes are holding the lines far enough away from Washington to allow for this, perhaps truly last, mile to be covered "with honor, decorously;" again the animal will be led on, like some sort of primitive sacrifice, high-stepping and maybe even jerking in panic at the bridle held by his handler; 45 will be there marching, maybe counting heads along the way with a discreet clicker (no, how could he hide that from the penetrating eye of the camera?), and ... I wonder what will be going through the mind of 49 as the caisson trundles past? Will he shiver with presentiment? "My son, my executioner?"

It was a long speech and even though it's not destined to go down in history like Kennedy's inauguration speech or that of Churchill in Missouri, the local paper printed the whole thing. I spent some time circling every mention of "God" and "gun" and "hero" recorded therein. "Hero" was mentioned sixteen times over the space of forty-three paragraphs, "gun" twenty-eight, and God, the overall winner, thirty-seven.

No surprise there, for anyone who's ever driven the great highways of America, especially south of the Mason-Dixon, where huge four-story Protestant metal crosses tower over the interstates, Protestant churches spend big money on billboards with phrases such as "Heaven, or Hell: Where Will You Spend Eternity?" and Protestant individuals spend more than they can afford on billboards with phrases like "Have Mercy On Me Jesus; Forgive Me My Sins" (decorously unsigned, of course. Why along a stretch of highway, like one of those "Gotcha! You looked!" advertising billboards? Do they reckon that, just maybe, God *is* somebody's co-pilot, and this is the best way to catch His eye between scrolling through the playlist for "In Memory of Elizabeth Reed" and cracking open a fresh can of Kodiak snuff?) But it's not just Protestants or Americans who have God constantly on their lips (in a brasher, and much different way, than the discreet Catholic at the communion rail) — there's never an atheist in a foxhole, as the saying goes, and everyone, I mean it, everyone invokes Him, especially in times of crisis. For, departing from speculative philosophy and theology for the moment, God is, at the very least, a bowl of popcorn after a hearty sob; a Linus blanket after a thunderous fright; a calm self-assurance that there is a plan for the world (meaning, "for me") and that everything is going to turn out all right (again, "for me.")

Boy oh boy, do people get God wrong, or what?

Or, on the other hand, maybe they get Him right, after all.

I don't want to get into a huge discussion about Adam and Eve — although I guess I probably could. They say that foreknowledge does not equal fore-ordination. They say that just because a person sitting on a high hilltop is able to foresee that the one truck barreling down the narrow, one-lane road and the other truck barreling up the same narrow, one-lane road, are going to crash head-on once they round the corner that's obstructing their view and get the surprise of their lives, that person does not *cause* the accident to happen. That may be true for you and me, but what if that "person" on the hilltop put the trucks on the road in the first place? Right? I mean, that's not the nicest thing to do, is it?

Then again there's that jokester God in the chapters of the Old Testament. The one that says to Abraham, "kill your son, if you're so faithful to me," knowing all the while that the *right* response is *not* "OK, here we go, lay down on the improvised altar, son, while I slit your windpipe for the greater glory of the Lord of Hosts," but "NO WAY! You want the boy's life, take it. You can't ask me to do evil. What's wrong is wrong, and even you can't change that."

You think that the experience that faithful Daddy Abraham put Isaac through didn't have *profound* consequences on that poor bastard's development? Maybe all of the subsequent cruelty in the Old Testament, and the New, in the Ages of Faith and the subsequent Days of Disbelief, can be traced to that one moment of pure horror to which a child was subjected, by his father, out of a blind and unthinking devotion to an absurdity. Yet no one calls the Divine Jokester to task for it.

The ways of God are mysterious.

"My thoughts are not your thoughts."

And so forth.

But who needs Abraham and Isaac, when we have Elvis.

Yep, you heard me right.

The King.

The biggest reason why the signs greeting you as you cross the border into Mississippi read "The Birthplace of American Music." And not just American music, after all.

"His measurable effect on culture and music was even greater in England than in the States," said Mick Fleetwood.

"He was the firstest with the mostest," said Roy Orbison.

"Elvis was the king. No doubt about it. People like myself, Mick Jagger, and all the others only followed in his footsteps," said Rod Stewart.

Can you see where I'm going with this?

Tupelo, Mississippi, January 8, 1935.

A woman is giving birth.

To twins.

At 4:35 that morning, Elvis Aaron Presley makes the first noise of a long and successful career, when he howls after being slapped on his rear end, suspended from his ankles. Next to his mother, on the bed, covered in a sheet, cools and stiffens his stillborn brother, Jessie Garon, who emerged from the same maternal darkness thirty-five minutes earlier, without, poor child, even making a peep.

The Lord giveth and the Lord taketh away.

Two brothers.

And the Lord had respect unto Elvis and to his offering. But unto Jessie Garon and to his offering he had no respect.

"Ask anyone," said Elton John. "If it hadn't been for Elvis, I don't know where popular music would be. He was the one who started it all off."

DING DING DING!

"Nothing really affected me until Elvis," said ... wait for it! ... *John Lennon.*

"Tell Elvis that if it hadn't been for him, I wouldn't be here." For McCartney, "Heartbreak Hotel ... was a magical moment, the beginning of an era."

Get it now?

So God decides to let only one of the twins live. He taketh Jessie, he giveth Elvis, and a direct line is drawn between that shack of a house in Tupelo to Liverpool where — had Jessie been the one unto whom the Lord had respect, John Lennon would be a frustrated Joycean poet spattered with oil in some Scouser's chippie and Paul McCartney would have grown into the UK version of Lawrence Welk, neither *Abbey Road* nor *Magical Mystery Tour* would have been composed, let alone famously for sale in record shops and iTunes Store, and the Second Falklands War would not have ended as it did, two days ago, with the Islas Malvinas reunited to their Argentine homeland, while poor John Bull looked on from afar, nervously wringing his hands in impotent rage. For what could poor England do, after the successful, opportunistic Japanese occupation of Australia, another "treacherous" act by a false friend?

Surely, God — who could have let both boys live, and the elder twin Jessie hook up his younger sibling with a job at the iron-works in nearby Alabama, diverting Elvis from his path to Pop Coronation and ensuring him a comfortable, though nondescript, biblical three-score-and-ten of marriage, children, illegitimate grandkids, union dues, and socially acceptable alcoholism — bears *some* of the responsibility for all that has happened?

Well, speaking of England, remember: it's where Billy got God. Or vice versa. It happened this way (to the detriment of Seattle and Portland, both in the crosshairs of North Korea and Japan, pawns in a Pacific Rim battle of nerves between the two Asian superpowers).

"Why did you do that?"

A firm hand fell upon Billy Kowalski's shoulder at the same time as the words fell into his ear. He jumped in surprise — but then let out an audible sigh of relief upon seeing that the person who was accosting him was not a Pennsylvania State Trooper sent over to England with the express mission of arresting him for murder, but rather a slight, blond man in a blue cardigan, jeans, and a clerical collar at the neck of his gray shirt.

"Do … what?"

"Give her your food," the priest said, nodding slightly toward the girl crouched on the sidewalk across from Paddington, who was pulling out the Whopper and onion rings from the paper bag he'd just set in her hands.

"Shouldn't I have?" Billy asked, wondering if he'd just committed another faux pas on foreign soil.

"You were very kind to do," the priest smiled. "As the Lord said, "I was hungry, and you gave me to eat, and inasmuch as ye have done it unto one of the least of these my brethren, ye have done it unto me."

Billy was struck speechless for a moment. Then, whether it was the kind smile of the priest — the first he had received in England from a person who was neither looking to lighten his wallet or had the power of admitting him to or expelling him from the country — the exhaustion of the long journey, or the strain weighing down his conscience since the fatal accident from which he was running, he burst out sobbing.

"Bloody knob," said the girl he'd just fed, disgusted at his unmanly shower of tears. She gathered up her styrofoam cup half-filled with spare change along with the Burger King bag in which she had replaced the meal and moved off down the street toward the turning that leads to Sussex Gardens. But the priest opened wide his arms, and pulled Billy close, gathering him to his chest, patting him on the back, until the fit of bawling passed.

"There, there," he said. "How about a nice hot cuppa?"

Billy had no idea what that meant, but he had nothing else on the agenda and so he allowed himself to be led away by the kindly man.

The priest in question was Fr. Jonas Carlyle, who was assisting the vicar at a High Church parish in Sussex Gardens. It was there, to the vicarage, that he took Billy for a cup of tea and a few odd, finger-longish sandwiches that the vicar's wife had prepared for lunch. It was there that Fr. Carlyle learned Billy's story — *No, of course, not all of it! although the poor bastard was so frazzled at the moment, that he just might have come right out with the whole thing if, somehow, something sparked the confession tensed on the tip of his tongue* — it was there that Billy had a bath (after painfully extracting his swollen feet from the python boots), got his clothes laundered, and was presented with two pair of clean used changes from the parish charity rummage bin; it was there that Billy found lodging for the duration of his stay in the capital; it was there he attended Mass, daily, even participating as a lector from time to time.

It was there that Billy embraced the Anglican faith after so many years of indifference to the Church he had been baptized in as a child.

Why?

Well, certainly, as we said before: here was God coming to tell Billy that "everything is all right" (at least for him; it's a bit more equivocal with that other poor bastard, Jason Bartosz, isn't it?) and what's more, it wasn't just his rationalizing conscience delivering the message, but *someone else*, and on top of all that, an *ordained minister of the Word*, a professional representative of God, who ought to know the lay of the land, right? "I, even I, am he that blotteth out thy transgressions for mine own sake, and will not remember thy sins" … "Come now, and let us reason together, saith the Lord: though your sins be as scarlet, they shall be as white as snow; though they be red like crimson, they shall be as wool." … "Repent ye therefore, and be converted, that your sins may be blotted out when the times of refreshing shall come from the presence of the Lord." … Such were the words of encouragement that Fr. Carlyle set before Billy at the odd moment when they were alone, at the breakfast table, or at the soup kitchen in Brixton, washing clean the cauldrons for the next day's gruel, or ladling out the cream of tomato as the grimy indigent filed past (more of that in a moment), for Fr. Carlyle was intuitive enough to guess that Billy had something on his conscience but British enough not to push the matter to an effective conclusion, encouraging him to get off the pot and confess his sins … All this was good enough for Billy, the seeming blank checks of the first two quotations (Isaiah and Acts, if you're keeping score). And truth be told, he wasn't all that well up on the theology of repentance, although he intuited that, in exchange for that forgiveness, God wanted something from him — and so he was happy to tag along with Fr. Carlyle and help out, every day, at charity store and food pantry. He knew nothing of the necessity of confessing his sins verbatim and expressing remorse for them, and Fr. Carlyle, who stuck with him to the very end of his stay in England and even delivered him to Grosvenor Square towards the middle of the week (where he got his passport) and Terminal 3 at the end of it (where he used it for the first time), never rubbed the quat to the sense, as it were. Had he done so, of course … as it is, he too must be called to account for the atrocities committed near Ocala (if atrocities they were and not just propaganda; with Photoshop it's never been easier to work the convenient political trompe l'oeil).

It should also be no odd thing to consider that Cranmer's liturgy should fall more sweetly into the ear of Billy Kowalski (he was an actor, after all, wasn't he?) than the flat post-Vatican II text he remembered from the boring Sundays at Mother of Sorrows parish in Sanantone …

Of course, none of this — the frequent Masses, the work in the soup kitchen — brought Jason Bartosz back from that undiscovered country from whose bourne, alas, no traveler returns. But it did bring Billy Kowalski back to the United States a profoundly changed person. Alas, again.

In the hot interior of his car in the long-term parking lot at JFK, he blessed himself before turning the key in the ignition. All the long way home to Sanantone, *the poor kid* (Jason Bartosz) was never far from his thoughts. In calling God to his rescue, Billy made a pact with him (in almost Mormon-like fashion, he believed that the peace and conviction he felt in his breast upon making that pact signified that it was acceptable unto the Lord). The pact went as follows:

1. I killed a person, but by accident, not by malicious intent.

2. I must take responsibility for this accident, but

3. Turning myself in will do no good. It will not bring the poor kid back to life, it will deprive the Lord of an eager, if late-coming worker to the vineyard (*he was speaking about himself, in case you're in any doubt*), and, in the case of my being sentenced to prison, it will merely add to the tax burden of the Pennsylvanians who will be forced to pay my room and board (*prison*).

4. But O Thou *Almighty God, unto whom all hearts are open, all desires known, and from whom no secrets are*

hid, thou knowest the truth of that fatal confluence when, all unknowing, I struck down my brother (*He was an actor, after all, beginning with Cranmer's second person familiar from the Collect for Holy Communion, he continued to use it*) Thou knowest as well that, not only did I not intend the tragedy, but I am heartily sorry for it, and thus I lay at the feet of Thy judgment (*his phrase; felicitous or not, he smiled inwardly*),

5. I shall return home; if Thou dost direct the agents of justice to my threshold, I shall answer their questions truthfully, even though it means self-incrimination, safe in the conviction that such is Thy holy will;

6. But, while I shall conceal nothing, and nothing prevaricate, I shall not come forward, and if Thou dost in Thy wisdom deem it seemly to let this cup pass away from me, I shall accept it as a sign of Thy great grace and forgiveness unto me, thy poor and wretched servant, and in my gratitude unto Thee, O Father, I shall devote myself to walking in Thy righteousness, now and forevermore.

In other words, Billy was saying to God, "OK. If you want me to face the music, start up the band. If I hear nothing more from you on this, I'll take it for granted that we're quits and I don't hafta worry about it no more." And he concluded his deal, not with a bloody signature, but the final sentence before the commandments passage, *Cleanse the thoughts of our hearts by the inspiration of Thy Holy Spirit, that we may perfectly love Thee, and worthily magnify Thy holy Name, through Christ our Lord, Amen,* by which what he really meant to say, "give me a Mulligan on this one, and I'll be a good boy from here on out."

I won't go into the theological niceties of this approach to the murder (I'm sorry, but as far as Jason Bartosz is concerned, such terms as "involuntary manslaughter" and "unfortunate accident" are just hair-splitting); I remember from high school religion class that St. Thomas Aquinas once said that no one life is of more intrinsic value than another — but he can't have had a situation like this in mind when he said that; this has nothing to do with a justified killing in self-defense, after all. But — *hey God, you listening?* — had God sent those agents of justice to Billy Kowalski's threshold, and had he (as he obliged himself to do) neither concealed anything nor prevaricated in any way, had, in short, the cup *not* passed him by and had he accepted a ten to sixteen-month sentence for involuntary manslaughter, increased, say, to twenty-four months behind bars because of the recklessness of his conduct, well, released on good behavior after, say, twenty months at an average rate of 15% or so of good conduct reduction, he would have been released from prison in 1990 at the latest, and the pogroms of Cuban Americans flooding north Florida and Georgia in fear of repression at the hands of the Dirección de Inteligencia (whose agents dry-footed Florida along with the Fuerzas Armadas Revolucionarias) would never have occurred some few short decades afterward.

But God, in His wisdom, not only seems to have accepted the pact offered Him by Billy Kowalski (did he or didn't he? we'll never know, will we? not in this life at the very least), but also as a sign of great grace and forgiveness unto His poor and wretched servant, said, in effect, "OK bub. Even Moses had a body; go and sling your arrows no more," to the undying regret of the ranchers along the Rio Grande, who recently experienced on their own skin the chagrin tasted by Mariano Vallejo in 1846 during the self-righteous Bear Flag Revolt.

'What goes around,' as they say, 'comes around.'

El que la hace, la paga.

Write that down for later.

And so, upon returning from London, Billy Kowalski pulled into his driveway in a much calmer mood from that in which he'd left it, a week earlier. There was no tiptoeing or soft-clicking of car doors, pressing down of trunks. He slammed the driver's side door as he always did, unlocked his front door, and walked in, after extracting a fistful of mail from his letterbox (no summonses, no notifications, adverts, and bills and a magazine in a brown paper envelope which he immediately tossed into the trash, firmly intending to cancel his subscription before the day was out), entering the cool interior of the living room he had left in such haste a week before, the screen door slamming (as the Boss once sang) behind him.

He felt a breeze from the back of the house; entering the kitchen, he found the door as he'd left it; hanging from one hinge at a crazy angle; no yellow police tape barring entry, everything in its place, the only evidence of intrusion being pecan and hazelnut shells left on countertop and kitchen floor by a squirrel (or squirrels) who took advantage of free access to the pantry.

Billy went out into the yard. He shivered slightly at the sight of those archery targets, but let out a sigh, took a deep breath, rolled his head on his neck, shook out his arms, and trudged slowly but steadily up to the dirt road running alongside the wood.

The body was gone, of course. There was no yellow tape there either or any other evidence of an investigation. There were none of those little plastic yellow wedges with black numbers you see on those CSI shows; no chalked outlines of the body in the position it fell; there were even a few fresh bike tracks passing right over the site where Jason Bartosz's life was stopped, suddenly and prematurely, just days previous to this; bike tracks and a flattened empty can of Schweinharn beer.

Billy didn't pause long there (he'd made his pact with God and fully intended to uphold his end of it, but why call needless attention to oneself?), rather, he walked down the dusty footpath in the cool of the evening woods, toward the south-west, where the orange sun was bleeding out calmly, pulled out the rosary he'd bought in the St. Paul's Cathedral gift shop, and began to recite as much of The Litany or General Supplication as he could remember. And he remembered quite a lot of it —all the way through, "In all time of our tribulation; in all time of our prosperity; in the hour of death, and the day of judgment, Good Lord, deliver us" — a prodigious feat of memory for most of us, I dare say (he'd been an Anglican for *less than a week!*), but you have to remember, Billy was an actor.

So you're too young to remember Flip Wilson.

That means you're too young to remember *Hee Haw*, right?

That corny and yet so comforting hour of Americana radiating from the Grand Ole Opry (by ricochet) each Saturday evening. KORN, Buck Owens and Roy Clark a-Pickin'an'a-Grinnin', the Joke Fence, Archie's Barbershop, Justice O'Peace ... *Everything is fine. The sunsets on Kornfield Kounty, of which we all are Kalm (sorry, Kouldn't resist it) patriotic and God-fearing locals, and upon us, it shall rise in the morning, after shedding its warming rays on the bacon-rind banner hauled up before the schoolhouse, now and forever, Amen.*

Some of us clutch our God (and guns), some of us have Junior Samples ...

Where O where, are you tonight?
Why did you leave me here all alone?

Because it turned out not to be forever, after all.

On the other hand, who knows, but if the Cubans are satisfied with Florida, and President Paz keeps his word and remains west of the Sabine River, we (those who wish to remain, for lack of a better term, Gringo Americans) actually *will* all be residents of Kornfield Kounty in saecula, to shift inappropriately from God's own KJV English, saeculorum? The good Christian folks at WSM in Nashville haven't skipped a beat despite all the chaos (seems like nobody wants Tennessee, or, at the very least, nobody can think up a good reason to justify in the eyes of the world the annexation of that marvelous city of Nashville), the Grand Ole Opry remains the longest-running, continuous radio program in the world, its offerings indistinguishable from the content of, say, 2018, 1988, 1978, and as far back as you want to go (*begatbegatbegat*), although these days, of course, they're charged with a far greater significance for the agitated faithful. "Courtesy of the Red White and Blue" alternates with "Swing Low, Sweet Chariot" with "That Aint' no Rag, it's a Flag" with "Give me Jesus" with "There's a Star-Spangled Banner Waving Somewhere," which these days might sound more ironic than it was ever meant to, if not for the fact that a walk down Broadway, or through Opryland, today would prove that it's business as usual in these (remaining) United States of America; the Star-Spangled Banner *is* waving there, and proudly; if anything, these last several months have only created an atmosphere of Bible-belt on steroids for all of Gringolandia stretching from the Great Smokey Mountains up to the tip of Maine and off to Cadillac Mountain "where God smiles first on America / each morning as the angels sing," (according to the refrain of a popular countrypolitan ballad written — not according to Wag-the-Doggish legend, after the sacrifice of its hero "Private MacElroy, the third-string high school fullback / who threw his burly body down upon / the IED along the dusty desert track / cried out 'God bless America!' an' was gone" — but, predating the present crisis, in 2004, in a Dunkin' Donuts in Milwaukee, by a frustrated Telecaster twanger who changed his name from Eddie to Trace, who was never in the military, and who, in strange despair, grew a beard, converted to Islam and died in a bus accident near Riyadh while making the hajj, never to enjoy the fruits of the success of his one hit song, as recorded by Jumbo Williams and the Eighteen Wheelers).

But we were talking about Billy Kowalski, who returned from London refreshed, calm in his new-found, sober High Church Anglican faith, growing calmer as every day passed without a single officer of the law, be it a local Barney Fife or a smooth Fed in dark glasses, showing up at his door or place of employment with inconvenient questions. God did not change His mind. (Which is, after all, one of His attributes, despite all your Nineveh yarns or Abrahamic bargaining "and should I find but one just man in Sodom?")

Day passed into week, week into month, month into year, and the unsolved, violent death of Jason Bartosz grew ever colder. The world moved on. Billy kept those archery targets up in his yard, although he never returned to the sport, for months on end, almost *inviting* queries from the authorities (did they never venture beyond the path where the poor boy fell dead?

Did they never look into Billy's backyard?

Did they never do those Sherlock-Holmsean CSI missile-trajectory computer recreations, which, as the never-lying TV assures us, would have led them right to the spot from which said missile had been launched? To find size 11 and 1/2 footprints still faintly bending the tender grass low?

I guess not.

Figure it out!

This is your bailiwick anyway …)

It was only in the next spring when taking advantage of
the Neighborhood Garage Sale!

Twelve Homes!

Come find your Treasure!

Billy dismantled the targets (it was becoming a bore to
mow the grass around them), set them up for sale, selling
every last one of them (to four guys in identical John Deere
baseball caps, a nervous blonde with a concealed carry
permit, whose breath stank of chewed fingernails, and an
old pack-rat of a woman in a flamingo mu-mu, who had
her dashboard piled with so many bobbleheads and lucky
Chinese cats waving one paw that it's a wonder she could
navigate the Tower-of-Babel-piled bed of her F-150 back
down the Rinnahannock highway to Norton.

He cleared $450, all of which he donated to the Emergency
Shelter program of the Episcopal Diocese of Bethlehem
(where his new parish, St. Erkenwald's, was located).

Nor was this the extent of the new straight and narrow
path he was treading. In his devotion to keeping up his end
of the deal struck with the Almighty, he:

1) volunteered twice a week at the St. Vincent de Paul
soup kitchen in Wixburn;

2) gave up his weekends to Meals on Wheels, not only
delivering food to the homebound, but sitting down with
them and listening to their bitching and moaning about
negligent offspring and grandchildren, giving then all at

least a full ten minutes of his time before excusing himself with "I'd love to stay longer, Dot, but I've got to get the meatloaf to Stella, you know;"

3) gave so much blood at Red Cross drives around the area as to endanger his health;

4) traveled to local hospices and retirement homes twice monthly to perform Shakespearean monologues in front of oldsters drowsing or more preoccupied with Digoxin and catheters than dactyls and Capulets (even though nobody really listened to him, this was the most satisfying of his charity works, so much so, that it made him feel guilty),

and

5) spending every vacation thereafter in London, with his friend Fr. Carlyle, continuing his good works among the poor and ragged of the capital. (Which also made him feel guilty, as he didn't spend all of his time in Hackney and Tower Hamlets, but also at the National Theatre on the South Bank and flitting from show to show in the West End).

Of course, none of this did poor Jason Bartosz any good. Perhaps Billy's prayers on his behalf did (although Cranmer removed all such intercessions for the departed from the Book of Common Prayer beginning in 1552.

Nasty old man.

Now, in my opinion, we ought even to pray for him.

And for number 49, believe it or not. Really!)

And this is where the matter gets sticky.

Not with prayers for the dead, but with Billy turning a new (and, reasons for the turning being what they are, what can he do about that? improved) leaf.

The first day back at work, as Billy strode down the produce aisle at Wartella's (it led from the front door to the back, where the employees punched in), and I and Jason (Hughes, the bass player) were rotating avocados and radishes, he responded to Jason's:

"Well if it isn't the old sod,"

not with

"Fuck you, asshole,"

but with

"Hello, Jason. Hello Ray. Nice to see you both again," smiling in what we could only take to be a sardonic manner (but all the same uneasily sensing something odd, like sincerity, behind it), before disappearing past the swinging metal doors.

We stood there, agape, I suppose, or flummoxed.

Then the world was jerked back into its usual grooves; I tossed a few more bags of radishes on the rack and Jason said:

"What a dick. What, is he acting like a *proper British fucking gentleman* now, or what? What a dickhead. The dick."

We thought it would pass. But this was the new reality. Like it or not, Billy Kowalski had changed, somehow.

"Hey fuckhead," Jason once called over to Billy, while the latter was transferring cellophane-wrapped trays of chicken fingers from his trolly to the refrigerated displays, "you still choking your own chicken in the shower?"

"Ha, ha," Billy responded, in what sounded like a genuine chuckle, then: "Jason, you still a baseball fan?"

"Um … yeah …" Jason responded, unsurely, whiskers twitching uneasily, wondering if the new Billy was setting a trap for him.

"Oh, great. Listen, this guy I deliver food to on my Meals route has a grandson who works for the Red Barons. He gave me these two tickets to Friday night's game. You want them? They say that Lenny Dykstra's being sent down for a rehab assignment ... Box seats, right behind the home dugout ..."

And he produced the tickets.

Jason (a huge baseball fan) almost drooled. But he couldn't take them. Angry at himself, and at Billy, and the whole concept of patience and kindness, he retreated to the backroom, slamming open the door in anger,

"Hey!"

almost breaking my nose in the process (it was me who shouted; I was coming the other way with half a watermelon I'd sliced and wrapped at the request of a customer), and adding insult to injury by tossing out an angry,

"Watch the fuck out, will you?" (This was Jason), "That's what the windows in the doors are for, you cocksucker!" (which admonition, I think you'll agree, would have been more justly directed at him, than at myself).

"Shit for brains!" he added, and I tensed.

I bit my lips.

I screwed my eyes closed so tight, I saw a white light. My fingers tensed on the underside of the watermelon half so tightly, that the tension pulled apart the plastic wrap and the damn thing tumbled down onto the floor and splattered. See what I mean about what that phrase does to me?

It's time to tell you about Axel Ross.

No, not Axel Rose — though it's both touching and encouraging that you recognize the name — Axel *Ross*. But to tell you the truth, it wouldn't have made much difference had it been the one rather than the other.

Anyway,

Axel *Ross* went to elementary school with me.

Yep.

Good old Washington Ave.

His father worked for the Marine recruiting center down by the prop airport and was active in the Toys for Tots program. I'm not sure why this has any bearing on the subject at hand, but it's the one thing I remember about him. That and his blue nylon parka with the fake fur around the hood.

Axel and I weren't friends.

We weren't enemies, either.

We just went to school together.

One day, out in the schoolyard, we were playing hockey with a crushed soda can. These were the good old days — the early seventies — before adults got all jumpy about soft playgrounds and no-child-left-behind-with-bacteria. The schoolyard was black asphalt. Somebody crushed a soda can flat and noticed that when he kicked it, it skidded across the asphalt like a hockey puck over ice. And so a bunch of us got together at recess, formed two teams, and started playing "hockey" (even though we were all wearing sneakers, and kicking the "puck" — we'd never call it "soccer" — because back then, soccer was for sissies).

Now, Axel was in one of the goals, marked with two knit hats, you know, toques — Robbie Yaneski's Packers hat, and Billy Drew's Redskins. The game was fun; we were all having a great time— you know kids, when they get into something, they lose track of everything. I wish I could concentrate like a kid playing hockey with a tin can on asphalt ...

So, the bell for the end of recess rings, the score is tied, and there's this scrum near Axel's goal. Two kids (me not among them) are scrapping for the puck, kicking each other's shins and feet, tussling with handfuls of each other's sweaters. Suddenly, the puck squirts loose, and it comes my way. I send it scudding towards Axel's goal; he comes out for it, then halts, so as not to leave a clear shot should I pass to someone on the left; Robbie runs up, and the scrum resumes, in front of the goal this time, me and Robbie. The puck is being mauled along the edges — now under Robbie's foot, now under mine; it squirts about, maybe six inches at a time, before one of us steps on it, scrapes it across the asphalt, kicks, and misses (whanging toes off the asphalt) ... Then, all of a sudden, Axel goes to his knees and covers up the puck with his bare hands!

Stupid thing to do, but logical — according to the rules, only he could touch the puck with his hands — but, stupid because we're all, what, ten years old? and wholly in the moment?

So, here I am, making no distinction between Robbie's Converse-armored foot and Axel's little, unprotected hands; I'm just kicking and kicking, trying to force that puck between the hats for the winning goal before Mr. Smedlie comes over (as he always did) to rush us lingerers into the school five minutes after the bell, and I'm kicking and kicking the puck, in the moment, not thinking of anything but that goal, not thinking, really, and here — what the fuck was wrong with him, anyway? — instead of just letting the goddam thing past him, who gives a crap about a children's game at recess? — Axel is pressing it down into the asphalt; the flesh on the side of his hands is getting pink, and then red, as the now warm and ragged can is beginning to cut into his hands, and I don't stop until some loud screaming pierces the frenzy in my head —

"What's wrong with you? Idiot!"

— it was Axel, getting up now, with the puck in his hands. Pissed off, he flung it at my chest.

"Shit for brains!"

he said, tears in his eyes,

and that's when I clocked him, as hard as I could.

Don't you agree that the day and age we live in is suffused with vulgarity?

I'm not just talking about TV shows, although, gosh, let anyone born after 1981 listen to George Carlin's "Seven Dirty Words You Can't Say on TV," and *they won't get it.* Because I'm fairly that sure that I've heard at least five of them, recently, on the broadcast networks. And "that sucks?" "You suck?" "It really sucks, that …" since when has it been OK to say that, anywhere? But now it's common parlance. Gosh, that used to be — considering *what* was being sucked — a top-of-the-list candidate for Saturday afternoon confession. Now, I've even heard a priest use it, during a sermon. I'm not just talking about popular culture. Pick up any novel, any highbrow writing, have a look at any ambitious film by any hot new *auteur* and you're sure to come across f-bomb after f-bomb; f-carpet bombing, you might say; and in those films, cripes! nothing is left to the imagination ... To think that once upon a time there used to be rules in Hollywood about one leg on the floor during bedroom scenes; tongueless kissing shot from the waist up; twin beds in conjugal bedrooms ... Well, I don't have to go on.

You go to the movies, right?

But I forgot. You *were* born after 1981; you *don't* know who Flip Wilson, or maybe even George Carlin, was ...

The point that I'm trying to get at is, although we're surrounded by vulgarity, and although we are creatures of our surroundings, and although I f-bomb as much as the next man and toss off, "the Phillies suck," without so much as a second thought, I have a problem about the phrase that Axel Ross used.

I mean a real problem.

An issue.

A friend of mine who ... well, that's neither here nor there ... but a friend of mine once said that I might have something called Intermittent Explosive Disorder. I once looked that up, online of course, and I must say that I'm not convinced. But the phrase that Axel used back then — the phrase I am carefully avoiding right now (although, if *I* use it, it doesn't quite affect me, maybe because it doesn't jump out at me like a bat swooping down from the curtain rod in the summertime — so, OK, the term you tossed out a while ago: id est, *shit for brains*) can be kind of a trigger for me. Just look back to that asphalt playground.

Axel got up shouting, calling me an idiot — and I stopped kicking the can. Then Axel threw the can at my chest — and I stood there stunned. That's when Axel called me *shit for brains* and a millisecond later he was out cold on the asphalt, immobile, with half the kids kneeling around him and pulling at his sweater (one kid pissing his pants crying, two others, believe it or not, laughing) and the other half of the kids running after Mr. Smedlie crying "Ray Verano just killed Axel Ross!"

I don't even remember throwing the punch, it happened so quickly.

No, I didn't kill him.

I punched him, he fell awkwardly and knocked his head against the asphalt and blacked out for a bit; then he came round, I got detention, my parents had a penitential coffee with his parents, and my mother never let me forget about Axel Ross and "Charlie," just waiting for me around the next corner, maybe, shaggy grandson of perdition that I may well be …

Why does this term affect me so much?

Why is it such a trigger?

Ask the arachnophobe why it's the sight of a spider that sends him into paralysis.

Ask the agoraphobe what happened to him that he suddenly became terrified of public places.

Is there ever a moment that can be pinpointed, long ago, in someone's childhood — say, a scratch and a nasty infection from Auntie Charlottes' tabby, or the sight of a kitty decapitating a struggling rodent, that the ailurophobe can acknowledge as "yep; my irrational fear of cats springs from that there, you betcha?"

Same thing with me. I don't know how it started. It must've been in me already, before the day that I "killed" Axel Ross. I can tell you that I don't like to dwell on the idea — one's head ... aslosh with feces ... *Brr.* That'll be with me now, all day long, like the refrain of a song you can't get out of your head. Not entirely thanks to you, but you didn't help matters any ...

But, as I say, when *I* talk about it, I'm, I guess, inoculated, prepared — it doesn't affect me the way, say, cats do to that person I mentioned before. He's not just afraid of cats springing out at him unexpectedly; he has a fear of cats, always and everywhere. He can't go up and pet a cat on his terms. And the agoraphobe can't just decide to handle a walk through the mall today, because he's prepared for it. Malls don't pounce on a person. He's simply terrified of being among people, period.

With me, it's the unexpected *shit for brains* that can set me off. I mean, I know about my problem and have struggled against it, with some success. For example, I did jump in my seat at the movies when it was first said — in the opening moments — of *LBJ*, but then I gripped the armrests with white knuckles, tried to think about something else — *Fried cod, fried cod, fish and chips, fried cod* sometimes works, and calmed down.

But then Woody Harrelson said it again! And so I tore up from my seat and marched out of the cinema and left my friend there without a ride home. But it was better than risking the trifecta, believe you me …

Well, this has gone on long enough.

When Jason tossed out over his shoulder the very worst combination of words that he could have uttered at me, fortunately, he'd already sailed up the produce aisle, out of reach, and the only casualty of that *shit-for-brains-cat* suddenly springing down from the curtain rod and sinking its claws into my neck in front of everyone, was a half watermelon.

To get back to the important stuff, the war of angry confusion and Christian patience went on for several more weeks. Jason just couldn't break through the "whole armor of God" wherewith Billy had dighted himself, prudently following the advice of St. Paul. To Jason's "Hey Billy — I just read this thing that said that Shakespeare was a faggot. He made the Butt with Two Backs with the Earl of Southhampton. Taking his ham down south, you know?" Billy replied, "Yeah, I heard that too. Of course, it doesn't matter, does it? It doesn't change the value of his writing. They say the same thing about Eliot. Who cares? The *Family Reunion* is the *Family Reunion* …" to which Jason could only reply, "Here, reunite with *this* family," while grabbing his crotch — the contradictory nature of this homosexual innuendo completely lost on my friend and a perfect barometer of the great degree to which Christian patience triumphantly held the field against all the assaults of angry confusion.

I don't know why Billy's transformation had such an effect on Jason. Maybe it was because he had been *sure* that Billy was bluffing about that trip to London. And then was proven wrong. Maybe it was because although Jason had big dreams himself, for his music, and — as we know now — the ability to realize them if he ever really tried, he'd never traveled farther away from the house he was born in than Binghamton, while Billy had already been to London and back. And even if Billy didn't land a spot in the stable of some theatrical agent "in the old sod," at least he went, tried, and left it on the field, as it were. Whereas for Jason, it was all still — always had been, and always looked to remain — a huge and increasingly unlikely hypothetical.

Whatever the case may be, it had such an effect on Jason, that *he* grew huge. First, he started eating meat again. And then junk food. And drinking oceans of beer. In the space of four weeks, he put on fifteen unnecessary and unbecoming pounds and showed no signs of slowing down.

It was then that it happened.

Somewhere, Jason found a hard-core pornographic photo shoot, with a Romeo and Juliet theme. Gleefully, he pulled it out of whatever magazine he grimed his fingers on thumbing for it, and, timing his break for five minutes after Billy took his, he sauntered upstairs and sat down at the table where Billy was picking through a smoked herring. Calmly, he spread the shoot out on the table, in the plain sight of his arch-enemy, and waited.

No reaction.

Nothing.

Billy calmly finished the fatty fish, wiped his fingers, and his mouth, with a paper napkin, directing such calm, but piercing, eyes at Jason that the latter couldn't take his stare, blushed, and dropped his eyes down and away to the left.

"Did you hear that McCartney's coming to Caseytown next month?" Billy said with a smile, "I know a guy who …"

"Fuck your guy!" Jason yelled, screeching his chair back across the linoleum with violence. One of the back legs of the chair caught against an uneven tile, and Jason, newly fat Jason, flopped over on his back and split his frayed and straining tan corduroys right down the middle seam.

"Are you all right?" Billy inquired with real concern, while Dora (she of the champagne glasses) laughed aloud and snorted Sprite out through her nose.

"Fuck you!" said Jason, clambering to his feet, "And fuck McCartney!" At which he gave the swinging break room door a violent shove. It was the wrongest moment possible for that, as that other Bill, the manager, was just on the other side of the door. Unlike me and my watermelon, Bill the Manager did not avoid the impetus of the metal door. Thwacked a nice thump, he somersaulted backward down the twenty-odd steps to the little alcove where the time clock was kept. There he landed bad and broke both his right wrist and his left shin (*I know! OUCH!*). To add insult to injury, the time clock also received such a thwacking thump that it had to be replaced — as did, of course, Jason, who was sacked on the spot, as soon as Bill controlled his Joe Theismann-like agony and was able to form the requisite, saltily-laced phrase.

And this was the last I saw of Jason Hughes until that phone call with which I began my account.

Having finished Hanskung, I went off to CUNY, from whence (why? O why?) I returned here and took up at Hanskung where I'd left off — on the other side of the desk, but just as despairingly bored and hopeless. And here I remained (*Lasciate ogni speranza,* as the famous quote begins) until … well, you know …

But Christian patience, and Billy Kowalski, hadn't finished with Jason Hughes.

Over the years that I lost contact with Jason, and Billy, and Alison, Billy had moved on from Wartella's Market, getting his AS in Service Industry Management, and moving on to a director's position at that pharmaceutical company on Pennsylvania Ave. that I'm not supposed to mention (because of the opiates class-action suit which has been brought against them, to tell the truth). But he never forgot the debt he owed to his deal-making God, so he kept on truckin' (he kept that shirt as a reminder of that particularly bad time in his life, although the python boots were chucked out long ago, along with the Jordache jeans), giving blood, declaiming the Bard to the uninterested elderly, ladling soup at a kitchen run by the rival, Catholic diocese, and carting around Meals on his (new) Wheels (a Tucson had replaced the Corvette, just as Danny Gokey had replaced Ted Nugent on his playlist).

It was due to this last charitable occupation that his path and Jason's crossed once more.

Jason, as previously mentioned, had taken a BA in Professional Writing from Hanskung. But he never used it; after he'd been fired from Wartella's, he never worked again. He found himself in a very bad place, what with the self-disgust that comes with dramatic weight-gain, the despair at being unable to control his urges to eat and drink, the greater despair at living still in a place he despised, but could not escape (that boat, seemingly, having set sail long, long before), and the shame that still seared him at the sudden recollection of that horrible day, when he'd almost killed Bill the Manager.

He still lived at home, or rather walled himself up in the bedroom he'd occupied since being brought home, an only child, from the Central Community Hospital as an infant, rarely changing his clothes, rarely shaving or cutting his hair, never touching his Kent bass, which slowly acquired layer after layer of dust and fly-spots over the years, and listening to music only when he had twelve beers and a tumbler of Triple Sec in him, and was oiled-up well enough to feel sorry for himself.

It's not true that he kept his mother's body in a freezer in the basement so as to keep on collecting her Social Security checks. That is a lie made up by some online "community journalist" following the latest assassination and picked up by the twenty-four-hour "news" machine that, like Saturn, his infants, nourishes itself by consuming the latest, and yellowest, sensations (whether they're true or not). It is however true that he sponged off his parents mightily, outliving them both, but attending neither of their funerals, having determined never to show himself to anyone who even remotely knew of his previous existence ever again.

One weekend, to get back to the point (are you aware of how you tap tap tap your ballpoint against your legal pad when you're impatient?), Billy was out on his Meals on Wheels rounds. Because he still lived on Upper Drummond Road (unlike Jason, or me, he had no NEPA complex; his home, as he would say, being in Heaven and everywhere on this earth only a place of pilgrimage), his one concession to convenience was to constrict his Meals route to the Yonder Mountain area. The address in the fifties of Maplehurst Drive had just been recently added to the list. An old bachelor (Good God! That makes *four* of us in this story, already! Is it any wonder that the demographics of this country are changing so fast? Then again, as Esposito would say, neither I nor Jason are really white anyway, so maybe our lack of progeny is evening things out for the Prickneys and Kowalskis?); an old bachelor, I say, with a lisp and a mean, mangy Labrador, who (the bachelor, not the dog) to the despair of neighbors for two blocks at least in each direction liked to pump out at max volume old Lawrence Welk classics on a Wurlitzer, must also accept partial responsibility for the mess we're all in. After all, if it hadn't been for his just having turned 63 and retiring early because of a heart-murmur, Billy would never have been up Jason's way. Because (if you remember), Jason, too, lived on Maplehurst Drive — as a matter of fact, right across the street from Dooley Tompkins (Billy's new client).

It was March again, that Saturday. There'd been a rather strong windstorm the previous night, sweeping up from Hurley's Lake, knocking out power for six hours, and downing tree limbs all through the oak-lined streets (*sic*) of the Maplehurst development.

Now, Jason, who had spent most of the intervening years (with or without his parents) sprawled on the living room couch between a Party Size bag of Swarthcut potato chips and a Jumbo Size bag of Cheetos, with a whole platoon of dead soldiers ranged on the carpet between his swollen ankles and the incessantly droning television (QVC. Always QVC. Later on, he said that this had been part of his self-imposed punishment), had to venture outside that day because one of the branches that had been cast down by the gale had torn away the cable connection that he had rigged to steal the TV signal. He had always been good with electronics.

The entry point for the cable was on the side of the house that was exposed to the road. And so when Billy was coming down the concrete steps leading to Dooley Tompkins' front door and caught sight of the pot-bellied guy in the grimy sweatpants with a patchy beard adorning his double chin and tangled tufts of greasy hair such as even lice would consider uninhabitable, he did a double-take.

No. Can't be him.

But, as he got closer, resting his hand on the driver's side door of the SUV, he thought, *No. It HAS to be him.* So he let go of the handle and moved, gingerly, into the middle of the road.

"Jason? Is that you?" he asked.

Jason, screwdriver, and cable in hand, paused in his thievery, straightened up, and looked toward the voice.

"Billy. Billy Kowalski."

And, believe it or not, he smiled.

"Yeah," said Billy, coming across the road and smiling himself. "Wow! Great to see you. It's been years."

He held out his hand, and Jason took it in his own.

"What've you been up to?" Billy asked.

Jason, wallowing in a narrow triangle between defiance, sarcasm, and simple frankness, chose the last of these. After so many years of giving up, he gave up. Christian patience had won through.

"To tell you the truth, absolutely nothing."

"Nothing?"

"Vegetating. Watching TV. Growing fatter by the minute," he said, slapping the hairy paunch that spilled out between t-shirt and sweatpants.

"That sucks," said Billy. (See? Even Christians say it all the time!)

"Yeah," replied Jason, uncharacteristically smoothing his hair with his hands. "It does suck, actually," and he laughed. He laughed as if he'd just figured out a particularly difficult crossword. A cheap satori, but a real one nonetheless.

"So, just hanging here at home? You're not working anywhere?"

"Yep," said Jason, expansively waving his arms. "All this belongs to me. An inheritance," he said, employing a British accent for humor, which he immediately regretted, "from pater and mater."

Billy laughed.

"Well then, the lord and master of your domain," he said, responding in turn with a BBC accent,

"I will be master of what is mine own:

She is my goods, my chattels; she is my house;

My household stuff, my field, my barn,

My horse, my ox, my ass, my anything."

Jason smiled.

"Still at the Shakespeare?"

"Always. The love of my life."

"Do you ever get a chance to do him on stage? I remember you went to London once to …"

Billy winced, despite himself, but recovered quickly.

"No. But I do get a chance to recite him. I … give small performances, twice a month, usually," he said, stopping there, afraid that if he went into more depth about hospices and old folks' homes he could be sinning by way of pride.

"I'd like to come by and hear you some time," said Jason, sending out dove after dove, like a Noah, stoned in love with the world on Cancun Gold.

"Umhmm," said Billy, non-committal. "But hey, you finished school, right?"

"Yep."

"English, right?"

"Sort of. Professional Writing."

Billy bit his lip.

"Would you like to put your degree to work, if you had the chance?"

Jason bit his own, involuntarily glancing toward the window, past which the Cheetos were beckoning like an impatient lover at interrupted coitus.

"I guess I'd at least consider it …"

And this is how Billy, who was managing the Advertising and Design department at (*.*.*) Pharmaceuticals, and who had been given the green-light from the higher-ups to expand (and fast! This was the Wild West when drug commercials were first being allowed on TV, now: "Possible side effects include partial blindness, growing a third leg, cannibalistic urges, and death. If you are fully sighted, four-limbed, alive, and if the ingestion of human flesh is prohibited you by your medical professional or your religious tradition, *.*.*ical may not be right for you …") offered Jason Hughes a job as a shill for dangerous chemical compounds, got him back on his feet, gave him the confidence to break the cycle of comfort feeding and self-hatred, got him back on stage (and how!) rocking and rolling, and precipitated what you and I call World War III, but the Mexicans a "revindication of a historical injustice," the Cubans "a liberation of the working peoples of the Ché Guevara Peninsula (Florida)," the Russians "a prudent police action to preserve the peace and security of Russian North America," and the North Koreans "a glorious ejaculation of the magnanimous might and victory-wisdom of the great leader, who has trod the senile viper of the inane imperialistic tycoons beneath his dancing heel."

Which brings us back to Alison Prickney.

The dancing heels, that is.

Time to get creepy.

Sorry, but there's no other way if you want to get to the bottom of it all.

But we won't get *too* creepy. Or rather, creepy in an antiseptic, Byronic sort of way.

Do you know what the most popular winter Olympic sport among males of the 25–50 year-old demographic is?

Hockey?

Wrong.

Ski-jumping?

Wrong.

Figure skating.

Female figure skating, that is.

Oh, sure, they'll wax poetic about the cross-checking ability of Sweden's third line; they'll talk about *da balls* it takes to launch oneself off that icy gantry; they'll make all the requisite and proper jokes about the butt-cheeks and fruity sequined jumpers of the male figure skaters, but the guilty little secret they'll never admit? Sitting enraptured before the boob tube (sorry, too easy), their eyes locked onto each gyration, Besti squat and fan spiral (to say nothing of the cantilever) of the shapely teens in the mini-skirts and makeup.

I'll stop there, and just say one more thing that the 25–50 demographic of leering beer-swillers reading this novel have already intuited that I'm leading up to:

Alison Prickney had just that kind of a body.

Oh yeah.

(Now, *that* was creepy. Apologies).

This was her glory and her curse.

Let's say that old Genevieve Prickney never experienced the second sight that had her look beyond the allowed limits of the conjugal bed, leaving stable (if morosely Calvinistic) Mike Prickney for fun-loving, duck-tailed (if ambiguously perverse) Tommy Watson, taking poor Alison with her. Alison would have grown up in a stable, loving if slightly overprotective household. In her teens, she would have been happily aware of her nubile form, would have rebelled against her parents' restrictions in a healthy way, had some normal physical fun with boys her age (remember Phil Rizzuto on the first Meat Loaf album …? Of course you don't. Worth a listen, though), broke a heart, and had her own cracked a little bit at least before age 17, gone on to college and contraceptives and real, healthy love (with Jason Hughes maybe. Why not?) Become an unconsciously MILFy mother, vacationing in Virginia Beach and touring colleges from Davison to Rutgers with her honor-roll daughter (who would be being courted by D-I swimming programs, who doesn't want to go to school at all, but try her luck as a late-come beat poet in the fourth … um, is it the fourth wave, already, of the Allen Ginsberg wannabes?) in a dank coffeehouse on Columbus Avenue in a San Francisco still pretentiously unbombed and unirradiated.

As it was, Alison was remanded into the custody of her mother by the divorce court, moved will-she, nill-she from (what was not only) her Dad's house in the Yonder Mountain to that small house on Roosevelt St. in Countyline, and into the unhealthy proximity of her mother's second husband, Tommy Watson.

While Genevieve slowly transformed herself into Esposito, filling her days with Ouija boards, tarot cards, joss sticks, voodoo, and cheap bourbon, Tommy would spend his free time:

a. mistakenly opening the bathroom door when Alison was stepping into the bath ("Oh, sorry. Didn't know you were in here. You, uh, want me to wash your back?")

b. *insisting* that he be the one to take her to ballet class, and sitting there, when all the other parents had left, entrusting their charges to the capable hands of the ballet masters, apart from the other (mother(s)) who may have remained, with nothing else better to do.

These latter parents would whisper amongst themselves, their eyes unconsciously and uneasily drifting over to "Alison's stepdad" from the parquet floor and barre … did I say unconsciously? Perhaps subconsciously is a better word as, truth be told, although they wouldn't admit it to themselves or others, the main reason they were now staying behind was to make sure that their daughters had as little unsupervised time as possible in the same general area as this strange *balletomane* with the greasy hair and cuffed jeans (who did he think he was? Fonzie?) whose dark eyes stayed locked onto each arabesque, battement frappé and cabriole;

c. spending way too much time in the bathroom himself, from which he'd emerge with the latest copy of the O'Rigen *Regent* under his arm (this was the yearbook we received from the high school each year. I think it wasn't so much the action shots of the football squad that caught his attention, but the class pictures of the undergraduates, with the lines of shorter pupils, i.e. the girls in their short plaid skirts and tight blue sweaters, ranged along the front steps leading into the school. But that's just an educated guess).

Alison was a bright girl. She noticed all of these things, and interpreted them correctly, if uneasily. And living in this environment, every day of her life, she felt all of the healthy sexual urges in her adolescent body being slowly choked and withered like a plant whose roots were scorched with hypersalinic, briny water.

And so.

When Janet Rymkiewicz and Liza O'Toole melted at the sight of Robby Warschauer's droopy lower lip, which gave his thin face a James Dean sort of perpetual pout, all that Alison could see was Tommy Watson's fly-catching mouth, a string of saliva dripping from it one night when, sitting on the couch and watching *Happy Days* after her shower, her terrycloth robe fell open unknowingly, revealing a good portion of her young right thigh, as she sat with her foot set on the couch cushion.

And.

When Colleen Reilly squealed in delight as Jim Haschek, the point guard with the curly hair, grabbed her quickly around the waist as she walked down the third-floor hallway toward the cafeteria at the break and pulled her into the empty shop classroom, Alison shivered at the sudden flash of memory of that birthday party two years previous, when Tommy grabbed at her and spilled the chips, in an attempt to pull her onto his lap.

And.

Even in her senior year, which ought to have been the highlight of her life so far, as she was driving Janet and Colleen to ballet and they started comparing the relative sizes of the packages of Jim Haschek, and Johnny Stiles, and Sid Karlovsky, as they ostentatiously paraded the hallway from the weight room to the football locker room, clad only in their tight base layers, all she could think of was being driven to ballet last year, before her license, by Tommy, who (supposedly) had a broken passenger's side door, which (for some reason) he could never get around to getting fixed. Out on the sidewalk, as she approached the car after ballet, she noticed that Tommy was already sitting in the driver's seat of his 1977 Cutlass Supreme.

"Climb in," he said, opening the door.

"How? You're already sitting there, Tommy."

"Come on, kid, don't make a fuss. My back is killing me today. Don't make me get out again …"

And she — as usual — was about to give in, resigning herself to the indignity of sliding over his lap with his hands gripping her hips to "help" her across, when something finally snapped. She closed the door with a furious kick and walked all the way home from Carbon St., which took her a full two hours.

When she got to the center of the Barter St. Bridge, she paused and looked down onto the surface of the longest unnavigable river — creek, rather — in North America. What crossed her mind? The fact that, a month earlier, a semi-retarded woman who had been arrested for attempted murder had sprung out of the cruiser that had been transporting her to the county jail, leaped the barrier, and after plummeting, only succeeded in breaking both her legs.

Yep, in Wixburn people even fail at suicide.

Not that Alison considered such a drastic step. Whatever we might say about Alison Prickney, the one thing that no one could ever say about her was that she was a quitter. If anything, she despised any and every one (rightly or wrongly, I speak only of her, I make no judgments myself) who took the easy way out. Another paper she'd delivered in Mr. Easton's AP English class dealt with Robinson Jeffers' "Suicide's Stone."

You know the one.

It ends with:

[…] life broke ten whipstocks
Over my back, broke faith, stole hope,
Before I denounced the covenant of courage.

Ironically, of course, Esposito "hungered long and pitiably / That way," but it is completely untrue, the rumor (bandied about amongst us who knew her, not by the national news) that Alison's paper on this poem was found on the night table next to the empty bottle of pills on the day her mother took her own life.

It is also untrue, in my opinion, that Alison placed this paper, or the poem itself, on her mother's dead chest before the lid of the coffin was finally lowered at Stuhr's. If I know Alison, and I think I do, she would never do any such thing to anything she valued so highly as Robinson Jeffers' poetry. (Parenthetically speaking, one of her greatest desires, besides becoming a surveyor, was to visit the poet's home on the coast in Carmel. Now, of course, she'll never get the chance. Not one, but two — and perhaps even three — dreams were denied her by the queer circumstances of this life. That too ought to be some sort of record).

No, she wasn't a quitter. She passed on through high school, stoical, unable, physically unable, to respond to the interest the boys had in her (and that interest certainly existed); bearing all the opprobrium particular to humans in the nasty nonage, their immature, but strong, desires stifled by the object after which they lusted; whispers and overt challenges tossed over shoulders unscarred by the lashes of perversity, like "lesbo" and "dyke ..." though they may have stung at first, they quite soon rolled off her back harmlessly. She hadn't a lesbian thread in her fabric. It wasn't that she wasn't interested in boys; the very urge to physical intimacy with anyone had been stifled in her, by her stepfather's perversity, and her mother's ever more perverse unconcern.

"Ah, he's only fooling with you," she once replied, belittling her daughter's tears when she worked up the courage to broach the topic. "Forget it."

Apparently, Esposito's "Keep your hands off my daughter" applied only to boys of Alison's age. Especially us, "Mexicans."

Another thing that Alison kept at was her dancing. Logically enough, perhaps, it was a necessary outlet for the physical energy of her body; one which required the participation of no other party; one which she could control. So, she danced, but always alone. She joined the local ballet troupe, but only accepted those roles (in the yearly *Nutcracker*) which did not call for physical contact with any male dancer.

And she danced in church.

The vicar of St. Erkenwald's once called upon his parishioners to "participate more actively" in the life of the church; not to be like that wretched servant who "buried the talent entrusted him by the Lord, rather than employing it so as to present Him with a five-fold, or even ten-fold, return on His investment …"

Be careful, as they say, what you wish for. (Cubans take note! Maybe the annexation of the Che Guevara Peninsula isn't the best idea?)

Anyway, the vicar's challenge led to a plethora of wild proposals, such as Daisy Rutter's colorful afghan altar cloth, and Swingin' Jim Mikolajczyk's once (and once only) Polka liturgy, with Charles Wesley's venerable hymns arranged for accordion and clarinet. One of the more cultivated, but nonetheless odd, ideas was that of Alison Prickney herself. Inspired by the example of David, who was said to have danced from joy before the tabernacle of the Lord, she prevailed upon the poor priest (who, having endured all of the above "returns on talent entrusted," as well as Rhonda and Reese Shoemakers' "interpretation" of the liturgy for "the visually attuned," with Rhonda as mime and Reese as circus clown) to allow her to dance down the main aisle of the church with a bowl of smoking incense for the Solemn Service to be held on Pentecost.

It was a more elevated concept than Reese's plopping down on a whoopie cushion before the main altar, in the pied costume of a sad little hobo-clown, during the reading of Pilate's "behold the man." It was also of short duration (after a grateful sigh, as Alison disappeared into the sacristy, after twirling about and censing the sanctuary, the much-tried vicar was able to get on with the service in peace) — but it was a sensation.

At least amongst the 25–50 male demographic. For Alison was comely (to use the Biblical phrase), and her white, gauzy costume (whether she intended it, or no), was fairly revealing; to remain with Biblical tropes, I guess the easiest thing to compare it to would be Salome's getup at Herod's birthday party.

And this was the third week that Billy Kowalski had been attending St. Erkenwald's.

At the time, he was right about 38 years old.

Do you think it's true, what CNN is saying about the Muslims of Florida? That they had "mysteriously disappeared from public life concurrently with the Cuban invasion and occupation of the peninsula?" Or is that "documentary" aired by Tele Rebelde, *¡Por fin liberados!* true, in which the imam of the Islamic Center of St. Augustine spoke of being "liberated" (odd name, that — "Islamic Center of St. Augustine." Odder still that Florida's been "liberated" so far up the peninsula. Will the tanks finally grind to a halt at the Florida-Georgia line?) "thanks," (him smiling nervously all the while), "to the victorious Cuban army of liberation, who have brought real security to the Muslim faithful in Florida, who had been living in the shadow of fear since 9/11"?

Which of these is propaganda?

Both?

Neither?

One thing's for sure. It's certain that number forty- … I forget which of the forties it was right now, there having been such a turnover at the Oval Office lately … but one of those ex-presidents tweeted: "If #MuslimsInFlorida think they had it tough when the #SunshineState was part of the #GreatAmericanRepublic, just WAIT until they get a taste of #LifeInCuba!!!"

I mean, the enemy of my enemy is my friend and all that, but now that they don't need them anymore, do you think the Cubans are going to risk *that* sort of front opening up in their rear?

They're not known for wringing their hands in worry over the niceties of civil liberties, are they?

A handful of pliant token Muslims in a masjid in Daytona, say?

OK. But for the rest of them, the *potential* dissidents ... there's the Combinado del Este, at best ...

Speaking of St. Augustine, I once turned down a job there. Well, it wasn't actually *offered* to me, but back then, last year of grad school, knowing little about my own country (the U.S., not Mexico, for your information!) let alone the world, except for Wixburn and New York, I had a silly prejudice against anything and everything south of 40 degrees north and west of 73 degrees west.

"Flagler's looking for a Byron specialist," Dr. Whittaker, my department head, informed me one day, in the fall semester preceding my graduation. "I think you ought to apply for it."

"I dunno ..." I said, kind of hoping, naively, that CUNY would, against all logic, decide to keep me on, incestuously, after I got my doctorate.

"What's not to know?" he said, peering at me over the rims of his bifocals with that lecherous Lancastrian toad drawl of his, which would have been more at home in an episode of *Morse* centering on a gay professor with a taste for Wagner than midtown Manhattan. "I know the head of the department down there. I'd write a great letter for you ... You're a big boy now; time to cut the umbilical cord ..."

Flagler? who'd ever heard of *Flagler?*

And *Florida?*

Who wants to live in hurricane alley?

This was also during the days I was getting all artsy and set my electric guitar aside for a Yamaha V3 violin (nope, never learned to play it, really) ... and I was going to live in Molly Hatchet's Gator Country among the Rebel-flag wavin', chaw-chewin', good ol' boys?

I left his office depressed.

Time to cut the umbilical cord?

That was the same sort of kick in the gut one gets when — out of the blue — *that girl* breaks up with you, at one blow, and you never seeing the kick or the blow coming ... I went down a few blocks to the Bread and Butter on 29th, where I drank some warm coffee and ate two stalish cinnamon buns, and then took the train down to Washington Square and defaced several books in the Strand bookstore by inscribing short poems along the clean lower border of page 39 (always page 39) of random volumes, when no one was looking, and re-shelving them, in hopes that one New York book lover would come across just such a book in the library of a friend, at a party in the Village, and say "Hey! I have the same thing in one of my books! On the same page!" and I would grow into an urban legend, and the hints that I'd left in each book (on page 39. Always page 39) would lead me to be identified, outed, lauded, famoused, wealthied ... fuck-you-CUNY'ed See-who-you-could've-had-on-your-facultied ...

I know, silly.

Just as silly as writing off Flagler (I applied to make Whittaker happy, but intentionally submitted only a partial dossier), which I once visited, years later, after landing the only job I could land, at my alma mater Hanskung, and experiencing the warmth of Florida, the narrow alleyways of St. Augustine, the *swimming pool in the middle of campus* ...

Shit.

But one thought leads to another and what I wanted to get around to was talking about other people landing other jobs: Jason Hughes and Alison Prickney, to be exact, at the pharmaceutical shambles on Pennsylvania Avenue, to be precise.

Have you ever had an eating disorder?

Or a drug problem?

No, I guess you wouldn't have. But if not, you won't be able to completely understand the 180-degree change that occurred in Jason's life thanks to that chance meeting with Billy Kowalski that overcast Saturday afternoon.

After Billy said goodbye and left, first leaving his business card with his old nemesis from the produce department at Wartella's, Jason went back inside his house. For the first time — was it because he had just returned from the ozone-fresh air outside, into which he had ventured for the first time in two and a half weeks? or was it because of something else? — he was knocked back by the odor of the place. *It stank.* He went over to the kitchen window, then the bathroom window, opened them, and thereafter all of the windows on his ground floor. He gathered up the overflowing garbage from the kitchen *poubelle* and lugged it outside. Returning to the kitchen, panting, he grabbed another garbage bag, went over to the sink, and dumped all of the dirty plates and pots and pans that had been festering in the sink for several days, and lugged them out to the trashbin as well. He went into the living room where smiling QVC-bots were still shilling continuously: *For a Limited Time Only* some useless gadgets or other *That Will Improve Your Life One Hundredfold Trust Me I Was As Skeptical About It As You There At Home Until I Tried It* promising *But Wait If You Call In The Next Ten Minutes* — and yanked the cable out of the back of the TV. An immediate peace fell upon the room and a breeze came through the front window — *Was it the TV that had been stinking up the place?* — Jason went back into the kitchen for another bag, scooped up the beer (the empties and the unopened), the Cheetos and the chips, dragged the clinking and crunching lot outside, where he yanked down the pirate cable connection (disconnecting at the same pull all the cable connections on that side of the street), stuffed the cable into the bag, and tossed that on top of the other two.

He never returned to beer, junk food, or TV after that.

And he shaved.

And he washed his hair and got it cut.

And that's when he started to puff down the street.

And his clothes started to be too big for him.

It's easy to change. The first time, that is. The pounds melt off; one sees the result on the scale daily as the runs lengthen, and this gives you the constant positive reinforcement you need to keep at it.

Nobody feels better about himself than the fat man who starts, really and consecutively, to shed pounds.

And nobody feels better about the world than a person who feels good about himself.

This is why Jason was constantly in a good mood at work, professionally writing fearsome scripts to accompany the innocuous stick-figures that *.*.* Pharmaceuticals used to entice the unwary people who *didn't* tear down their cable connections, to use, and like, and depend upon — their witch's brew of chemicals in merrily colored "quick release" capsules.

This is why Jason returned to his bass — by himself, never thinking about a band, just enjoying the physical delight of making the air vibrate with music, like Samuel Pepys, for example, alone, in the evenings, for his pleasure and satisfaction.

And, this is why Jason greeted Alison with a, "Hey, Alison! Great to see you again! You're working here now? Cool!" when Billy introduced her to the rest of the department on her first day, and this is why he ignored or didn't notice, really, her distaste of his person, which continued undiminished since their Bishop O'Rigen High School days — a distaste so strong that had she known that *Jason Hughes* would be working a couple of cubicles down from her, she would have, probably, turned down the job offered her by Billy.

Had she done so, of course, there would have been no reason for Jason to offer her a ride into town that fateful morning and the Texas legislature would not be debating today between:

a. resuming a desultory attack upon the Mexican army from beyond the DMZ on the Colorado River,

b. declaring the re-establishment of the Republic of Texas and recouping the territorial losses in the south-west with a push into northern Louisiana, Oklahoma, and Arkansas, with the blessing and (hopefully) the support of President Paz and his armed forces, and

c. seceding from the United States of America and soliciting re-admission into Mexico, as a state, within its historical boundaries (but with respect for English as an official language of the state, and with the proviso that enforced conversion to Catholicism not be required of the Texican Gringos, this time. Truth be told, they were willing to negotiate on that latter demand, but recognition of English was something, without which, the whole conversation was a no-starter, or so I've heard).

Of course, all of this is academic, because, three weeks after her delightful prancing with the incense down the nave of St. Erkenwald's, and two weeks after she and Billy began, tenuously, to hang out together, Billy offered her the job, and Alison accepted it.

He was dying to offer her more, of course, but theirs was doomed to remain a Platonic relationship. From the start,

Billy knew that Alison would be a tough nut to crack, but he was patient and determined to concentrate on the long game. Not that he wasn't a-rarin' to go, as the old-fashioned phrase puts it. Right after service that day, Billy popped into the sacristy and, maugre the giggling servers, came right out with a salivating, "Father! Who was *that*?"

Billy was overwhelmed.

It was Alison, as you might have guessed, who was in no hurry to make intimate acquaintance with Billy Kowalski, or anyone else, for that matter. It took two weekly sessions of spiritual counseling (Fr. Ramsey was not as smells-and-bells as Fr. Carlyle; "spiritual counseling" is what he called auricular confession) for him to convince her to give it a try. "Think no longer about it but accept," he urged her, when she told him about Billy's invitation to the movies "up da mall," suggesting that she consider it an active, therapeutic penance for her confessed sin of looking down on people.

Now, Fr. Ramsey did have ulterior motives for assigning her such penance. As we have seen, that sermon on the talents, and his encouragement of his parishioners to take a more active part in the worship service, had backfired rather badly. It's hard to cram the genie back into the bottle, and once he's been released, he gets pretty ornery banging against a reimposed lid. So, for some time after his gentle, but firm, prohibition of the Children's Choir, Cabbage Patch Saints, and Archie's Home Brew Altar Wine ("I c'n walk behind you wid a tray," Archie said, "an' ask'm, discreetly-like, after you slip in the wafer, *Red, White, or Rosé?* — Hey! I got it! I'll ask'm *Father, Son or Holy Ghost*!") he had been pestered by a consolidated front of angry Parishioners for More Lay Participation, headed by the Mime, the Clown, and the Accordion Player, miffed at their pastor's sudden anathemas of Polka Services and Visual Interpretations of the Liturgy).

Billy's after Alison?

Well, there was a way to relieve the pressure a bit — to *pry the leech off his leg and sink her fangs into somebody else* — such was the formulation that he beat back from his conscious mind as soon as it surfaced there.

The history of their tête-à-têtes would be long to tell and rather anti-climactic.

Billy had the hots for Alison.

Big time.

But the pact he made with the Lord obliged him to right action, and so — alarmed as she was in the movie theatre to suddenly feel an arm draped around her chair-back in the dark, and fingers sliding down onto her shoulder, and as soon as she recognized the appendage to belong to Billy, who was not playing the childish trick of ghost-tapping her shoulder, but trying to edge his way near her erogenous zones, she shied away ... and the arm disappeared. There was no fuss, no testosterone-fueled second try. There was a movie and a good-night handshake and that was that. *Right thoughts, right words, right actions.*

Alex Kapranos might have had Billy in mind when he wrote that.

Who?

Never mind.

Billy was *frus-tra-ted!* — *She's gettin' to 'im* — to explosion, but, as we said, he determined on the long game, patiently listening to Alison's rants on Mexicans and terrorists (to whom she referred interchangeably when speaking of immigration and the existential threat to American culture), suffering his arms to be gently sloughed whenever he ventured to embrace her on a walk along the dike in Koi Carp Park, his hands to be firmly pushed away whenever they ventured a bolder recon near her knees or breasts on the picnic blanket on the riverside pull-off near the bridge in Rinnahannock, all the time nodding and saying "you may be right about that," or "I've never thought of it that way, myself, but," and so on and so forth.

For her part, Alison was pleased with the way things were turning out.

Maybe Fr. Ramsey was right after all?

Maybe this penance of hers was therapeutical?

All men, it seemed, were not like Tommy Watson after all. With his tolerance for her ever more extreme politics, his habit of saying grace before meals (even in restaurants), and the pliant way he *obeyed* her when he got too frisky and she let him know where he ought to get off with that (sorry — infelicitous expression!) well, *she* was in control here, and, who would have expected it? (Or, actually, why should we not?) her feminine amour-propre was titillated and … who knows how far it would go? One night, after a quick bite at the Harvest Moon barbecue (there was a *real bitchy* waitress there with way too familiar speech habits and a butchy shock-top haircut), when Billy endeared himself to her by replying "Both" to her question "lemon with your tea, or milk?" mixing both (the milk, of course, curdled immediately) and then gulping down the nauseating brew in two quick mouthfuls, she even allowed him to kiss her goodnight at the door of her house (But "no tongue!").

Neither Billy nor she got any sleep that night. Billy, from arousal (had he finally split the alabaster?) Alison, from worry (had she let down her guard?)

So, anyway, as I say, who knows, especially from that point, where things might have headed for Billy and Alison? They might have inched towards Boring White Protestant Marital Comfort and Respectability if Not Bliss, for their own good, and that of the world, had Billy not hired her at the Pharma factory and, in the process of doing so, introduced her to Buck ("Call me Jarhead") Toth.

Follow me carefully here, for we are now getting very close to the reason why Maine has recently debated articles of secession, and (if what we used to call the alarmist mainstream media says is true) sent annexation feelers out to the provincial authorities in Fredericton.

Gaylord ("Buck, but call me Jarhead") Toth was one of two graphic artists employed by that poison plant on Pennsylvania, the other being the new hire, Alison. His parents, immigrants from the Lake Balaton region of Hungary (they escaped over the bridge to Austria after the Hungarian Uprising of 1956), struggled with the niceties of American English, which can be most spectacularly seen in their choice of name for their youngest son, born in 1967. His other siblings had nothing to complain about; Ferencz, Béla, and Imre were straight-line normal names, such as even the most inventive of high school punters could do nothing with. Not that anyone would ever try to mess with the twins, Ferencz and Béla, quarterback and flanker, respectively, for the West Valley Trojans. They were called the Hungarian Hurricanes because of their speed and destructive potential on both sides of the ball. Big, mean, and seemingly sharing one consciousness between them, they were so flawless on offense that Punk Pirelli (the West Valley coach and former CFL standout, which explains, by the way, his preference for aerial attack) gave up calling plays midway through the boys' freshman year. The Trojans even stopped huddling on offense; only Ferencz and Béla touched the ball; both of them knew, instinctively, what route to run and where to place the ball, and, even though every team that played West Valley knew who to key in on, the Toth boys just couldn't be stopped. The pace imposed by the truly no-huddle Trojan (or, really Tothian) offense was so taxing on the defense that, even though they didn't score on every series, West Valley was usually up by 21 before six minutes of the first quarter had elapsed.

The Toth boys were the only two Trojans to play every down. On defense … now, was Ferencz a linebacker or a safety? Was Béla a lineman or a linebacker? It didn't matter. What did, though, was that uncanny intuition that existed between the two boys. If one was involved in a tackle, you could be sure that the other was too. They would arrive at the poor ballcarrier simultaneously, and when they did, well, they hit him with such force, that they held an unofficial PIAA record for inflicting the most broken bones, torn spleens, and concussions resulting in temporary cognitive impairment in a single season of Quad-4 football.

Receivers were known to let eminently catchable passes sail right past them when coming across the middle — and sometimes even this didn't restrain the Hungarian Hurricanes from cleaning clocks more expertly than Aaron Becsei. You didn't make fun of these guys' names.

It was no different for Imre. He, blue-eyed, dark-haired, with his mother's olive skin and the good looks of a young Johnny Depp, succeeded, in the words of the gushing editor of the West Valley Hellenist (the school yearbook) in "giving new meaning to the term Hunky, Wowee!" His mother's pride, Imre played varsity baseball since middle school, regularly hitting 98 on the JUGS gun when on the mound; he remains the only pitcher in PIAA history, or, for that matter, the history of baseball, to toss eight perfect games over the course of a four-year career, striking out 27 batters in a single game three times during that thrilling run. He also holds the record for home runs in a single season (71) hits (2012 over four years) and batting average (.879).

It's not hard to imagine that the Major League scouts drooled over him with the same ardor as every female creature in West Valley, from his nubile classmates to his teachers (Yep. Different times). But baseball was not his real love. He was an actor. Especially fond of the Elizabethan era, it was he who chose what was to grace the stage at

West Valley; I remember *Edward II*, *'Tis Pity She's a Whore*, *Volpone*, and *The Spanish Tragedy*, a tall order for teenagers, but Imre's performances were so Olivier-spectacular that the faults of all the others were overlooked, nay, went unnoticed, and for this reason only, the years 1973-1977 are still considered the high point of theatre in NEPA. When Imre graduated and went on to his stunning career under the stage name ... well, under a stage name that you would recognize, but I won't reveal, it all went back to *Guys and Dolls*, *Don't Drink the Water*, and, well, *Guys and Dolls*, for Pete's sake.

Billy Kowalski was Imre's classmate at West Valley, which is a matter of great import to our story. But of that in a moment.

Gaylord Toth had none of the athletic prowess of his elder brothers, who had preceded him at West Valley by seven, and six years. He was hopeless at baseball, too slight for the smallest pads moldering in Punk Pirelli's football tubs under the gym bleachers. He had none of Imre's good looks, inheriting neither his mother's olive complexion and classical features, nor his father's thick black hair and stocky build. He was a skinny child, with a tic; when nervous, he jerked his head to the right and winked his left eye. His *gaucheness* as a sportsman was acutely disappointing to his mother, who, like all Hungarians (and especially Hungarian women) was an avid supporter of the San Francisco Giants. It was her passion for the national pastime of her adopted country that decided her youngest son's name. You guessed it: he was named after Gaylord

Perry, the first pitcher to win the Cy Young Award in both American (Indians, 1972) and National (Padres, 1978) Leagues — even though both awards were far in the future when he was born. Zsófia was living in Tacoma during that year when he burned up the PCL, and that was enough to clue her in on what was in his future. Which just goes to show you how expert she was at spotting talent. Another Esposito. A baseball Esposito. Alas, it was different with her son. When ten-year-old Gaylord broke out bawling at the plate after getting pegged in Little League, Zsófia Toth got up out of the bleachers, and without taking a second look back towards her sobbing offspring, left the field, got into her Fury III, and drove away, leaving Gaylord to navigate the five miles home on his own. That one look, too, was enough to tell her all she needed to know.

And he so wanted to please her. When he thought he'd finally found the solution by joining the cross-country team as a freshman, she said:

"Running? Running is what you do when the Russians invade your country, and even then, it's a hard shame to live down. Running is not a sport."

She had even less appreciation for his other school activity: playing clarinet in the marching band.

"The clarinet is not a musical instrument for a man. The *koboz* is an instrument for a man. The *dobolás* is an instrument for a man! Men do not put their lips around such a thing."

And yet both running and music were outlets for the nervous child, who had so little else. There was no one around him when he ran (literally, for everyone pulled away from him quite soon after the start), and he was unconcerned with time and place and results, so that he soon developed the loose, loping pace of a marathoner who forgets his body, lets his physical reactions take over, and goes on auto-pilot as it were. When he achieved this state, his mind sank into cogitations that made his already sensitive imagination even more receptive to creative impulses.

He composed poems.

He hummed clarinet riffs.

He imagined what it would be like to find a girl who loved him, and the girl he imagined during his runs was so real to him that he could not only recall her image at will, but he even knew her specific quirks. For example, that she was a Kansas City Royals fan, and often snuck a Kent cigarette from her dad's pack and smoked it alone on the roof outside her bedroom window in the evenings when she and Gaylord weren't out, and she liked buttermilk —

"Hey, Gaylord. Gaylord!"

It was Augie Thomas, a bully from the tenth grade, who shook him out of his reverie on the orange disk of the cafeteria table at West Valley one day at lunch.

"I got a secret to tell you," Augie said, leaning closer.

"What is it?" Gaylord asked, kind of proud that such a distinguished Trojan as Augie had taken notice of him, a freshman, in such a confidential manner. But as Gaylord drew his head closer to Augie's, the bigger boy straightened up, spun around, bent over, and broke wind right in Gaylord's face.

No one at the table — not even Gaylord's best friend, Miles Schoof, a trumpeter in the band — did anything more than laugh nervously. For his part, Augie shot a long, intense leer in Gaylord's direction that, had a psychiatrist witnessed the scene, would have given him or her a capital reason to diagnose Augie's behavior, not as a sick practical joke, but rather an incipient mental illness with a fundamentally scatological, erotic basis. The only person who noticed the disgusting, infantile exchange was Mr. Brown, a substitute History teacher who was monitoring that half of the cafeteria that lunchtime. As the extraordinarily long period (it dragged on forever for Gaylord) ground to its end, and he took his tray over to the slot in the kitchen wall where dirty dishes were collected for washing, Mr. Brown came up to him and said,

"Are you going to let him do that to you?"

Gaylord turned his eyes, widened in surprise, up at the young substitute, who had been a second-line winger for the university that shared his name and could think of nothing to say. He blushed, shrugged, and shuffled, jerking and winking, out of the cafeteria, toward fifth-period geometry.

This is not to say that Gaylord didn't learn anything from what had happened. Chiefly and most importantly, he learned that it's therapeutic to seek out the weakest person in the room and shove the figurative knife in, giving it a nice, slow, sadistic twist while you're at it.

In short, it's no wonder that Alison Prickney and Gaylord ("Buck, but call me Jarhead") Toth got along so well with each other from their very first meeting.

How did that meeting come about?

Well, that too was the direct result of the unfortunate and sudden proximity of Gaylord's face to Augie's hind parts.

Gaylord, the kid who wanted to fit in, but couldn't, decided that it wasn't worth the trouble trying anymore. He withdrew from band (and from his friendship with that traitor Miles), remained in cross country (achieving still worse results, but at the same time an even more intense interior life), and, what is more important, he began to lose himself in transferring the images of that interior life onto the pages of his notebooks. He began drawing them.

These were, at first, rather elementary likenesses of Gaylord's cartoon and wrestling heroes, such as The Incredible Hulk and Bruno Sammartino, distinguishable only from a bushy-haired, trunkless elephant or Winston Churchill in tights by the identifying captions he provided them with. But then he got better, according to the exaggerated 10,000-hour rule, and under the influence of love. When he began putting Megan down on the page (Megan was that imaginary girlfriend of his), the dogged, extra care he took to transfer the image burned into his consciousness onto a sheet of paper resulted in a progressive, but all the same miraculous, mastering of perspective, shading and cross-hatching, rounding through chiaroscuro and the proportions of the human form (which, when exaggerated, were so for obvious reasons) that resulted in such a flair for naturalistic drafting that he could effortlessly create a photographic image of any person or thing, on-demand.

It would have made him popular with his classmates if they weren't scared to death of him. But more of that later.

In short, Buck Toth (he jettisoned the Gaylord early in his sophomore year, choosing Buck in homage to Russell Keaton) could draw, and Billy Kowalski, who needed an artist in his department, turned to the younger brother of his former acting idol Imre — who realized the dreams he never would, landing leading roles at the National Theatre in London. And so, if you needed any more evidence that the much-derided "butterfly effect" is a real thing, let me state unequivocally: the stream of unhealthy air that Augie Thomas expelled from his backside at the naively trusting face of Gaylord Toth precipitated the blast wind that flattened so much of North Beach.

Before we move on, there's one more thing we need to know about Buck Toth's high school cartooning career.

One morning two years later, when Buck was a junior, he was shaken out of his early creative trance — depicting Megan in jorts on a palomino, waving a lasso above her head — by a sobering announcement of Principal Headstrom's that came over the PA during homeroom.

"Fellow Trojans, I have very sad news to share with you. Augustine Thomas, a senior, took his own life last night. This is a hard blow for all of us at West Valley High, his friends and classmates, and teachers. I wish to remind you all of the duty we owe to our fallen friend, who, in the face of a personal crisis, the seriousness of which none of us can fathom, decided upon such a drastic and tragic step. Let us respect the feelings of Augie's friends and family by not indulging in idle gossip, or doing anything at this time that would make the unspeakable pain they are going through even more unbearable."

There were gasps and exclamations of disbelief and even horror from the pupils ranged around Buck in Homeroom 3C — or, rather, ranged *before* Buck in the classroom, as he had taken to sitting in the back row, pushing his chair as far away from everyone as possible.

Caroline Van Ness even began sobbing (because that's what she thought a pretty and sensitive girl *ought* to do at a time like this. Finally, a tragedy to mark her young life as a transition-point to the "real world" she was still eighteen months away from entering …!)

"Although we will be going on with our normal schedule today …" Principal Headstrom continued (at which the exclamations of disbelief and even horror, not to mention tears, were all transformed into groans of disappointment) … but Buck was no longer listening. He returned to his drawing pad, carefully adding the mangled body of Augie Thomas beneath the trampling hooves of Megan's palomino.

Later that day, Buck was called down to the principal's office. When he got there, he was surprised to see his father and mother seated at chairs drawn up before Principal Headstrom's desk. His father's head was bowed down as if he were inspecting something riveting on the corner of the educator's poorly stained walnut desk; his mother turned a worried expression toward him, gripping the hoops of the purse she held on her lap.

"Gaylord," the principal said in a serious voice, "is this your work?"

He held out a notebook to him — the red-covered notebook he'd lost a week ago.

"Yeah," Buck said, without a moment's hesitation.

"Oh, God," his father groaned, silently.

It was only then that Buck glanced at the sheet to which the notebook was folded open. It was a drawing of Augie Thomas in the position Buck remembered from two years ago: bent over, hands on his knees, face turned to the spectator with an expression of ecstasy ... for Augie was wearing no pants, and was shown being fucked by a dildo of prodigious dimensions, emerging like a snake from a pile of car tires (Augie's Dad ran a gas station on Colorado Ave.) charmed forth by Jimmy Josephs (his equal in idiocy) sitting on the ground like a fakir, unmanly clarinet in his mouth. The drawing had been passed around from hand to many a hand, to which the copious scrawled commentaries bore witness.

Buck smiled.

"You're smiling?" the principal exclaimed in real (or maybe pretended?) ire (Was he really upset, or was this how he figured he should react in this situation?)

"Can I get it back?" said Buck. "I mean, it is my notebook."

"It's your notebook," Headstrom said, "And are you aware of the fact that Augie saw what you drew as well? And that it was found next to his suicide note?"

Buck's father drooped his head even lower and his mother burst out crying.

"And that Jimmy Josephs hasn't come into school today either? The police are on their way over to his house right now!"

"Cool," said Buck, smiling an even broader smile, and turning to go.

"Come back here, young man!" Headstrom called after him, as Buck closed the door. "We're not finished here yet!"

But how wrong he was. At that moment, Buck Toth's education was complete.

"Mom, I gotta go!" said the little cartoon bee to its cartoon bee mama.

"All right, honey," she replied, "but bee quick!"

The mama bee buzzed round and round the blossomless bushes until the little bee came back.

No sooner were they reunited than the little bee said:

"Mom, I gotta go!"

This scene was repeated twice more, at ever shorter intervals, while the Bee mama was getting more and more exhausted with her fruitless buzzing around sterile grasses and naked branches until, finally, arriving at a pollen-thick bloom, she fell asleep on the job, and knocked her arm against her bucket, at which all the honey she had gathered (it's a cartoon, poetic license), spilled out and was lost. Then came the voice-over:

Losing time and energy because of your child's frequent urination problems? Ask your doctor about Bloxomochisine. Bloxomochisine is a one a day urethral repressive, that lessens your child's overactive bladder dysfunctions, giving you, and your child, more time to get on with the more important things in life.

"Come on, Mom!" the happy little bee cried at the end of the commercial. "Time to get busy!"

Ask your pediatrician if Bloxomochisine is right for your child. Common side effects include constipation, shy bladder syndrome, headaches, dry mouth, and irritability. In some cases, Bloxomochisine has caused tuberculosis, blurred vision, hearing loss, suicidal thoughts, cancer, and death. Use only as directed …

I once used this very text in a meeting with one of my advisees at Hanskung College, who announced her desire to switch majors from English to Professional Writing.

"This is the sort of writing you can look forward to doing with a Professional Writing degree," I told her. "The major is *not* going to make you into the next Ernest Hemingway."

"Who?"

Hmm. "Never mind. Point is, you do know it's not *creative* writing …"

"I know but … you know …" she replied, with all the eloquence of someone wanting to tell you to *fuck off and sign the papers* without being so impolite as to actually, honestly state what was going through her mind at the moment.

Which is exactly why Professional Writing graduates create texts about Bloxomochisine, which inhibits urination, and Plynolatvic, which encourages urination and never become the next Ernest Hemingway. Whoever he was.

When I used the Bloxmochisine commercial shill, I had no idea that it was the work of my old bandmate, Jason Hughes. Yet this was exactly the sort of thing that he was doing for that cynical petri-dish of side-effects on Pennsylvania Ave. since accepting Billy's offer of employment, and, it seems … he was enjoying himself at it.

And why?

The answer has already been given. Twice already he'd had to travel to Hollister's *up da mall* to buy jeans to fit his shrinking waistline, his hovel no longer smelled of dirty dishwater and Shopping Channel, and he had begun fooling around with his bass again. With some nostalgic regret, he'd traded in his battered old Kent for a fifty-buck discount on a second hand P-Bass (what action! What tone! And how smooth the hand and fingers glided over the varnished neck and fretboard!), dusted off the old Peavy amp that he *thump-thump-thumped* up the cellar steps into the living room (where the cord-cut TV now stood, black and useless) dove into the wonders of Songsterr and Ultimate Guitar Tabs and was patiently re-building the callouses on the tips of his fingers, which had grown soft with years of disuse.

A run in the morning, a day filled with idiotic challenges (*How can I subliminally convince aging men to accept a boner in exchange for the distinct possibility of a disabling stroke? Is there a cheery way to foster in over-protective moms the conviction that little Billy's animal spirits are symptoms of ADHD, and that the one and only "safe" (haha!) corrective is Obesalix, which is potentially the chemical equivalent of a lobotomy? And what's the answer to the question of how to put Pellimastic into the hands of the 25–45 male demographic, that wonder drug that promotes not only hair growth but the development of female breasts?*) and a peaceful evening of thumping and slapping the old round-wounds to backing tracks ranging from Buddy Holly to Ministry — is it any wonder that Jason was as peaceful and composed as Gautama beneath the bo-tree?

The day that Alison began working at the place I'm not supposed to mention by name, was a week after Jason had come across a guy in a clerical collar only partially obscured by his long-braided beard *Holy shit! Rick?!* scrounging through the old Yamaha bodies and discarded Strat necks in the projects box up at the Music-Go-Round, *Jason? How've you been! Shit, how long has it been, man?* and one thing led to another, *We oughtta call up Dave* (and Ray? Did they remember me, maybe, too?) and had the first OHP-Reunited jam session in Dave's mousy basement, which led to the dogfight above Portland and that messy B-1 incident that eliminated a whole generation of hipsters from the Pearl District.

Not only did they start jamming again, but they also began discussing *gigging*. And so, when that other Billy (whose "drug of choice," as he once told Alison in a desperate attempt at closer intimacy than a dry swipe of closed lips, "was Jesus") introduced (or so he thought) Alison to Jason, our friend (am I assuming too much? As I said at the start, he's *not* the monster he's made out to be! After all, who is?) Jason, the latter replied with a hearty

"Hey, Alison! Great to see you again! You're working here now? Cool!"

Now, she responded with the indifferent shrug of distaste (*Here? I'm supposed to be working with him?*) that you, by now, would probably expect of her. However, her mood brightened perceptively (and involuntarily, I might add — which is further proof of the fact that you can't completely stifle nature; a healthy erotic womanhood was lurking deep inside her repressed psyche after all) when a deep voice boomed

"Well! Who do we have here?!"

and a burly chap of about 5'6" with close-cropped (though thin) hair and a tattoo in Arabic and English reading "infidel" on the outside of his veiny right arm came up, and assumed his position, legs spread, hands-on-hips, as if the next words out of his mouth were to be *Halt! Password!*, grinning a broad shiny grin.

"Alison," Billy began unsurely, "this is …"

"GAYlord," Jason lobbed in, which made the meatstick turn his face slightly to the right, and his grin devolve into a sneer of distaste aimed at Jason, before he wheeled it around again, and re-formed those lips of his into an even grinnier grin (aimed at Alison), to whom he extended a beefy right hand with,

"Buck. But call me Jarhead."

"Or Gaylord," Jason piped up again, "His name is Gaylord."

But Alison wasn't listening. She was gazing deeply into those brown eyes of Gaylord (Buck, but call me Jarhead) Toth. Believe it or not, it was almost like that moment in *Le Gendarme se marie* when Louis de Funès' character — (you don't know Louis de Funès? Oh, what a pity. Look him up) bends down to kiss the hand of the chic widow and a crackle of electricity stuns him so, he tries it again, with the same result ... Well, it was that instantaneous, for Alison at least, and, it seems, for Billy too, who

> *Alas I am undone, by fickle Cupid*
> *Whom — treacherous babe! — I'd taken for my friend*

slumped visibly in a despairing satori, cursing the day he overstepped his mark by offering her the job, which only introduced her to a rival triumphant.

Perhaps you are wondering about Gaylord's transformation into Jarhead. Well, it happened like this:

When Gaylord / Buck (as over the previous year he had become known to his classmates, who took him to be a sort of voodoo priest for his stunning illustrative talents; caricatures were his specialty: he could create the most vicious portraits of despised pedagogues or classmates — hilariously exaggerating a well-known trait or for a certain clientele of spotty boys with a nascent pornography addiction, render the pretty girls of West Valley in erotic poses with striking naturalism — in either case, if the sketch fell into the wrong hands [accidentally or intentionally] it was sure to have *devastating* effects [witness the case of Augie Thomas]; in short, you didn't want your picture drawn by Gaylord,

I mean, Buck Toth,

and you wouldn't, as long as you paid him more for *not* drawing what a nefarious classmate had promised to pay him *for* drawing it); when, I say, he *left* Principal Nordstrom's office on that fatal day, he kept on walking down the hall, out the front door, and into freedom. A frightening freedom. Because, despite the fact that it was an effective bit of drama, such as his famous (under another name) brother Imre would appreciate, it was a spur-of-the-moment kind of thing, and … now what?

Well, for one thing, he couldn't go home again.

Ever.

So he disappeared.

So completely did he vanish, and for so long, that the folks of Wixburn who happened to follow the local news, especially in the aftermath of the suicide of a local high school student, began to slowly become convinced that they had *another* teenage tragedy on their hands — this time (*I tol'ja it'd end dis way, hayna?*) the boy who had caused his classmate to kill himself, seemingly unable to bear the guilt of it all, had done himself in as well. The river was dredged (well, metaphorically. Except for the odd flood every fifty years or so, the local river is so shallow you can dredge it with a rake), the police of all surrounding boroughs looked high and low and were left scratching their heads. It seemed like Wixburn had, anachronistically speaking, another cold case of an unexplained tragic death on its hands.

Anybody remember Jason Bartosz?

He wasn't dead back then, but he is now, and still is, and nothing that Billy Kowalski does as far as penance is concerned will ever bring him back to his still gently grieving family and friends. Principal Nordstrom lost his job, of course — the Toths (especially Zsófia) saw to that; I mean, didn't he handle the matter that day in the office a bit too harshly, for a sensitive child like our Gaylord? I mean, he disappeared *right after* he left the office broken, in tears (Oh, our selective, skewing, creative memories!

He was *smiling*!

He said "Cool!" at the news of his sketch being found next to the suicide note.

And unconcerned!

"Can I have it back? It's mine," is all he said before closing the door behind him — presumed dead he was, until, eighteen months later, an envelope from Keeler AFB arrived in the mailbox of the Toths with a terse note: "In case your [*sic*] wondering, I've joined the Air Force." This note was accompanied by a (flattering, of course) self-portrait in pencil of Buck Toth in an airman's jumpsuit, standing next to a truck with a flat tire and Hellfire missiles piled up high in the bed, one so akilter it looked like it was about to fall onto the potholed dirt road beneath the wheels of the truck — something, which could only have been drawn by that sensitive child Gaylord.

This news, that their son was alive, actually caused some consternation to Zsófia. For she had filed a wrongful death suit against both Norman Headstrom and the West Valley School District, to the tune of ten million dollars, and it had been progressing through the shysterly locks of the legal system quite nicely until the letter arrived — which more or less cut the legs out from under it. Zsófia (*tsk tsk TSK*) considered secreting the note until the settlement had been reached … but thought better of it, in the end.

Whether this was good or bad news for Norman Headstrom, we'll never know. The only job he could find after his pillorying in the local press was at Gerschwin's Pool Hall, where he worked nights and developed throat cancer from all the secondhand smoke.

Anyway, this is why the next words out of his mouth directed at Alison were:

"Helped kick Saddam's sick ass out of Kuwait."

"With an oil filter wrench," sneered Jason, "and from afar, truth be told."

This got Gaylord's (sorry, Jarhead's) Irish up. He snapped back with

"Oh yeah? Where the fuck were you, cunt? When I was in Riyadh, all the bombs falling around me?"

"Here, Gaylord, here," he replied. "Where nary a bomb was a-fallin'" he lilted, with a credible Burnsian brogue.

"Sorry for the French, ma'am," Jarhead said, turning back to Alison who (saints preserve us! Wasn't offended at all!) "But we vets sometimes get a bit touchy with comments like that from stay at home flag-burners."

"I never burned a flag," Jason said, turning to a skinny kid with long hair sitting at a desk to his right, "Jim? Did you ever burn a flag?"

"Not me," replied Jim, "But I did stay at home. Safe in bed. Who needs missiles?"

Speaking of which, before we go any further, you need to understand something about Jim Krywicki.

At the time we are now describing, Jason, who had happily rediscovered his enthusiasm for the bass, was in his psychedelic phase, easing himself back into the saddle, so to speak, with the uncomplicated, yet still funky, patterns of Jack Bruce and the (unjustly, often overlooked) Noel Redding. (He had not yet moved on to, God bless her! Kathy Valentine!) It's the latter, Redding, that springs to mind because the album *Axis: Bold as Love* (with the cool little runs at the bottom of the neck along frets two and four in "Spanish Castle Magic," which suddenly jump up to frets eight and ten) kind of reminds me of the office vibe that existed between Jim Krywicki, Buck Toth, and our Jason Hughes.

When we think of three people linked together, it's seldom a good thing. Setting the Holy Trinity aside (which is actually a Unity, though of Three Distinct Persons, for those non-Trinitarians among you, it's ... ah, forget it) or musical trios like The Jam or Jason's incomprehensible favorites, Dizzy and the Primos, or Jason's own, (sigh) re-formed, One Hour's Practise or Noel Redding's Jimi Hendrix Experience,

what else have you but jealousy and tears?

I mean, for example, a love triangle?

That's never a good thing, is it?

Which (sorry for skipping around like this) by the way, really sets apart that title, *Axis: as Bold as Love* as one of the truly great titles in history, right? I mean, playing off the whole "love" theme, which must, as a matter of course, allude to the love triangle and the sixties' innocent popularization of the catastrophe of free love, it's the "axis" that holds it all together, ironically, pregnantly, smelling of the disasters to which all such *menages à trois* inexorably lead.

Because, what does the word "axis" conjure up for you?

Surely, the evil Axis Powers of Nazi Germany, Kamikaze Japan, and Fascist Italy. (How *bold* it was of Hendrix to make an Axis reference, just twenty years or so after the end of World War II!) And let's not forget nr. 43's "Axis of evil" speech …

So, like three angry dogs in a perpetual, spinning, snarling fight, with the fangs of each snapping at the hindquarters of the other, Jason and Jim, and Buck formed a perpetual Axis of Bile in the Advertising and Design Department of the big pharma slaughterhouse at 5 Pennsylvania Ave.

Come to think of it, though, my simile of the wheeling dogs does not accurately cover the situation between the three. Because in the simile, you have three dogs, out for themselves only, snapping at each other's butts — kind of like the ouroboros — you know, the ancient symbol of the snake devouring its tail? That's not what was going on here at all. It was rather like — to use a simile from young, twitchy, Gaylord Toth's aberrant juvenile interests — an uneven tag-team wrestling bout, with Jason and Jim as the tag team, one of them leaping down onto the shoulders of the solo-act, Buck (Call Me Jarhead, *please!*) Toth, from the turnbuckle when he was engaged with the other.

Oh, don't feel sorry for Jarhead.

Ever since he'd bulked himself up on creatine and calf-brain protein, acquiring thus the swagger that complemented so well the sadistic streak discovered earlier in high school, he'd only grown bolder in his need to emphasize his self-worth by seeking out the weaker party and denigrating his. Oh — it's like another adolescent fetish of Buck's — remember the TV series *Highlander*, about the Scottish samurai Duncan McLeod? The 400-year-old "immortal" who is fated to seek out other "immortals" and fight them to the death (by beheading, another sick fetish of Jarhead's)?

Remember how, after the obligatory, choreographed fencing match (who's gonna win? Oh, gee, I hope it's not … *Oh come on, don't even pretend to be so effing naive!*) Duncan sees his opening, swings for the fences like Sadaharu Oh (*samurai*, man. Who did you expect here? B-B-B-Barry Bonds?), and when he separates evil immortal's head from evil immortal's torso, a freaky life force of some sort emerges from the corpse before it even hits the ground and enters into Duncan's body as a "quickening" lightning bolt, that makes him stronger?

Well, that's how it was for Buck. (Gosh. Now there's a really good metaphor. Isn't that what happened, literally, with Augie Thomas? That bully feasted on Gaylord's abasement in the cafeteria that pungent lunchtime, and then when Gaylord brought about Augie's death — literally — he experienced his first "quickening" into a bully himself!) Because no thing made him feel better, stronger, more spring-heeled, than when he was able to assert himself in that unlovely way that bullies have of denigrating a weaker person, in the "best" case, publicly.

And there was no one at the toxic pusher's palace on Pennsylvania more suited to the role of whipping boy than Jim Krywicki.

Short, thin to almost brittle proportions, ungainly and socially awkward, timid (you name it), he was, well, *Gaylord Toth* before his transformation into Buck-call-me-Jarhead. In preying upon Jim, Buck was hammering, and hammering, away at himself — at that awkward, twitchy geek who still and all lived somewhere, deep inside the burly Desert-Shield-And-Desert-Storm-Vet-And-Proud-Of-It-You-Betcha Buck.

Buck couldn't let pass a single opportunity for putting Jim down.

And because they worked in the same stuffy office, he had plenty an opportunity for doing so. On the very first day of his employment at Mengele and Sons (that's *not* the name of that pharmaceutical place on Pennsylvania, by the way, but it's one of the ways I can denote it and still obey the law), which was Jim Krywicki's last day of peace, Buck picked up the Darth Vader figurine from Jim's desk and turned to Billy with.

"Hey, Boss! I didn't know that you could bring *dolls* to work! Is this *bwing youw toys to wowk day?*" he pouted, while Jim laughed as nervously as Buck's friends at lunch that day way back when, glowing beet red and thinking, *Oh crap! Is it going to be like this from now on?*

The answer to that question obviously was, 'You-Betcha.' He couldn't even escape from Jarhead on break.

One day, as he was pouring himself a cup of coffee at the urn in the break room, chatting and just gaining traction with Lana (the slightly chunky, but pretty girl from accounting), he was blindsided by Buck who approached him from behind, grabbed the mug out of his hand, and read its inscription with a critical eye. It said "World's Greatest Something or Other."

"World's Greatest Fuck-Up, maybe," said Buck, with a wink toward Lana, who blushed and laughed …

So, when Jason arrived, at last, it was like a godsend for Jim Krywicki. Because although Buck-Call-Me-Jarhead tried the same shit with him, Jason would have none of it.

"Why don't you suck my cock?" Buck once said, with all the wit he could muster, in response to a jibe from Jason.

At which Jason stood up, putting a radiant expression of joyful surprise on his face,

"Why, fuck, Buck," he smiled, "you're queer!"

"Fuck you! I'm not …"

"Hey, listen up everybody," Jason called, expansively, in a voice that could be heard throughout the floor, "Buck here wants to have oral sex with a man!"

"I di—"

There were titters and snorts of laughter from several cubicles; this time it was Jarhead's turn to blush.

"Buck, you're, you're GAY!" Jason continued, at which Buck blanched, his eyes grown wide.

"That's not my name! That's not my name! Call me Jarhead!" he stammered, before beating a hasty retreat toward the men's room.

"I'll be there in a minute, honey! If you can't wait, remember to use a tissue to clean up, and then be sure to wash your hands!"

It was, admittedly, a scene right out of middle school. But it was a huge release for Jim Krywicki, who had delighted in the denigration of his denigrator, and from that moment on, he began to surface, slowly, until he reached the point where he could join in the repartee, as we saw him do (tentatively, but still, what a big step for him) above, when Alison was introduced into the office mix.

Now, as you might remember from earlier on, in his relations with Billy Kowalski back at Wartella's Market, Jason had a nasty streak himself. He could smell blood in the water too — which is not a very attractive personality trait, but, again, I have a hard time feeling sorry for Buck.

The blood in the water this time was Buck's panicked babbling about what his name was, or wasn't, as he abandoned the battlefield. It didn't take Jason too long to discover Buck's given-name — Gaylord — after which it was the only way he would ever address him — almost always shortening it, of course, to "Gay."

"Hey, Gay," Jason would greet him, loudly, in the morning.

"Call me Jarhead, asshole."

"Hey, Jarhead Asshole."

It went on kinda like that.

The tag-teaming, too, started rather early. Whatever you want to say about Jason's behavior as being as unseemly as that of Buck himself, it did help Jim Krywicki, who had undergone a personal Gehenna for the six months that transpired between Buck's hire, and that of Jason, to fight back, to win the sea-legs of self-confidence necessary to navigate our world. (And so, isn't Jim being Duncan McLeod himself? Don't we have here an unholy succession of bullyishness, in an unbroken line from Augie to Gaylord/ Buck/Jarhead to Jim? Why, I guess we do. An … axis.

Doesn't the world suck?

And who's to blame?

Who brought sin into the world?

All of this, then, including the poisoning of the Detroit drinking-water system, which everyone's blaming on fifth-columnists from Dearborn, is the fault of Adam and Eve. Or, of God Himself, who knew what they would do with that sole daughter of his voice before it was uttered, and yet utter it He did).

"What's that book on your desk, Jim?" Jason once asked, theatrically.

"Why, it's *The Kingdom and the Power* by Gay Talese," Jim responded, just as theatrically.

"By who?"

"By Gay Talese?"

"Who?"

"GAY. TaLESE."

"Gay Talese," mused Jason, looking over in Buck's direction, whose neck, then cheeks, then ears, were growing progressively redder by the second. "That's a funny name. Tell me, Jim: Do you think that 'Gay' stands for 'Gaylord,' like in the case of our good friend Gaylord over there?"

"Could be, Jason," Jim replied. "Then again, it could be self-descriptive."

"Come again?"

"I mean, maybe it's because he's gay and proud of it."

"Like our good friend Gaylord over there?"

"Could be, Jason."

The pencil he was clutching snapped in Buck's meaty hand.

And Jim asked Lana out, and Lana accepted.

Sometimes the baiting of Buck Toth took on more subtle forms.

As I'd already mentioned, Jim was the computers-guy in the Advertising and Design Department. His job covered all aspects of computer layout, at which he was quite good (in the bad business of pushing drugs, but still and all), because not only did he have a journalist's (I'd cringe to use the term artist here) sense of "new media," but "mad programming skills" (as one of his awestruck college friends, as skinny and nerdy as he, used to put it).

One day, Jason connived to break into Buck's e-mail account, with Jim's help, and to send out the following e-mail "to all:"

AS MEMORIAL DAY APPROACHES, BEING A VETERAN OF THE IRAQI CAMPAIGN WHERE I HELPED KEEP KICK-ASS SCHWARTZKOPF KICKING ASSES BY MAKING SURE THE AIR FORCE'S NUTS WERE NICE AND TIGHT (ON THE WHEELS OF THEIR VEHICLES, THAT IS!!!) I'D LIKE TO REMIND EVERYONE TO HONOR THE BRAVE MEN AND WOMEN OF THE ARMED FORCES BY GREETING EVERY ONE OF THEM WITH A HEARTY HOO-AHH!!! WHEN YOU SEE THEM AROUND TODAY!!!

GAYLORD (IN A. AND D.) TOTH

HOO-AHH!!!

Gaylord, er, Buck, was shocked to see this show up in his mailbox, sent from his account, no less … He knew he didn't write it, but … why wouldn't he have? It expressed his heartfelt sentiments (*Look at me! I'm a vet! I'm a big tough old SOB vet, and you're not!*) and so, he kept his mouth shut, and … rather uneasily, but still and all … took credit for it.

"Hoo-ahh, Gaylord!" Jason greeted him, snapping to attention.

"Hoo-ahh, Jarhead Asshole!" ventured Jim (proud of himself, although, vide supra).

And so on, all day long, like all the other employees of the place, except for Billy, who was still suffering inwardly from having thrown his love to the lions, and who did his best to avoid Buck, greeted Buck with a big

"Hoo-ahh!" every time he passed them in the hall.

It was around three in the afternoon that Buck sensed that, maybe, he was being made the butt of a practical joke, after all …

"Hoo-ahh!" piped Alison with a smile — and it was such a pleasant smile, such a genuine *hoo-ahh* out of that pretty little thing with those tits like firm apples and that tight little ass, that Buck's chest swelled with pride.

Ah, but the genuineness and pleasantry of the budding relationship, to which we have surprisingly alluded before, was about to come crashing down.

Alison, then.

Let's get you back in that car.

You know, *Jason's* car, on *that* day.

If you can remember back to the very beginning of my explanation, or testimony, or what have you, the whole scene played out something like this:

The Beatles were on the car stereo, and more or less out of habit, Jason began going over his imaginary fretboard, the wrist of his left hand set against the steering wheel, mimicking Paul's funky skips over the top three strings, and exclaiming:

"God, he fingered well,"

at which Alison's eyes got big, moving from those four swaying fingers of his left hand (like so many fat wriggling worms) to his eyes and his mouth (with its pooling saliva), as he added:

"I wish I could finger as well as him."

Now, Alison was just getting up the courage to say something like *I don't feel very comfortable with this conversation,* which, had she done, the *Manuel Azueta* would not have opened fire on a North Korean submarine in San Francisco Bay, sending it to the bottom with its entire crew and putting us all on edge — the occupation and disintegration of the United States of America is one thing, but who wants World War III — the Atomic Conflict, which they've been scaring us with since 1945? But never in this configuration of combatants? — getting up the courage, I say, because she'd just accepted a ride from a coworker, and it wasn't like he'd placed his hand on her knee or anything, but then:

"Oh! Do you hear that?" he asked, with authentic enthusiasm now, as the pattern repeated, and *for want of a nail the shoe was lost,* and all that shit that turns out to be *spot on,* WHY do people not listen to their poets? he reached out and *gave her a nudge with his right wrist against her thigh!* And who would have thought that a pretty, forty-ish girl in Nowhere, Pennsylvania, by simply demanding: "Pull over into Burger King, please," could ever be the efficient cause of Fra Angelico Chavez being dusted off and used for propaganda purposes by the government of Nuevo México as a mouthpiece for a campaign called "Bridges to the Future," intended to assuage the fears of Gringos in Gallup and Santa Fe and Albuquerque that everything was business as usual, for New Mexico, the land of their birth, after all, predated politically *both* the United States and Mexico?

Was she overreacting?

Was her #MeToo moment just a bit too stretched?

You might think so.

But if you go back over her history, both the recent and the more distant past, it all does kind of make sense.

Remember: she had grown up in a fractured house, with a crazy woman for a mother, and a stepfather who was always trying, and that overtly, to get into her pants (with no place to turn for help, as her mother simply bagatellized the whole matter, and she had practically no contact with her real dad until after her mother's death — but that's another story, which we may not have time for now — seems that neither the Cubans nor the Mexicans did stop at their predetermined lines, and, who knows? maybe in two weeks or so, they'll be *right here* and our present situation will have been dramatically altered? — in short, men, and sex, had become repulsive to her at an early age. She had been deprived of normality (not just erotic normality, although that is a big part of most people's normality, *hayna?*) at an extremely early age, had channeled her repressed urges into fascist-leaning (let's call a spade a spade) political activism (remember Esposito? "Keep your wetback hands off my daughter?"), and had *only just* begun to crack through that thick, thick shell thanks to Fr. Ramsey and good old (well-meaning, and heartbroken, though never innocent) Billy Kowalski, who, though he wanted to be the end-station for her journey to orgasm (I see your heart, and call your spade a spade) was only a stepping stone towards (of all people! Alison!) Gaylord-Buck (Come on, fellas, CALL ME JARHEAD!!) Toth.

Backstory, please.

The Courtship of Eddie's Father — remember that show?

From the good old days when who among us knew that California had a Spanish and Catholic past?

… Ah, why do I bother?

Sorry, this is how my mind works.

I know you're in a hurry …

The courtship of Buck and Alison, if you could call it that, lasted a mere two weeks, and was carried out entirely at their workplace. It consisted of a wink here, a high-five there at the completion of a project, a shared coffee, and one intimate lunch at Triangles on the Circle, over Broccoli and Cheddar soup and what passes for sourdough bread in NEPA, at which time Buck bared his soul to Alison by showing her his sketchbook.

I don't know what his exact reasons were, for bringing it along, or for showing it to her in the first place.

Was it a premeditated act?

Or mere coincidence?

Whatever the case may be, he hit the bullseye. The pages of his newsprint tablet were covered with pencil drawings of sexy American superheroines, now beheading Arabs, now treading them underfoot ("That's what they hate the most, you know? they consider the sole of the foot to be unclean," he explained), now planting an American flag, Okinawa-like upon the summit of a mountain of turbaned skulls.

"You're not grossed out, are you?" he asked, milking it (I'm sure he was, for he saw her eyes shining with emotion), "but you know, after 9/11, I just, I mean, I just wanted to kick some Arab ass," (although truth be told, Jason was right: this ass-kicking was circumscribed by an auto-service pit outside Riyadh, into which he would descend several times a day to change the oil of Humvee, LAV-AT and "Deuce and a Half"),

"No, not in the slightest," said Alison, reaching out and squeezing his wrist of her own accord (DING! DING! DING! The attentive listener will note that this is the *very first* time she ever initiated physical contact with a member of the opposite sex in her entire life!)

"You're a hero," she added, her eyes welling with tears of pride and ... maybe something else ... Which she noticed herself, and — maybe it was a bit too forward? That wrist-squeeze and all? — so she turned the page to the drawing of a buxom Megan in way too tightly fitting digies, bending over and blowing a provocative kiss toward the beholder, encircled by Arabs in turbans and blindfolds and dirty underwear, hanging by the neck from nooses suspended from long rows of I-beams.

"Abu-Ghraib," explained Buck, lying through his teeth. "That's where we kept the baddest of the bad. Now," he hastened, taking the opportunity of reaching out and laying his hand on *her* wrist, which (Alison! O Alison!) she left right where it was, shivering at the thrill (Thank you, Fr. Ramsey!)

"That's not what we *did* to them," (which is true — Buck had nothing to do with Abu Ghraib or anything closer to the front lines than The Gap at Al Nakheel Mall), "but that's what those bastards deserved. And the girl I drew there," (here he paused for effect, and — Imre would be proud — choked back a fake tear) "well, she was ... she was ..." He hid his eyes behind his hand, "I'm sorry ..."

"That's all right," soothed Alison, soft and moist in all the right places at this moment (I'm sorry, I know it's gross, but it's the truth! and it does tell you something about poor Alison, doesn't it?) — she would have fucked the whole "heroic" battalion at that moment, to the strains of "God Bless The Yooo Ess AYYYY!" — instead, she said, "Thank you for your service," which, truth be told, she might just as well have said to the guys who sucked and pumped the 5W-30 down at the Jiffy Lube for her, because that, in reality, was the extent of his "service" in Desert Shield/Desert Storm (in all actuality, ONLY Desert Shield) ...

Buck (*call me Jarhead!* even though the closest he ever came to the Marines was in the mess-hall movie theater, and what the *fuck* were they showing that to the troops for, some of the Airmen bitched before walking out) uncovered his eyes at that moment, which was a VERY GOOD THING for him to do, considering his intentions, because *Oh Shit!!* Alison was about to turn the page of his sketchbook ...

"Sorry, no more!" he said, slamming the cover closed, and pulling the book down off the table and onto the bench he was sitting on ... "Sorry," he continued, with wet, hangdog eyes, "I really shouldn't go back to those places ..."

And he picked up the tab. And even though she had insisted on going Dutch, Alison *let him,* which, had Buck known as much about Alison Prickney as I, and Jason, and poor, heartbroken Billy Kowalski do, he would have said, deep in the depths of whatever shriveled soul he possessed, BOOO-YAAAHHH! because, that was actually, like, the equivalent of *second base.*

Why am I going on with this?

Be. Patient.

Alison, as we have said, was on proverbial Cloud Nine.

And good for her, right?

I mean, considering her past, even Buck was a good place to start. A nice initiation to that Crazy Little Thing Called Love (doesn't Queen suck? I mean, besides Brian May and "Bohemian Rhapsody," and maybe, maybe *Sheer Heart Attack*, what do you have? This is Jason's opinion, mind you, although I heartily concur. "Another One Bites the Dust —" come on! Crap with a capital K!)

BUT!

There's always a BUT.

What was the drawing that he didn't want her to see?

… That sensitive, big, manly man …!

When they got back to the office, Alison made sure to note where Buck put the sketchbook. And, discreetly, but continually, she kept her eyes on his cubicle until she saw him get up and leave for the pisser. Then, quick as a flash, she hopped over to his desk, pulled out the sketchbook, opened it up, leafed to the place he wanted her not to see, and saw:

A very, very, salacious, I mean pornographic, I mean Larry-Flynt-Would-Blush drawing of …

Her.

It could be no one else.

That face, in that moment of down and dirty ecstasy, was *hers.*

Yep. Now, this was no bespoken portrait. This was something that Buck had done for himself, after meeting Alison. Alison had supplanted Megan, *big time*. Because Megan was, really, a sweet little thing, an affair of the heart, a first, puppy love. Alison, on the other hand, was associated in Buck's mind with, *ahem*, another part of the human anatomy. Yeah, enough said.

Confused, broken, sad, dashed to the earth, chopped in pieces, you choose the descriptive here, Alison looked up from the sketchbook just at the moment she saw Buck returning from the little boys' room. Quickly, she closed the sketchbook, put it back where she had found it, and slipped out of the cubicle and into her own, unnoticed.

Needless to say, she got no more work done that afternoon. When five o'clock rolled around, she gathered up her stuff, sailed past Jason and Jim and Billy and Buck, beet red, without a word, went out into the parking lot, and, safe in the hot and stuffy interior of her Prius, she locked the door and allowed herself ten seconds of tears and one scream (punching the steering wheel) before she steeled herself anew in the armor of irascibility, turned the key in the ignition and slid out of the parking lot (calmly, flicking on her blinkers) and drove up the Cross-River to her home in Sanantone.

And do you know what she did when she got there?

She poured herself a big glass of pinot grigio. She sat down on her front porch. And she calmed down, and felt ... no longer violated, but *confirmed*.

Because you know what?

She was right.

All men ARE shits, like Tommy Watson.

Fuck you, Fr. Ramsey.

She drank down her pinot grigio and poured herself another. One more, that was it. She didn't need any more. She'd made a determination. Tomorrow, first thing, she'd walk into Billy Kowalski's office and introduce him to the dark side of Buck Toth. She pictured his incredulity — "Buck? Really? But he's, he's an *American Hero* for God's sake! Fought in Desert Storm! For his country! Sets aside 10% of his paycheck for the Wounded Warrior Project!" — and then his stunned reaction when she would lead him to

Buck's cubicle and take down the sketch pad and show him the drawing.

This was to be her authentic, well-documented, and righteous #MeToo moment.

And who could blame her? *Hayna?*

But then Jason Hughes gave her a lift to work, and (quite, quite unconsciously and with no ulterior erotic motives) tapped her on the leg.

Rob Westover worked at the Ferry Building. He had just been dropped off on the corner of Washington and Embarcadero by his wife, six months pregnant, when the ICBM struck San Francisco and obliterated him, and her, their unborn child, and thousands of other San Franciscans, resident and tourist. Now, Rob was a good fellow, and I'm sure he's been welcomed by Jesus with open arms into a place even more lovely than the City by the Bay, or — at the very least — into a mild and brief purgatory, so, I'm sure he wouldn't say what springs immediately to my lips at this moment:

Fuck you, Alison Prickney.

Of course, our good friend — sorry, my good friend — Jason Hughes knew nothing of the backstory leading up to his dismissal from you know where. If you remember, his first thought at Alison's strange and sudden leap from the passenger seat in the Burger King parking lot was:

What, she don't like the Beatles?

He shrugged and drove on.

I mean, what would you have done?

And then came his coffee break, and then came Billy Kowalski showing up at his desk with two uniformed security guards, saying:

"Jason, take your things and come with us."

Jason stood up, looked at Billy, then at Jim, and then back at Billy, and then over at Alison who flushed crimson and turned away, and at Buck, who smirked, and snorted a chest-heave that said *Heh!* The security guard with the long nose hairs held out an empty cardboard box. Jason looked down at his desk. There was his *Free Paul!* coffee mug (remember when they arrested him in Japan for possessing a couple of grams of grass?) his *Bass Aerobics* book, and a dual edition of *Animal Farm* and *1984* which he picked up on the mistaken assumption that the song of the same name from *The Village Green Preservation Society* was based on it, or vice versa (but he got into it anyway, and Orwell (how aptly!) had become his favorite author. Those three items hardly required a padded envelope, to say nothing of a box. So he just shrugged (again) and with these few possessions in hand, followed Billy into his office, the security guards striding officially to his left and right.

"Wait out here," Billy had said to the guards, as he opened his glass office door and let Jason in before him. Jason looked back at the two security dudes — who both looked as if they only took this job because they'd failed out of Mall Cop Academy, as they stood to both sides of the door, backs to the office, one with legs wide spread and hands on his hips, the other, slouched a little bit with an incipient hunchback, still holding the empty cardboard box in front of him — and burst out laughing. Jason, that is.

"What's so funny?" said Billy, irritated.

"Your Dick Tracy out there," he replied, sitting down on the chair in front of Billy's desk, "He looks like he's begging canned goods outside of Walmart."

And then "Oops!" he sloshed his coffee onto the large desk calendar from Maaco Auto Parts. "Sorry, Billy."

"No worries," said the latter. "That's last month anyway."

And he tore the damp top leaf off the calendar, with a dramatic flourish that made Jason cough with laughter again. And now it was like a case of the giggles in church. Despite himself, Billy couldn't suppress a snort of laughter either.

"Maybe you should give it to him?" Jason continued, nodding over his shoulder toward the guard with the box, "Maybe if he gets enough old paper, he can redeem it down at the recycling plant?"

And Billy laughed again, although that wasn't all that funny.

"Stop it," he said, "this is serious."

"What?"

"Ahem. Sexual misconduct."

But Billy, in an effort to control himself and establish the requisite gravitas demanded by the situation, had said these words in an unnaturally deep voice that sounded like Pee-wee Herman trying to do James Earl Jones.

He and Jason looked at one another for a millisecond of silence …

... and then burst out laughing so loud that the two guards exchanged uneasy glances ...

...and Alison turned a shocked face toward that glass door, where she beheld her "abuser" sharing a belly laugh with her supervisor, who was supposed to be laying down the law! She grabbed the two arms of her chair and was about to push herself up, but then thought better of it; an angry snort of wind rushed out of her nostrils, she tightened her lips and tried to concentrate on the layout book for Neandrosil Eyebrow Enhancer, angrily flipping pages that might as well have been blank.

Back in the unfortunately transparent office (although, with the door closed, little could be heard outside — except for those inappropriate bursts of laughter), Billy Kowalski was taking deep breaths and trying to get control of himself.

"What the fuck are you doing?" Jason asked, knowing nothing of the tricks actors use to get control of themselves before going on stage.

"Deep breaths, asshole. Actors do this shit to get a grip ..." and to get his mind on something else and stop the uncontrollable laughter, he returned to the last lines he was preparing (in his bedroom in those ugly new houses, as Mozz would put it, where he danced his legs down to the knees) ... unfortunately, it was Act V of *Richard III* — "'Jockey of Norfolk, be not so bold / For Dickon thy master is bought and sold ...'" he whispered.

"Get a grip on the Dickon in my jockeys," responded Jason — and once again they were back in the Wartella's Market breakroom — again they exploded in laughter and suddenly Billy jumped up from behind his desk howling in hilarity:

"Stop it! Stop it!" hopping the while from one foot to the other, gripping tight his crotch, (he'd drunk about a *quart* of coffee that morning, and was on his way to the pisser when Alison stopped him with her complaint) "I'm gonna fucking piss my pants!"

Jason was caught in such a paroxysm of laughter that he doubled over in his chair and started pounding the desktop with his fist.

"Ooh! Ooh!" whined Billy, "Really! Shit, Jason ...! Wait here!"

And Billy was gingerly hopping around one side of his desk, his hand tightly throttling his Johnson, when the door to his office was suddenly flung open — it rebounded from the wall so hard that the upper glass panel cracked diagonally from corner to corner — and in the door frame stood Alison, shaking, livid, like Megaera on a bad snake day.

"I QUIT!" she screamed, turned on her heel, and stomped back out to her desk, where she grabbed her purse and her raincoat and headed for the exit under full steam.

And this is why New York City canceled Puerto Rico Day for the first time in anyone's memory — *One thing leads to another*, in the immortal words of Cy Curnin of The Fixx ... or was it, Adam Woods?

Sorry.

Anyway, Alison Prickney is to blame (along with Billy, along with Jason, along with ... yep, all the way back to

You Know Who) for the angry riot that began just south of the park and led to the looting and destruction of at least one tall building across Fifth Avenue from the Presbyterian church, and ... well, it wasn't a good day to be blond in New York, was it? And, come to think of it, will the looters be tried as enemy combatants, since Puerto Rico had declared its independence from the rump republic of the old USA a week previously? And if so, well, Guantanamo Bay is out of the question these days ...

As is the presidential funeral. The horse never left the stable; the backward boots needed not be polished to reflect the brilliant southern/Tidewater sun, which has been rising in the morning over the Chesapeake and progressing calmly through the Washington skies to disappear in the evenings beyond the hilly environs of Russell Road in Alexandria, stately and unconcerned, as it always has, since before there ever was a Washington or a Fairfax County, or even Chickahominy or Powhatan harvesting shellfish from the pristine Potomac ...

Yep.

State of emergency.

No parades.

DC under lockdown.

Well, *Anacostia* under lockdown; the rest of DC under curfew because it was raining a couple of weeks ago in Northeastern Pennsylvania and Jason Hughes was running (naturally!) without his eyeglasses; the former Commander in Chief was buried with skimpy honors, back in his hometown of Shubuta MS, with nobody in attendance at the funeral service at New Canaan United Methodist except for his grieving immediate family, his uncle Blind Orange Jim-rag (*the* best Dobro player you've never heard of!) and the Mexican Military Envoy for the Gulfshore Region (whom, rumor has it, is just days away from being named Governor, once push comes to shove and the Cubans are made — gently — to recognize the fait accompli) — which is just as well I mean, the small funeral.

Good ol' 48 was a kind of hometown sort of guy, wasn't he?

Never much for the pomp of big cities.

And I *know* he was smiling down from Heaven (why not? *De mortuis nil nisi bonum*) when the down-home choir struck up "Peace in the Valley." I mean, can you imagine the Marine band doing justice to that one? To say nothing of "Save a Place for Me" or "Will the Circle be Unbroken." *Bury my body. Bury me …* All because of *Abbey Road. Goo goo ga joob.*

Alison's dramatic appearance in the office doorway, and subsequent theatrical exit from the building, quashed the giggles that had been plaguing Billy and Jason.

"Well," was all Billy said, closing the door and sitting back down at his desk, having regained control of his bladder. Just weeks before this, he would have raced after her, begging and pleading her to calm down, to stay, etc., etc. — not because she was indispensable to the company as a layout person (it wasn't her thing, let's admit it, finally, she'd have been much happier in a fluorescent vest and hard hat) — but because … well, you know why. But ever since his error in introducing her to Buck-Jarhead, he had come, not slowly, but ever more definitely, to the knowledge that *it was not meant to be.*

Alas, and like the steaming summer rains,
So doth my love escape me, to the skies.

Or to her lonely house in Sanantone.

And so he sat back down at his desk and he pulled out the HR folder, as he was trained to do for circumstances like this, reading through the boilerplate of Jason's Dismissal for Cause, with the Severance Package generously added, although since it was "for cause," it was up to the supervisor's discretion whether to add it or to just pull the lever and send Jason hurtling downward through the trap door to unemployment.

And of course, the name of Jason's accuser was (for reasons of privacy and out of concern for the complainant's safety) not to be revealed to him, and so it wasn't. Not that it needed to be, after all. Even without her storming the office like that, he would have figured it out: Alison.

Who else?

Jim Krywicki?

Gaylord?

And it was explained to Jason (word by word, as written on the page) that the Termination was Final and that there Was No Appeal, (Do you find this unfair? Bless your innocence! Where have you been hiding throughout, gosh, even 2017!), and Jason accepted the hand that Billy stretched out to him over the desktop, and shook it, genuinely, after which he gathered up his few belongings, and went out into the warm noon sunshine — taking a deep breath in the parking lot and wondering, suddenly, at how much he'd missed over these past months, sitting at that desk, when large honeybees were hovering over the yellow squash blossoms and purple hibiscus, and a long black salamander with yellow spots was soaking up the warmth by the side of a road it should not cross. (Jason walked over to him, picked up its soft, dry tube of a body in his hand, and carried him to the little wood across the street, which was where he had been thinking of heading).

After which a speeding car beeped angrily at him, the driver of which rolled down the passenger window to bellow,

"Asshole!"

at him, for having the nerve to stand by the side of the road, before crossing back to the parking lot.

But that didn't bother Jason.

He'd helped a salamander; it was sunny out, and just the thought of his P-Bass at home made him smile. He was trying to figure out some Jimmy Haslip, believe it or not, on a regular four-string bass.

Speaking of Jimmies, Jim Krywicki had got up from his desk and walked outside, for lunch, just as Jason was pulling out of the parking lot. Then something hit him in the back of the neck, as he stood there on the hot macadam in front of the side door, watching his friend drive away. His hand flew up and brushed at it, thinking it to be an insect, but as he walked over to his car, he felt something hit him in the back again and turned around.

It was Buck Toth, from the sidewalk in front of the building, flicking paper clips at him from a rubber band.

"Hey! Shit, man!" said Jim.

"Hey! Shit man!" Buck mimicked with a singsongy voice. "Don't you say bad words like that! I'll tell your Mommy you used the S-word!"

"Fuck you, Buck," said Jim.

"Looks like your boyfriend got bounced," said Buck.

Jim had his hand on the door handle when Buck said that. If you had been behind him, you would have seen his shoulders slump. But then he turned around, walked over to where Buck was standing, and, without so much as a word, buried his fist into Buck's solar plexus with such force, that Call-Me-Jarhead regurgitated that twitchy spazz named Gaylord who was always just under the surface of his skin, jackknifed toward the pavement, gulping air like a stranded fish, in a panic, trying to get his respiratory system operative again.

"Buck, I said *fuck you*," Jim repeated, and, grabbing the gasping man by his ears, he brought Gaylord's face into swift contact with his right knee — making his nose explode in a bloody torrent.

"I get the last word, Gaylord," and with this, he opened his car door, got in, and drove away.

Nah. It didn't happen like that. It never does.

If you were standing behind Jim at that moment, you would have seen his shoulders slump. And then you would have seen him open the car door and slip inside, as fast as he could, so that you wouldn't see the tears welling in his eyes. He was crying, not because Jason had been fired, or, not precisely: but rather because, since Jason had been fired, things were now sure to go back to that awful normal of his being the undying prey of the immortal Duncan McLeod that was Buck-Call-Me-Jarhead Toth, who would grow stronger and stronger from the daily quickenings he would imbibe from the never-quite-severed jugular of his helpless victim.

Am I being a little over-dramatic here?

Well, what's the difference between a bully in a cubicle with a pencil in his hand, and a bully in a cubicle at the controls of a drone?

But — in case you're feeling sorry for Jim — be patient, he shall have his revenge.

You'll see, in just a moment.

But now, d'you want to know what was I doing at this juncture?

I was trying to get my aching fingers around "This Charming Man."

Ha, ha!

Lower your judgmental eyebrows.

That's a song.

By The Smiths.

Hmm.

Blank stare.

Well, you do sorta look like a Marty Stuart kinda person.

I was patiently (more or less patiently) trying to get down the opening, ringing couple of bars to that song, because, as I've mentioned before, this was one of *my* songs during the first iteration of One Hour's Practise and I was about to join the reunion tour for their gig at Hanskung College.

That got your attention, right?

Yes, we're almost there, at the very conjunction of fibers organic and alloyed, so to speak, that is of most interest to you … *Almost there.* As you've already noticed, there is a chain of events behind every Event With A Capital E and backstories are important.

So, anyway, when Jason dusted off the Kent and then traded up for the used P-Bass and was having such a good time in the evenings that even the loss of his day job couldn't quite faze him (he was so looking forward to cracking the jazzy scale runs of his hero Jimmy) he wasn't just playing with himself of an evening.

Oops! Sorry. I mean playing *by* himself — playing *alone.*

Marginal note about unconsciously onanistic English references. Do you know that I was once publicly slapped across the face for using the word "ejaculation?" It was at a conference in Steubenville, Ohio, and I had agreed to act as an interpreter for a redhead from Medellin who was presenting her paper in Spanish, and the dude who was supposed to do the honors hadn't shown up. Smart dude. In the session just previous to hers, I had presented my paper on Sor Juana and Donne, and for that reason, the chair of the next session, in which the Columbian chick was going to bore the assembled eggheads for twenty-five minutes on "Las notas de pie de páginas imaginarias en las novelas de Borges," approached me.

Now, translating is no simple matter, and when you're pressed for time, especially when you're *interpreting orally* (which despite my being fairly bilingual, I have not been professionally trained to do), you need to spit out the first equivalent that comes into your head — so that a twenty-five-minute speech, say, will last no longer than thirty-five minutes, and not be dragged out to sixty-five. This is fairly easy to do with words such as *agua* and *perro* and *cerveza*, which — I see from your face — don't even need to be translated (take heart, gringos! When *la revolución lingüística* arrives in your neighborhood, you're already prepared to curse out bartenders with a reasonable facsimile of "You dog! This beer is watered down!") or when you're acting as an intermediary at Easter breakfast for your abuela who speaks no English, and your girlfriend/boyfriend who speaks no Spanish — "My grandmother says that when she was young, all the boys chased her, and you're so good looking you probably have the same problem"— sure, that's simple enough.

But when you've got a little firecracker of a Columbiana, who despite being 65 or so is still wearing short skirts and (you get this five minutes into meeting her) thinks she's the cat's meow of any feline wearing pajamas and reminds you that "you are dealing not only with a masterpiece of criticism but also with the greatest Spanish author of the modern ages. So please be on your toes and be aware of the subtleties of both Borges' text, and my own, which Carlos Fuentes' second cousin himself once told me is 'written with élan and a passion that would make Borges himself fall to his knees'"), and then, just as you're doing your damnedest (not because of any humanistic, altruistic impulse, but because the dude who asked you to do this also offered to refund your conference fee *and* your travel expenses! — Did he buy into the self-serving spiel of the spoilt little redhead? Or did he just want to get her to *go the fuck away already* before she burns down the whole school?) you're catching dagger-like glares of disapproval and frustration from Herself the Almighty She Nearly Anointed by Carlos Fuentes' Second Cousin and a silver-haired guy in glasses, with a Van Dyke and a bad orange tan, sitting in the front row who is probably the Royal Consort of Herself the Almighty She, well ... that's a different story altogether.

I know, I know, I'll get a move on!

So, it all came down to a passage from Borges' short story "El evangelio según Marcos," which reads:

Espinosa, en el campo, fue aprendiendo cosas que no sabía y que no sospechaba. Por ejemplo, que no hay que galopar cuando uno se está acercando a las casas y que nadie sale a andar a caballo sino para cumplir con una tarea. Con el tiempo llegaría a distinguir los pájaros por el grito.

And, coming to the end, I translated *grito* as *ejaculation*.

Now, in my defense, remember: I was translating, or trying to translate, with as much immediacy, and accuracy, as I could. Second, in English, we do not "distinguish birds by their cry," we distinguish them by their *voice*. Third, I had just finished presenting my (rather well received, by the way) paper on "The Substrata of Baroque Catholicism in the poetry of Sor Juana and Donne," in which I had *used this very term* in its acceptable significance, according to none other than the Oxford English Dictionary, of "the putting up of short earnest prayers in moments of emergency; the hasty utterance of words expressing emotion." Fourth, for us Mexicans (I give up, already! I've been defined as such from Esposito to the latest CNN windbag, and so I'm formally "dropping the hyphen." No longer Mexican-American, OK, OK, Mexican already!), for us Mexicans, I say, *grito* is associated with the *Grito de Dolores* of 16 September 1810 — which is our *real* national holiday, by the way — "Cinco de mayo" is more of a Gringo thing — but you'll get used to it, eventually, which *pronunciamiento* was delivered by Fr. Miguel Hidalgo y Costilla, a priest and thus it all fits together like the pieces of a *rompecabezas* (look it up, Gringo. But context helps! You can already buy your wet dog a beer …) and so I said that "With time, Espinosa arrived at being able to distinguish birds by their ejaculation."

WAS it a bad translation?

Well, it wasn't a *good* one.

But nobody in the audience (fifteen people; there had been forty-three for my group!) tittered or noticed or seemed to care — except for Herself and the Silver Haired Consort. As soon as I'd said the word, there was so long a pause, that I looked over at her, wondering if she had finished. She hadn't, but there was such a look of horror on her face, that — well, we've already used a Megaera reference, so I won't do it again, but you get the idea. Silver Hair *ejaculated* some vocables in no language known to me. He said:

"Hrrrumphan!"

As if a dog, getting his belly scratched, had suddenly noticed a cat in the yard, and was torn between chasing off after his mortal enemy, and remaining there, on his side in the warm sunlight, enjoying the ecstasy of the massage.

But the wheels of the universe began to spin again, and the redhead

I'm.

Too Sexy for my Shirt.

Too Sexy for my Shirt.

blundered on to the end, visibly editing the text for length as she progressed, which made my task all the more difficult, "Borges … upon the pyramid … World War I in the Philippines, if you remember the 'Garden of Forking Paths' …" in such fashion did we stumble on to the finish line, and I was about to sit down, red-faced, amongst the auditory, or leave the room completely, when the chair halted me with the obligatory, "Any questions?" directed at the audience.

Now, lunch — a free lunch — was already in full swing in the halls outside our room (you could hear the throaty chuckles of the naturally gray, pashmina scarved vegan whales in free-trade huarache sandals who carve out ever-smaller niches for themselves by becoming THE expert in Female Masturbatory Semiotics in *Jane Eyre* or the Earl of Oxford as William Shakespeare AND Christopher Marlowe) so there weren't many.

One fellow asked the first presenter "Can you not say that Paz's time spent in India led to at least a tentative adoption of Gayatri meter in his later poetry?" and, after a long, long reply, another, female, academic with the hair and voice of Barbara Walters circa 1974, directed her query at the second presenter (the only grad student on the panel): "So. Quintana Woo. Is it not twue that he actuwawy despised the poetwy of Wamawtine?" and again, a long answer, but then, stomachs overcame politeness (you could *sense* the Smoky Chickpea Wraps with Dill Tahini Sauce and Sesame Quinoa Spring Rolls disappearing down the gullets of *others less deserving!*) and there were no more questions; the star of the whole shebang (in her own mind and that of the Consort, at least) broke out into uncontrollable sobbing, alone at the long desk on the dais, and I (after hesitating, twice, between saying "thanks," "bye," "have a nice day," "can I get you a Kleenex?" and just splitting) was immediately confronted by the Man With The Beard Like Kenny Rogers And The SprayTan Like John Boehner at the foot of the little steps, and Whacked Across My Left Cheek By His Open Right Hand!

"Wha …?" was all I could manage, in astonishment.

"You nasty man!" he began. "Look you make her cry! What with jerking this off stuff?"

"What are you talking about?"

"You make her birds whack off? You *ejaculate* the birds?"

"I …what? …" and here *I* had my giggling in church moment; I burst out laughing, which caught Kenny Boehner off balance, it seemed; here I was, slapped across the face, challenged, and — I suppose — the proper response in his mind was for me to jut out my sharp Sevillian chin and wrap myself round in my flowing velvet cape (no, I'm only speaking figuratively; I was in khakis and Ralph Lauren buttondown, like everybody else) and challenge him to a duel, with his choice of weapons, but, here I'm laughing uncontrollably!

"You think this is full of humor, no? You funny man? You play birdies' peepee?"

He just turned on his heel and walked out, not even waiting for Herself Queen of the Fucking Universe (Peter Townsend, "I am an Animal," from the same album as "And I Moved," cited earlier) who brushed past me, uttering through her tears, *in English*:

"*Grito* means cry. The bird's *cry*, God damn it!"

which got me pissed off; because if you know English well enough to be insulted by my translation, why the *fuck* didn't you translate it yourself?

Or deliver it in English?

The answer, of course, is, she wanted to look more important, with a translator at her side: just like President Paz, who was educated at Oxford and taught at Northwestern, still speaks only Spanish in his pronouncements, and has his interpreter at his side for the Gringos.

Well, water under the bridge.

So, I was practicing "This Charming Man," because a few days earlier, Jason had called me up again, and said:

"Hey man, we're playing your school. How about you join us on stage this time? For a couple of songs? It'd be a blast for your students."

And I wasn't about to let this opportunity slide by again. It *would* be cool to shred a bit (although I was only a rhythm guitarist, still, from my veiled references to my past in classroom — yeah, I guess I can be just as vain as a redhead from Columbia— you'd think I'd taught Eddie Van Halen all he knows) before my students, especially ... well, never mind ... *And* OHP had scored a recording contract! Yeah! Believe it or not and a *single* getting airtime on WNKR 106.5 "The Rock!" I said, 'yesyesyesyesyes!' this time, with visions of sugar plums dancing in my head, thinking this, oh, this would be my ticket out of Hanskung College and Freshman Comp (turned out that I was right about that, but in a different way!) and soon my iPhone *dinged* and there was a text from Jason with some songs to brush up on, all the ones I knew from way back when, like (besides "This Charming Man")

"Turning Japanese" by the Vapors,

"Bully Bully" and "Stay in Time" by Off Broadway, and

"You Are Like A Hurricane" (which I sort of knew we wouldn't play, because Jason hated that song; he probably added it only because it had an easy solo that I was able to do — nice kind touch there, actually), along with directions to Dave's new split-level, where we would jam together for the first time in — Cripes! Over Thirty Years! —in preparation for the gig at Hanskung in two weeks.

So I was whanging at the Epiphone for hours on end now. I even carried it into school to whang at during office hours (making sure it was placed with strategical prominence in a stand near the window for my advisees to notice, although my participation in the gig was to be a total surprise), and who knew that we'd call down a storm just 'Like a Hurricane,' to sweep away Yankeedom from New

Orleans, where the tiled street names had already been in Spanish, anyway, for some time previous to the present Mexican occupation?

Ding-dong (cliché, I know. Don't you hate'm? But there was a doorbell at Dave's split-level in Hannover Heights, and I rang it, and it sounded like that).

The door was opened by a thin, scrawny kid in a Kansas t-shirt two sizes too big for him (Kansas the band, not the school), and black horn-rims that had a band-aid wrapped around the nose-piece — he looked like the King of the Land of the Geeks.

"Hey," I said, unsurely. "Are you Dave's son?"

"No," he said, blushing. "I'm with the band."

Uh-oh.

"What—" he began, but then he noticed the guitar case in my hand, and said "Oh. You must be the new guy. Come in."

"Thanks," I said, pushing past him, a little peeved.

New guy?

"Hey, Ray!" came Jason's voice from somewhere down below. And I noticed that right before me was an oddly-placed door leading to the cellar. "Come on down, man!"

"I'm one of the *old guys*," I tossed over my shoulder to King Doofus XIII. "I played with them back in the eighties." And I trotted downstairs, the confidence which I had been lacking during my drive over across the river again in full flood. (We've all got a little bit of Jarhead in us, I suppose …)

"Ray!" said Dave, getting up from behind his kit. I gave our drummer a hug and turned to the right, where Rick, doing some pastoral crap on his phone, sent a nod and a smile in my direction.

"I know, Mrs. Wallace. But you must remember that Methodists are Christians too. And there is only one baptism … Yes, yes, I will pray for him to return to the fold … Yes, Mrs. Wallace. No, Mrs. Wallace, if she were a Mormon, it would be an entirely different matter. Yes, Mrs. Wallace. May He always be praised. And you too, Mrs. Wallace. Yes. Goodbye!" after which, he rolled his eyes, came over and gave me a big bear hug, then said,

"Strap in, gentlemen!" which almost brought tears to my eyes, as he always *used* to say that, slung his Frankenstrat over his shoulder and plugged me into the center amp.

"Raymond, if you please?" he invited.

And of themselves the fingers of my left hand found the fifteenth fret and in I plunged with the opening *faux Japonais* riff of "Turning Japanese," and … a miracle happened.

Not only Dave (who, as a drummer, you would expect to find the beat immediately) but Rick and Jason slammed in seamlessly, and we were off — I mean, they were *good*. I made a few stumbles as the song went on and I tried to regain that mystical balance of being able to sing over playing the guitar, the mind separated in halves, or, the muscle memory of the hands and arms and fingers taking over while the conscious mind goes on with *No sex no drugs no wine no women no fun no sin no you no wonder it's dark*, reasonably in the proper key and at the proper tempo … but they were so *good* that even I couldn't spoil them; they were like the goddam *Wrecking Crew* or something!

"Still got it!" Jason smiled from my right when the song crashed to an end. How kind of him to say so. I mean *really*. If there's one thing that you must put down, you must put down this: *Jason Hughes is kind.*

Anyway, things sort of went downhill from then on — less badly on "Stay in Time," which I was to begin with a rather simple up-fretboard ringing strum of twenty-odd seconds; turns out I was just a little sharp — twice, two false starts; I got confused (I've never been able to adjust a riff once I've learned it in the wrong place; stupid, I know, but my mind just locks in on that pattern, and …)

"Never mind," said Rick with a smile and a quick look towards Jason. "Do it there. We'll bend it in."

And so I began again, sharp and — dear God, were these dudes my old friends? And if so, had they spent the intervening thirty years at Muscle Shoals or something? — Rick and Jason played sharp along with me, and made *me* sound good!

A few beers and I got relaxed; Jason (Jason is *kind*) suggested his much-despised "Like a Hurricane," which I nailed — as he knew I would do, and this set me at ease — as he knew it would — and so when it came time for "This Charming Man," I only screwed it up *once.*

And then more beers. The guitars were latched into their stands; Dave turned on *Dark Side of the Moon,* and His Royal Nerdness turned out to be cooler than he appeared, as he pulled out a baggie with some ganja and I was suddenly transported back to Wildwood Crest, 1978 or thereabouts, smoking weed with these three guys in a cheap two-level motel by the shore, in the room of a stranger (represented, in this instance, by the kid in the Kansas T) who suddenly knocked on our door one evening as he passed by and saw Rick twanging away at his Les Paul and said,

"You dudes wanna get high?"

And so we sat there on the stringy carpet of his room listening to *Dark Side of the Moon* on a portable record player and passing spliffs around, crunching roaches between our molars, and laughing like crazy in a world that was warm and brotherly and *what the fuck is a record player doing in a motel?* was all I could think of, growing happily dizzy as my eyes followed the tip of the prism on the center sticker spinning round and round ... life was good, once.

Turns out that the Nerd King was Jim Krywicki (whom you've already met),

"My friend from work," said Jason, introducing him to me, finally — as I'd completely forgotten about him once I came downstairs and we started hugging and jamming,

"The newest One Hour Practiser," he went on. *Uh oh!* "He's putting together a wild video projection behind us for Hanskung. Shit, man," he said, unable to hold his inhale longer, expelling the smoke and passing the joint to me with a friendly nudge to my bicep, "this is gonna look fucking *big time!*"

So, he's with the band, but he's not *exactly* a member, new or not, so — I could almost sense Esposito smirking knowingly from the other world — so maybe it will all be OK.

How wrong I was, as we all know.

That was it; the whole extent of my jamming in the days leading up to the rally at Hanskung for the recently departed 48 — and what more could I do? Now, it wasn't like all my dreams came crashing down on my head; I'm a big boy — like I said, as close as we were to one another, talent-wise, in the good old days of garage jamming in Dave's cellar off Jefferson (a rather pretty girl once bent down at the ground level window, trespassing on the lawn, to say "Hey, you guys are pretty good!") there was an *ocean* — or, at least an inland lake the size of say, Huron — between us these days; that much was apparent from my very first artfully disguised stumble through the Vapors' hit.

But it was going to be a full set, I was told, which is something like twelve to fifteen songs (how was 48 going to stand for that? But what do I know about rallies, anyway? A bigger question is: how did Mick and Keith allow 45 to use "You Cain't Always Git Whut You Want" during the runup to his four felonious years?) and I only knew — more or less well — four, songs that is … so, I learned that I was going to be invited on stage after the first couple tunes, do my bit, and then retire to the wings and let the Real Men carry on (that's not how Jason put it, of course, but that's the gist of the situation, and I was *totally* OK with that; what's true is true)! — of course, they invited me to stay on and jam some more with them, but, like, what's the point? I mean, Blur? Muse? Above my pay grade, as you all say.

And so I packed up my Epi and trudged up the stairs, in a mood that wasn't sadness, really, but a kind of pleasantly depressing awareness of reality … you know what I mean?

No, I see you don't. No matter.

I drove home buzzed.

So buzzed, that, after running a red light on Jefferson, I stopped the car and looked backward, waiting for it to turn green again — and only when the crossing traffic began beeping did I realize what I was doing, and broke out into hysterical laughter for what seemed an eternity, before I moved on up towards the Yonder Mountain.

So, the big day arrived. (At the time, of course, nobody knew *how* big). Although I only had a 9:30 that day, I stayed on campus all day long. The whole couple blocks surrounding Hanskung were cordoned off by the Secret Service and the local turtles (that's what we called the cops back in the day. They were big and fat and if you knocked them on their backs, we used to say, they'd lie there wriggling their little arms and legs in a futile Gregor Samsa-like frenzy to turn over; not that we'd ever knock them on their backs to begin with — they were the fathers of our friends, oh, like Dave Wilcott, and the worst thing they ever did was to confiscate our sixes of Schmidt's at the old collieries or interrupt awkward juvenile coitus alongside the Creek Road; turtles — never *pigs*.

They were the fathers of our friends.

OK, I'll stop the sentimental bullshit) and if I had gone home (which I would have, if not for the gig; what the fuck did I care about any of the forties, or thirties, or twenties for that matter all the way back to The Father Of Our — *ahem* Your — Country?) I would have driven out past the checkpoint on River and damned it all to Hell. But since my

presence was required at the gig, I didn't want to be caught in
the traffic or the checkpoints on the way back *in*; so I stayed
in my office, which had a nice view onto the Tertullian Center
— no, not Turtle Center, the *Tertullian* Center — and I saw
the motorcade pull up, and 48 get out and be greeted by Fr.
Barth in his lime-green soutane of the Pelagian Order.

I still don't know why 48 chose Hanskung to announce
to the world his determination to increase funding for the
Healthy Tobacco Research Initiative (or "Hearti" as some
dyslexic genius anagrammed it for the propaganda boys);
the rumor is that no other school in these (those?) United
States of America would host the event, but could he have
approached *all* of them before the good fathers of St. Pelagius
said yes? Now, Fr. Barth is from Mississippi himself. Maybe
he and old 48 were old chums? I mean, the spread he set up
in the room off the upper corridor in Tertullian was a good
ol' boy's dream smorgasbord. Before, and possibly after, his
announcement, the Chief Executive of the United States of
America would be able to fill his copious belly with:

1. Biscuits and gravy
2. Burgoo (you don't want to know)
3. Collared greens
4. Shrimp and grits, and (alas)
5. Chicken and waffles.

I do know why One Hour's Practise was booked to play
the StudentFest leading up to the rally. They were next up
on the Rolodex at InaPo Music.

No kidding.

And it gets better.

If you remember, the twist to InaPo Music bookings was, when you called tone-deaf and clueless Bob Bartosz to hire a band for your event, you didn't necessarily get the most appropriate group for the gathering. You got whoever came next on the Rolodex. I won't go over that again, but, you also remember that, against all odds, this *always worked out*. There's something in us that never dies, that excitement of plunging one's hand into the CrackerJack box (well, not literally, those boxes are small, but you get the metaphor, right?) and pulling out the mysterious toy … It made Bob Bartosz the go-to guy for music bookings in NEPA, it made him the Brian Epstein of Wixburn and its surroundings (as we've already said), and everybody always left happy … until

… Yeah, but how long could that crazy streak of good luck last?

Anyway, the three bands booked *literally hours* before OHP grabbed the Presidential brass ring (and, giving it a good tug, unleashed fire and fury on the Bay Area), were 1) The Bobby Daniels Newgrass Group, 2) the Gospel Choir of the Meshach African Methodist Episcopal Church, and 3) Holly and Dolf — an *ahem* right-wing folk duo who dressed in lederhosen and sang things like "Eidelweiss" and (believe it or not!) the "Horst-Wessel-Lied" — *all three of which acts* would have been much more to 48's tastes than OHP. But how was Bob to know?

The rally was scheduled for seven pm, the StudentFest for six. So at five-fifteen I took a deep breath, picked up the

Epi — put on sunglasses, *I know, I know!* — wearing black jeans and a tight-fitting shirt patterned after the Japanese battle flag which I bought back in '83 and feverishly dug out of a box in my attic the night before, after being reminded of it in a dream

(no kidding! Esposito? Who knows?)

and walked out of my office building, turning right for the alley that runs up behind the Tertullian ("Come to the back doors of the gym," Jason had told me. "Sound check at 5:30.")

Now, I said that I saw the motorcade drive up; despite my digression, almost no time passed between then and now, when I looked out my window and saw a rather curious scene being played out across the way. After exchanging a few words with Fr. Barth, I saw 48 gesticulating wildly, spinning around on his hefty axis, arms akimbo, raised to the heavens, pointing vigorously at a little black dog that — was that Ol' Beau, 48's famous First Dog? Always seen on TV romping around the White House grounds and clambering into Marine 1 after his master (and before the First Lady), pissing against the leg of the saluting Marine in dress blues at the side of the steps? — but if so, gosh, he sure was small! I know that television adds ten pounds, they say, but that dog looked positively tiny compared to the Ol' Beau I thought I knew from the telly ... But what really surprised me was, he was being held on a leash by three guys who looked suspiciously like Dave, Jason, and Rick! The Rick-looking fellow even had a long-braided beard ...

What were they doing with the president's dog?

I admit I felt a little jealous at that point. I mean *I* didn't get to meet the president's dog ...

But then I saw the three turn around, as the president marched off towards the Tertullian Center, and head the opposite way, toward a white van at the end of the parking lot with something written on the side ... Canine Cruisers? Canine's Able? Ahhh ... those weren't my boys. That was the expensive shuttle service the American taxpayers were bilked for, whenever the Prez was on a junket of fewer than three hundred miles ... Weird (and expensive), but it seems that the Secret Service has some sort of wacky rule about pets in official armored vehicles? As if it's cheaper to rent Canine Cruisers, getting all the dog-handlers their security clearance, and paying the surely exorbitant transport costs of "air-conditioned doggy limousine service, with treats and toys and companionship every mile!" than a Dirt Devil vacuum cleaner and a box of disinfecting leather wipes, well ...

Anyway, I locked the door to my office, and, as I said, I walked — or sauntered, rather — down the steps, came out into the sunlight, and turned on my heel, right, towards Buchanan St. and the Tertullian Center.

"Hey, Doctor V!" someone called from across the street to my left, "Where you going? Is that a guitar?"

It was a group of students playing frisbee.

"Come on over to the StudentFest at six and find out!" I called back, my voice almost cracking with excitement — I felt like a *fucking rock star*.

And then reality, again.

"Whoa, chief. Only band members back here!" a pot-bellied, long-haired guy in a black Slipknot t-shirt that barely covered his flab said to me as I approached the doors.

"I'm part of the band," I said.

"You are? What band? Not OHP. They're on stage at sound check, dude. And OHP is a trio, you know?"

I hoped I wasn't blushing as brightly red as I felt I was.

And ah — I'm usually not this brassy. Not too long before this I might have just shrugged and turned around, my tail between my legs, skulking past the frisbee-players on the quad and gone home, had a beer or twelve, and … the roads around the picturesque Monument Valley Tribal Park would not be clogged with cars chock full of persons of diverse hues who can lay dubious claim to at least one unadmixed Native American ancestor in the his or her pedigree, even if six to ten generations ago, clamoring for the mythical Navajo Nation Passport with which to avoid the mythical Gringo Internment Camps that the Mexicans are (rumor has it) setting up in a string running from Farmington to Grand Junction. (Just in case you're wondering, 1/32 Indian is just as useless in this regard as 1/1024. There are strict legal requirements for laying claim to any sort of tribal citizenship).

I could have cut and run. Alas … alas!

"Look," I said, as a skinny kid in cargo pants and a white polo came out the back door and glanced our way, "I'm Ray. I founded this *fucking* band!"

That's better, I thought (how wrong I was). *When in doubt, profanity.*

"You're Ray?" the tall kid asked.

"I am."

And he whispered something in the fat guy's ear, at which the latter said,

"Oh. OK. Sorry. Go on in then," extending his left hand toward the doors and letting me pass — but giving such an eyebrow-fart at my battle flag T-shirt as if he wanted to say,

"Just don't touch anything, asshole!"

The rear doors led right out onto the stage; the guys were already there doing the sound-check that I thought I was invited to — but, ah come on. This was no time to be peevish. And anyway, what did I know about sound checks? We never had mixers at the high school dances we played when "I founded this fucking band ..." And double-plus anyway, I didn't have time to be peevish or annoyed — I was knocked off my feet. OHP had *Marshall Stacks.* OHP had *Roadies.* OHP had —

"Hey, Ray!" said Jason. "Look up there!"

OHP had a big screen behind them, over which the videos were going to be projected, and over which was now being cast — *an old grainy VHS video of OHP, MY OHP, on stage back in the day, and front and center, there I was, in this same shirt! Windmilling like Peter Townshend through "Modern World" by the Jam ...*

"Cool, eh?"

I could only smile in response;

God, God, all was forgiven.

"Fucking *big time!*" I blurted when the capacity of speech was once again returned to me. "Fucking big time."

And big time it was.

You've got to remember that Wixburn is a nowhere place not known for music; it's neither New Orleans nor Detroit nor Chicago nor Jacksonville nor Nashville; it's true that back in the seventies a local group had a national hit with a song about some coal miners being trapped in a cave-in and emerging after all hope had been extinguished, minus one of their number whom — the rumor went — the survivors had eaten ...

And then there was Ben Ding Franklin, who got their start on the college circuit here before exploding into a hemispherical, if not global, popularity; One Hour's Practise, miraculously miraculous after thirty years of inanition, was *popular* among the young-and-soon-to-be-despairingly-prematurely-old-Wixburnians.

I mean, shit — their single "What do I Care about Crows?" was getting airplay on WLS in Chicago for Pete's sake! The same station where I first heard, late at night, parking with ... never mind ... on the Creek Road, The Vapors and Off Broadway!

The place got PACKED as soon as the doors opened and — Morrissey like — there was no opening act; instead, Jim had put together a fifteen-minute warmup playlist and video show — the place was *jammed* with young people *screaming* for OHP!

My OHP!

Well, no longer *my OHP,* exactly, but ... and again I felt that sweetly depressing sense of reality hit me.

But before I go any further, I've got to tell you about the graduation speaker at Hanskung back in 2002.

Somehow, the Pelagian fathers got hold of Johnny Scrimshaw, yes, the actor who played the lead role in the *Hidden Christ of India* — that controversial movie about the "lost years" of Jesus. Well, you probably know that Johnny Scrimshaw is a Third Order Pelagian Lay Brother.

Yep.

So, anyway, he comes in and gives this long commencement speech about overcoming this ADHD and that ODD and the occasional OCD — and all before his seventeenth year, mind — I mean, it was a long speech about free will and fasting and unaided moral good works and an almost Norman Vincent Peale insistence on positive thinking. Then he ended his speech with a rousing,

"And now, brothers and sisters, let us send the devil back to Hell!"

accompanied by a theatrical fist pump in the air.

Why am I telling you this?

Because the reaction was just what you'd expect from a hundred or so hungover twenty-somethings, a demographically appropriate percentage of whom were suffering from chancres and herpes.

The silence was deafening.

This is not to say that there is anything *wrong* with sending the devil back to Hell, and I'm sure if you polled those oversexed and alcoholic throngs, you wouldn't find a single soul amongst them who would say, "No, let's let him stay right where he is."

The point is, nobody likes commencement speeches in the first place. The gym is hot, your head is pounding, some bald dude (the rule; they're hardly ever as comely as young Johnny) is misquoting Bruce Springsteen, and one platitude shoots out over your head after another. And here — he's making you sit through a *sermon*?

So, before you start talking about the choice of OHP being inappropriate to the occasion, well — shit, you were there! — OHP got ol' 48 a nice ol' crowd. (That they were there for OHP and not for 48, and only stayed there because — what happened to fire code? — the doors were locked until he wound down his uninspired drawl about safe cigarettes and tariffs and jobs just waitin' for all y'all so come on down an' join in our revitalizin' o' Dixie, only proves my point about Johnny Scrimshaw's tent revival speech).

But back to our regularly scheduled programming.

I wasn't on stage with the boys when they sauntered out there, cocks of the walk, to the frenzied, screaming crowds — but even in the wings, I felt the adrenaline rush as if I had been.

Now, OHP got its start as a cover band. And so the first couple of tunes were party crowd-pleasers:

"Boys and Girls,"

"Smokin'" (Boston. Remember them? Done *without* keyboards. Good gracious, Fr. Rick's true vocation is shredding!), and then — I mean, it *did* pass through my head, *what was Jason up to?*

"Nüguns." That *really* got the head-banging going, and then — masterful, masterful! — the band segued into their new-metal originals:

the nationwide hit "What do I Care about Crows," with Rick rapping up the fretboard like Eddie Van Halen *and* Jason's blurringly complex bass solo that would have made Geddy Lee's jaw hit the floor —

after which (where did they get the stamina?) their bitter, but blistering "Fucksquehanna," which, taking into consideration airtime on college radio throughout the Northeast, will be the sort of thing that ushers them into that building of I.M. Pei's on Lake Erie some day.

If it's still there.

After that song boomed to a close with the Dave's final tattoo on the toms and double basses, a sweaty Jason looked over in my direction, beaming, and nodded. I nodded back, and he turned to the crowd.

"Wow! Thanks! I hear we got some Hanskung students here, huh?"

And the crowd exploded in shrieks — and from the mosh pit, *panties* began to flutter onto the stage at the feet of Jason and Rick, who glanced at each other and laughed.

"So, you guys may not know this," Jason continued, "but this group was founded, way back before most of you were born, by a guy named Ray Verano!"

Again, wild cheers. Of course, not for me. There would have been wild cheers if Jason had said "Milk is for baby cows. Join PETA now!" (which would not have been out of character for him, as you know).

"You know this fellow as Dr. V here at Hanskung. We know him as the rhythm guitarist and front man of the first iteration of OHP. Ray," he said turning to the wings, "get out here!"

And so I did, bouncing as if I had springs on my feet, in my battle-flag shirt, with my Epiphone over my shoulder, to the enthusiastic screaming of the crowd, much of which was made up of Hanskung students, and quite a few of whom (I was never very popular, but *everybody* has to take Freshman Comp) were my own. Of course, they would have been screaming and throwing their panties if Jason had said something like "Spam may be popular in Hawaii, but it's not very popular amongst the porcine population!" — they didn't give a shit.

It was a party!

But of course, I felt like I was Eric Clapton, being called out onto the stage as George Harrison's surprise guest.

"Smiths," Rick mouthed over to me with a smile, as I fumbled the phone plug into the Epiphone's jack; and *Oh shit* — but — have you ever been on stage? It does something to you. There's a rush you get from the eager, indulgent crowd (again, they don't give as much a shit about you as they do about the bacchanalic release of primal screams) — whether it be tens of tens of thousands at Wembley or fifteen spotty chicks in a high school cafeteria on coffeehouse night.

They *help* you.

The adrenaline rushes into your over-fat fingers and — you plink your way effortlessly into "This Charming Man" as if you were Johnny H. Marr himself.

And the band kicked in behind me and we were off.

It was going so well, it suddenly crossed my mind — is my amp off? Maybe Rick is the only one playing? And I almost stopped picking through the chords to check when I said to myself,

What the hell. Enjoy yourself, idiot.

So I'll never know if I was pulling a Milli Vanilli or not.

But it doesn't matter.

What a splendid fifteen minutes it was.

Me, front and center, on stage, OHP.

See the Grand Canyon and die.

We ran through "Turning Japanese," and "Stay in Time" and finally "Bully Bully" (at the line in which "I picked up my guitar and busted out his teeth. Oh yeah," I looked over at Jason and saw a funny kind of look on his face.

Wistful?

Sad?

At the risk of sounding blasphemous, he looked kind of … *Ecce homo*, you know?) But then he laughed, the moment passed, and as the song wound down, the band paused; and I paused with my fingers set for "Like a Hurricane," when Jason raised his hand in my direction and called out into his mike:

"Ray Verano! Let's give it up for Doctor V!"

That was my unspoken cue; I unplugged the Epiphone, lifted it over my head, took a bow, and trotted back to my place in the wings.

Sad, sure.

But sweetly so.

I had kind of expected to do "Like a Hurricane."

Since I didn't, maybe that meant my amp wasn't off, after all?

"Good job," said the flabby guy in the Slipknot shirt, patting me on the back. But then he said "cue the video" into his headset, and it all seemed like what he wanted to say was "glad that's over," but it didn't matter to me.

It was a splendid fifteen minutes.

So, no, I wasn't on stage when all hell broke loose. Figuratively. I watched from the wings as Jason led the band through a series of provocative tunes, like Rainbow's "Can't Happen Here," Morrissey's "I Bury the Living," and both "Reapers" and "Revolt" by Muse. It was during "Reapers" that Jim Krywicki got his vicarious revenge on Buck Toth. He'd worked up a video montage of some raw military footage, from the horrid Auschwitz films to grainy smart bomb footage beamed back as the missile draws near its target, before the screen goes black and snowy, to napalmed children in Viet Nam and Israeli bulldozers and soldiers relaxing with video-games; when Jason began to shriek "Here come the drones!" a series of official portraits of the American presidents, from Kennedy through nr 48, flickered across the screen in time to the music, interspersed with slaughterhouse scenes, it all ending with that cheesy and sloppy North Korean propaganda Photoshop of a missile taking out the White House.

Did he go too far?

Well, he also collated the photos of the "Hometown Heroes" — head shots, all in uniform, all against a background of Old Glory — of all the soldiers, sailors, and airmen from NEPA who had died since Desert Shield (he got these from a Veteran's Day spread in the local paper) ... gosh, maybe he did.

Go too far, that is.

Did Jason know he was going to do it?

I don't know.

I am fairly sure that Jim's real target was Call-Me-Jarhead.

I am fairly sure that Jason's target was the same. Otherwise, what did his dedicatory remark about "all our glorious warriors, from the Commander-in-Chief down to the lowliest USAF grease monkey" mean?

So I think it was just a stab at catharsis.

Target.

Stab.

Unfortunate choice of words. Do our everyday idioms not prove good old Robinson Jeffers right about mankind?

But gosh, I mean, if Jason had *known* that the upshot of it all would be the accident in the silo in Naxkohomen, which has all the seismologists in the world biting their fingernails about the "trigger reaction" (no conscious irony) that might release, at last, that apocalyptic volcanic eruption beneath Yellowstone, he wouldn't have gone on to sing "Fortunate Son" at which point, I believe — but you know better than I — nr 48 is said to have left the upper box in a rage he could only assuage with two — large — tumblers of Cutty Sark, over the protestation of his holiness-tabernacle wife.

For sure! Jason is *kind*. Jason is a *pacifist*.

But Jason was exorcising demons.

That's why the band ended up with "Bad Girl," another Off Broadway showpiece for Rick (who sparkled like John Ivan himself) — for which I was on stage, as you know. Back during that jam session at Dave's, Jason had asked me if I remembered the words. In the cannabis haze that followed, I'd forgotten all about it.

But then I heard him say to the crowd,

"We have time for one more tune before You-Know-Who comes out to take over — Sorry for the involuntary shudder," he joked "too late now! So, how about we shift gears a bit? I'd like to ask Dr. V to come out here again — without his ax this time," he said, just as I was taking my first step forward with the Epiphone, "to sing a little song I'd like to dedicate to a girl I know. It's an Off Broadway tune called 'Bad Girl.' So, this is for Alison."

(Wild Cheers. Even though none of them had ever heard of the song, or the band, or Alison, for that matter).

"Ray!" he called "Get your wetback ass out here!"

And, caught up in the moment as I was, as soon as Rick tore into the opening riff, I did my best Cliff Johnson impersonation by cartwheeling out onto the stage (landing just half a yard away from the center mike — and finally tearing my too-tight battle-flag shirt so that — on the spur of the moment — I decided to do a Morrissey, tear the rest off and toss it into the crowd.

Yeah, I know.

But Mozz looked better back in '86, too, and he still does it).

Alas, even that couldn't save those brave boys of the Alabama National Guard who tried to oppose the Cuban landing party at Spanish Fort.

And Alison, of course, wasn't even there.

At Hanskung, that is, not Spanish Fort.

Why would she be in either place?

Speaking of Hanskung, I have been described by some as a "frustrated employee of the college." If I were grading a term paper that included this phrase — and paying attention to it, not just glancing it over (do you know we sometimes have thirty papers to read at a pop? and if they're all ten pages long, that's three hundred pages of drivel?) and making a mark here and there for honesty's sake, so it *looks* like I'm paying attention to this rubbish, I would mark "frustrated employee of the college" as that fallacy known as "distinction without a difference." I may sound jaded, but — survey the faculty yourself. You'll probably find out that most of the people who teach here are "frustrated" to say the very least.

There was only one hero among us. It's an overused term these days, but as I see it, appropriate.

He was a colleague of mine several years ago, name of Harold Johnson.

No.

The ballplayer's name is *Howard* Johnson.

As is the restaurant chain you've never eaten fried clams at.

Married to a hag of a woman who also teaches here, and son-in-law to the dean (another pill).

Mysteriously disappeared ...

wonder where he is ...

Anyway, he *up and quit* one day.

Slammed the door in his father-in-law's face, and "took a powder" as they used to say in B-movies.

More of him later.

But I once read — because he asked me to — an article of his on T.S. Eliot. I don't think it was ever published. It was about Eliot and the weight of the decisions we make every moment of our lives. Supposedly, it is a Leitmotiv — sorry, a common theme — in Eliot's writings, that every act of ours here on earth, grand or trivial, is fraught with moral weight. Everything we do here on earth determines our future life in Heaven. (Sounds like something St. Pelagius would say, though Eliot would disagree, probably, with the old duffer, on the role of grace in those decisions.

But let's move on, shall we?)

That one thing stayed in my mind, from the whole paper, the rest of which I've forgotten. Because it seems to me that, grace and karma and the future life to one side for a moment, everything we do *can* have, and maybe *does* have, a motive significance for acts we never imagine might be related to them.

Think back to Billy Kowalski's arrow and poor Jason Bartosz.

Or think back to June 28, 1914, in Sarajevo. Did you know that, not only did Franz Ferdinand and his wife Sophie *survive* an assassination attempt that morning, with a *bomb* thrown at their car but that the assassins would not have got their second attempt at him, which turned out to be successful if his driver had not made a wrong turn on their second outing that morning?

And that the driver — Leopold Lojka — would not have made the wrong turn had Erich von Merizzi, the governor's aide, who might have told him about the change in route, not been in the hospital that morning, and incommunicado? And that the Sarajevo police officer Edmund Gerde, who was supposed to tell all the drivers about the new route, had been frazzled that morning, and forgot?

And why was von Merizzi in the hospital? Did he, against his better judgment, eat a spoiled herring the previous night?

Why did Gerde, who was *concerned about the lack of safety along the route*, forget to tell the most important thing in the world to the drivers of the motorcade? Was his wife nagging him that morning about something? Did he complain about his coffee being cold, and did she burst out crying at the breakfast table, and did he slam the door and rush off to work after complaining about her "Damned theatrics," only to feel so bad about berating her *over nothing*, that he could think of nothing else?

And so, because of a fishmonger who prized a few hellars over the health of her clients ("Fresh catch, just yesterday. Hasn't even had the time to take on all the brine it should, Your Excellency"), or a too hastily poured cup of java (*Why*, we might ask, did he take so much time shaving that morning?) the world was turned upside down; three empires were riven apart on stupidly ethnolinguistic lines, and an unknown and unremarkable Austrian painter, who otherwise might have remained unknown and unremarkable, save for his inability to successfully render the human form in his otherwise capable draftings of architecture, went on to destroy at least six million lives during a twelve-year spree — and how many others, over the years, posthumously even, well, your guess is as good as mine.

And here, because Willy Jones (that's the name of the fat roadie/Slipknot fan) wanted to beat the traffic on I-81 and be on the road to Lesser Orechsville before the entourage set off, clogging the damn road all the way back to DC, as he was sure they would, he hustled OHP (myself included) out the *upper* corridor of the Tertullian Center (a shortcut to the parking lot on the hill next to the fine arts center, where the vans were parked), rather than out the *lower* corridor, which was jammed with journalists and lobbyists and other hangers-on, and where the lines through the metal detectors snaked up and down and up and around like the worst TSA jam on Thanksgiving weekend.

Ah, had he only played by the rules, Oakland would not be smoking still with the fires of the riots! No, concerned only for himself, he led us up the steps and along the corridor, *past the room where 48 and his entourage* were getting ready for the big speech with teleprompters and makeup girls and Cutty Sark, and because the door to the room happened to be open, and 48 was heading over to the table for another plate of burgoo, he saw us pass, and, nearly apoplectic, called out:

"Theah they ahh! Git those fuckahs in heah!"

That's how he put it.

You were there.

The biographies will say something else, as the talking heads are doing right now, but you and I know how it really was.

There they are, get those fuckers in here, to translate out of the Shubutian.

It was a surreal moment, that's for sure. Standing in a small room smelling of down-home foods, with men in suits lounging here and there— some with plates in their hands, others, more officially, with their hands behind their backs — and the person we used to call the Leader of the Free World right in the middle of it all, whiskey glass in one hand, a plate of yellowish goo in the other, and an angry scowl on his face.

"What the FUCK do you boys think you're up to?" exploded 48, his round head swiveling on his flabby neck, turning his face now to me, now to Jason, now to Rick and Dave (the latter doing his best to become as small as possible, and hide behind the back of the former).

"Mr. President …" began Jason.

"Mistah President!" huffed 48, "Don't you Mistah President me, boah!

I need an explanation of your supreme royal fuck-up, and I need it now!"

I remember looking around the room.

Jim Krywicki was nowhere to be seen.

Figures, doesn't it?

I wish he was.

I would have thrown him right under the bus and clapped my hands clean.

It was his fault anyway, wasn't it?

I mean, do you think that 48 — whatever part of the concert he attended — was able to make out the words of any of the songs we'd — er, they'd — sung?

Wasn't he famous for greeting the rapper Li'l Jaymee after a command performance at Kennedy Center with, "Son, I don't know whut in hell you wuz up theah talkin' about, but if the young folk like it, tha'ss good enough fah me?"

But that video montage!

Those body parts and gore, interspersed with the official portraits of all the presidents, going back to 35 at the least and ending with none other than the Pride of Shubuta, well — who can blame him, if they burned themselves into his retinas?

I looked over at the calm face of Jason Hughes, who was about to start talking music, and free speech, and artistic expression, and that calm, kind, reasonable expression on his face infuriated me.

New guy in the band!
I wanted to holler over in his direction.
I told you so!
This shit is on you!
But then the president swiveled his face back to me, and there was, it seemed, an expectant pause. So I started in with:

"Mr. President, if you please …"

"If *Ah* please?" he said, moving in on me in that domineering way they say he has, er, had, growing taller, it seemed — was he standing on his tiptoes? — as he backed me up against one of the long tables covered in tablecloths in the Hanskung colors of lime green and violet, stained now with grits and gravy and waffle mix, "If Ah *please?*"

"If you please, Mr. President, this isn't our fault …"

"This isn't your *fault?*" he bellowed, looming over me like a wave about to crash, blocking out the sunlight. And, did he always repeat everything anyone ever said to him? Without backing up an inch, he turned to one of his detail and snarled,

"Bring that piece of shit in here, Roy!"

Roy went out, and 48 turned his glare back upon me.

"Mr. President, I can understand if the music was not entirely to your liking, but as far as the video program goes …"

"What the *fuck* are you talking about?" he bellowed, the smell of burgoo on his breath positively unbearable at the short distance between us, and then, "What do you call *that*, boah?!"

Still, without shifting or giving an inch, he swept his left arm behind him. Gingerly shifting my neck to the right, to peer past his large shoulders,

I saw that he was pointing at Ol' Beau.

Or what I took to be Ol' Beau ...

"That, sir?"

"Yes, *that* suh! What do you call *that*, suh!"

"That — that's a dog, sir."

"Listen, you smartass, I know that that's a dog. But it ain't *mah* dog! That ain't Ol' Beau!"

Still at sea, I had the pleasant feeling of having my suspicions confirmed.

"I thought he looked small," I said, with an unconscious smile.

"You thought he looked small? When did you 'thought he looked small?' When you picked him up at the White House? No, because you didn't pick that dog up at the White House! You picked up Ol' Beau at the White House, Ol' Beau who is a Giant Schnauzer, about yea tall, and who weighs more than my two gran chillen taken d'gether — an' they's sixteen an' foahteen, boah! An' that there, that there's a *miniature piece of shit schnauzer!* What the FUCK do I pay you for, to lose my dog in the space of six hours, and right before I have to go out on stage and talk about a new social program that ..."

He grew red in the face, coughed, thumped his chest, and one of the guys in suits said,

"Mr. President, a glass of water ..."

" ...A new social program that ... aw, fuck! What good is tryin' to explain this to you! What foah? Problem is, son, you lost my dog, *Shit For Brains*, and ..."

I felt my hand close around the handle of the waffle press on the table behind me.

But I don't remember swinging it.

And do you know how heavy those things are?

But that's adrenaline for you, I guess.

So, that's that. Where do I sign?

I see that the Mexican Military Envoy for the Gulfshore Region has been named governor of the *Región del Golfo de México* as had been foretold ... Cuba remains Cuba.

Posers!

All that heady propaganda bullshit about the little Island of Righteousness taking on the Evil Empire and beating their pants off. They got no farther north in their occupation zone than the Tamiami Trail (the St. Augustine video was a bluff after all), and wouldn't have even got that far, wouldn't have dared to thumb their nose towards Florida, if not for the Mexican advance ... And now President Paz has not only snubbed the President of the Cuban Council of State and Council of Ministers when he flew into what used to be George Bush International, but he also directed the Army of the Northeast to take over "peacekeeping duties" from the *FAR*, which, after some face-saving photo ops featuring the Mexican general and his Cuban counterpart, embracing, smiling, got back onto their outdated tubs and leaky amphibious vehicles and retreated to the tatty little beachhead of a political system that no one's believed in for more than fifty years now, the only advantage that they won is the right to put the *torcedores* of Ocean Drive out of business since all embargoes on Cuban cigars have now been lifted. At least in those parts of North America reunited with the Mexican Republic.

And how that Republic has grown! All of what had been the western United States has been reunited to the Mexican motherland, as President Paz said it would be, several weeks ago, with his repudiation of Guadalupe-Hidalgo. Since then, of course, "extraordinary circumstances" and "the wishes of the peoples (plural!) inhabiting the more easterly-lying regions of the old (sniff) USA" have pushed the frontiers of *Los Estados Unidos Mexicanos* to the western bank of the Mississippi, with all of the Gulf now in Mexican possession, including all of Florida, and the panhandle west, effectively cutting off Alabama and Mississippi from the sea ... The unofficial grumblings coming from Cuba seem to indicate a rather serious state of nerves on the island, which is only, as we know, ninety miles south of the most southerly lying portion of El Estado de Florida and the rest of the imperialistic (?) Mexican behemoth ...

All of this has been rationalized based on old maps, of course. You know, the maps of Spanish possessions in America, which all Gringo schoolchildren ignored after first encountering them with a flash of incredulity — after all, the only map that was *real* was that depicting the Lower 48 (Ha! there's a bad pun in there, somewhere, but I'll be nice, out of respect ...) and good luck with getting *them* back, right? Who knew that the Gringos of the twenty remaining Anglo States of America would be wiping their brows — *phew!* — at the generosity of President Paz, for not blowing the dust off the old *mare clausum* treaty map ...

In other news, as they used to say, it turns out that North Korea only had two submarines in their entire fleet.

Both of them now lie in the depths of San Francisco Bay after experiencing mysterious explosions — which some of the cognoscenti ascribe to mysterious Chinese maneuvers off the Golden Gate right about the time that the Korean peninsula was formally annexed to the Chinese motherland (with the South promised a measure of autonomy as a Special Administrative Region).

President Paz and Tsar Vladimir are to meet on Vancouver Island in a few days to finalize the recognition of the Republic of Alaska as part of the Transbering Siberian Autonomous Region, and all the talking heads on all of the remaining Anglo news outlets are blaming the "present catastrophe" on "Mexican fifth-column insurgent Raymundo Verano, whose fatal bludgeoning of the forty-eighth president of the United States provided the necessary platform for the joint Mexican-Cuban-Russian invasion of North America."

You will not be surprised at the fact that I take issue with this presentation of the matter.

First of all, I was never known as Raymundo.

Secondly, I have been apolitical since I first emerged into the daylight. I'm certainly no insurgent, for God's sake, never a fifth-columnist or any sort of sleeper-cell member.

Thirdly, if I'm Mexican, it's because my parents hailed from there. You don't get to choose your parents, or what people call you: and that's the term that everybody's used to bludgeon *me* with since ever I can remember.

And about the bludgeoning of the president — you'll notice that they never mention the weapon I used.

I assassinated the Leader of the Free World with a waffle iron?

Can anybody say that with a straight face?

Finally, that concerted Mexican-Cuban-Russian invasion.

What about North Korea?

I mean, if you look at the chain of events as they unfolded, the assassination of 48, following hard upon the assassination of 47, is what gave the North Koreans the idea — *now is the time* — and they lobbed that ICBM over the Pacific, at which point the Mexicans decided — crisis on the East Coast, crisis on the West, *now is the time, hermanos!* and then — well, I mean, how could the Russians keep their hands off Alaska, with such land grabs going on?

Come on!

It looked like freaking Oklahoma there, for a while, no?

Now's the time, bratya!

But poor old North Korea is left out of the mix. Maybe it's because they were punching above their weight? And now they are just an insignificant, though better fed and industrializing, part of the red empire of Beijing?

And are there any bigger whores than journalists?

I mean, they're *so quick* to sniff out where today's truth is tending, no?

Wait a few weeks, and you'll see all the pink faces at CNN and Fox toeing the same old party line as their cronies across the Mississippi in the studios of Telemundo and Univisión.

And now, really finally — it's not my fault at all.

I didn't set this chain of events in motion.

I would never even have been in shouting distance of the 48th president of the United States if not for a rainy day in Sanantone, and my friend, good old Jason Hughes — who feels *terrible* about all this, by the way — buying the wrong Beatles album.

And if Alison Prickney was not such a bitch, and if Billy Kowalski never shot Jason Bartosz (still dead, although that's somebody who deserves to be brought back among the living) and ... shit, if not for all that, and more, the world today would have been no worse, and no better, and certainly not changed, from what it was, say, around November 2016.

As if it were Jason's fault that he's got hyperopia.

Thanks a lot, God, for farsightedness.

That, and mad cow disease.

And cockroaches.

Oh yeah, and those caterpillar wasps.

Way to go.

To say nothing about original sin.

What's up with that?

AUTHOR BIO

Charles Stephen Kraszewski is the author of four books of poetry: *Beast, Diet of Nails, Chanameed* (in English) and *Hallo, Sztokholm* (in Polish). He is a literary translator from Polish, Czech, and Slovak.

www.ingramcontent.com/pod-product-compliance
Lightning Source LLC
Chambersburg PA
CBHW032137270626
47172CB00008B/211